PETE
YOU'D

REGINALD Evelyn Peter Southouse Cheyney (1896-1951) was
born in Whitechapel in the East End of London. After serving
as a lieutenant during the First World War, he worked as
a police reporter and freelance investigator until he found
success with his first Lemmy Caution novel. In his lifetime
Cheyney was a prolific and wildly successful author, selling, in
1946 alone, over 1.5 million copies of his books. His work was
also enormously popular in France, and inspired Jean-Luc
Godard's character of the same name in his dystopian sci-fi
film *Alphaville*. The master of British noir, in Lemmy Caution
Peter Cheyney created the blueprint for the tough-talking,
hard-drinking pulp fiction detective.

PETER CHEYNEY

YOU'D BE SURPRISED

DEAN STREET PRESS

Published by Dean Street Press 2022

All Rights Reserved

First published in 1940

Cover by DSP

ISBN 978 1 914150 95 1

www.deanstreetpress.co.uk

CHAPTER ONE
THE GIRL FRIEND

You'd be surprised!

Maybe you guys have got a good vocabulary of your own. Maybe you can find just the right cuss-word when you want it. But I'm tellin' you that even if you was listenin' to Doctor Goebbels talkin' to himself about Winston Churchill after dinin' on an ersatz *filet mignon,* you would still not begin to understand some of the expressions I have been gettin' off on this trip.

Me—I am a neutral. I am so neutral that even if I do think that Mister Hitler is so crooked that he would make the leanin' Tower of Pisa look like a plumb line, I would not say such a thing to any guy who was deaf. Because I am a neutral guy, every time I see a picture of Mister Goering in a swell new uniform I make a noise which, while intended to denote deep admiration, sounds just like tearin' calico.

I am one big innocent sucker. I am prepared to believe that Winston Churchill sank the *Athenia,* that Poland invaded Potsdam, that J. Stalin is just a big sissie tryin' to work his way through college. I know for a fact that the Czechs declared war on themselves outa spite, an' that Austria likes bein' Hungary. I know all these things, because Mister Goebbels has told me so; an' who am I to say that he is such a one hundred per cent. liar that he would make Ananias look like a two-bit amateur tryin' to four-flush a ten cent jackpot from a couple of screw-eyed old lady members of the Big Fork Temperance Sewin' Bee.

What I mean is I am a neutral.

I am also very fond of Swedes. I go for Swedes. I am very fond of the Swedish captain of this passenger an' cargo steamer who has been turnin' same round an' round in order to keep topsides up with some "U" Boat guy who has just shot a torpedo off at us so'd we shall know that he wants to be friends. I would like to have a long talk to this "U" Boat guy about neutrality—with a piece of lead pipin'!

It is so goddam dark on this boat that any time somebody strikes a match it looks like Independence Day celebrations. Nobody can see a thing an' even if they could they wouldn't like it. Every time I try an' walk around the shelter deck some dame throws her arms around my neck an' asks me if I know where her cabin is. I inform this momma that I do not know because, havin' taken one quick look at her in the dinin' saloon, I am also neutral so far as she is concerned.

Maybe you guys will agree with me when I say that it is always dames with homely faces an' figures that look like the child's first problem in geometry who are the ones to get themselves lost on a dark night. Other dames who have swell shapes an' what it takes both in feature, walk an' have-you-got-me generally, do not get themselves lost on the slightest provocation, an' even if they do somebody usually finds 'em before you do.

But maybe you are wise to dames. Maybe you have known *femme* trouble yourself. An' if this is so you will know that dames are always without logic an' are always doin' things that are not in the book of rules. I would go so far as to say that ever since the world began dames have been tryin' to get a stranglehold on guys, beginnin' with Eve, who would not even lay off that poor mug Adam an' let him get on with his fruit business. Every time he tries to concentrate on apples she is pesterin' him to turn over a new leaf. Did that dame put the fig in figure or did she? I'm tellin' you she started it an' every other baby has carried on with the good work since.

No guy who is born without his fingers crossed an' an extra helpin' of grey matter, ever knows where he is with a dame.

Believe it or not, one night I was tellin' the story of my life to some honey-blonde in Saratoga an' she was eatin' it up like a cat in a creamery. Suddenly she slings me a hot look that woulda made Casanova do a couple backfalls, an' she says:

"Lemmy . . . You have *got* somethin', honey. You slay me completely. To me you are Marc Antony. You are my dream man!"

Then she slings her arms around my neck an' put a half-nelson on me that woulda made Hackenschmidt jealous, an' she puts her little mouth up an . . . well, just then the telephone starts ringin'.

When she comes back she stands there lookin' at me like I was a piece of stale drippin'. She says sorta icy:

"You get outa here, Lemmy Caution. Get out before I take a smack at you!"

An' when I ask her what this is all about she says:

"That telephone call was from my husband. He rang up to say what a swell time you an' him are havin' at the fight down at the Maybury Ring. Ain't *nothin'* sacred to you guys?"

All of which will show you people that the amount of logic that a good-lookin' dame possesses could be stuck in your eye an' you wouldn't even notice it.

I give a big sigh an' heave myself off my cabin bed, grab off a shot of Canadian rye an' ease up on to the main deck. The wind has dropped a bit but it is black as hell an' we are ridin' without lights. As I go past the Captain's cabin I can hear him swearin' in Swedish an' I think it sounds just like I am feelin'.

I pull into the wireless room. The operator is a good guy named Larssen with blond hair an' big blue baby eyes.

"How're we makin' out, Larssen?" I ask him.

"I donno, Meester Hickory," he says. "The Captain he say we make Le Havre arondt nine o'clock to-night. He say we are O.K. now. No more torpetoes . . . yes?"

I do some quick thinkin'. Maybe I can still do what I want. Anyhow I'm goin' to try because I do not believe in wastin' time.

"O.K., buddy," I tell him. "You send these radiograms for me an' make it slippy." I write 'em down for him.

To Miss Geraldine Perriner Hotel Dieudonne Paris France stop

Arriving Paris to-night from Le Havre stop Urgent you meet me twelve thirty to-night Siedler's Club vestibule Rue Des Grecs stop Wear spray of three gardenias so I recognize you stop Tell nobody stop Meeting at request of your father stop Hickory Transcontinental Detective Agency stop End.

To Rodney Wilks Hotel Rondeau Boulevard St. Michael Paris France stop.

Arriving Paris to-night stop I am Cyrus Hickory of the Transcontinental Agency employed by Willis T. Perriner to find Buddy stop I have radioed Geraldine to meet me twelve thirty to-night Siedler's Club Rue Des Grecs you be there stop So long stop Caution stop F B I Identification B47 stop End.

He says he will send these right away an' I ease back to my cabin an' proceed to do a little sleepin' because I should like to tell you guys that I am not at all pleased with this job I am on an' when I am not pleased with anything it is my usual habit to sleep which is nice an' restful an' don't cost anythin'.

When I wake up I get the idea that somebody has poisoned me in my sleep because my tongue feels like a piece of carpet, but after a bit I conclude that this must still be the rum. I flop outa the bunk and doll up a little, put on my big coat an' go up on deck. All around the place, standin' by the dimmed deck lights that they are now showin', are the passengers, with that sorta hopeful look on their clocks that comes to guys when the journey is nearly over.

Away in a corner I find my steward standin' by my luggage. He tells me that we will dock in fifteen minutes. I give him a tip an' light a cigarette, then I walk over an' look over the rail down on to the shelter deck. Right in the corner, sittin' sideways on a deck chair, is a dame.

I look at this dame very deeply. Because I am askin' myself how in the name of heck I can be kickin' around on a one-eyed boat like this for days an' not even know that there is a baby like this one aboard.

She is dressed in a swell travellin' coat with a big fur collar that is caressin' her pretty face like it was fond of her. Just above her head is a stanchion light an' I can see her cute little suede hat tipped over one eye, with a very tasteful coiffure doin' its stuff over one ear. And boy, has this baby a line in ankles or has she!

Me—I have always gone for ankles. Some ancient history fan once told me that some Roman blonde named Messalina had such a swell shape that guys committed suicide about it. Well that ain't nothin' because this baby's ankles would have made the entire Gestapo jump off the end of the pier.

If I had a pair of nether limbs like this dame has got I woulda rushed over to Berlin an' sent in my card to Adolf after which he woulda declared peace on everybody an' given Upper Silesia to the Esquimaux just outa sheer boyish fun.

Just as I am indulgin' in these deep ruminations the baby decides to light a cigarette. She flashes on a lighter an' I have to stop myself squealin' because this honeybunch is nobody else but Juanella Rillwater, one of the cutest an' toughest babies that ever helped her husband—Larvey Rillwater—to blast the time-lock off a bank safe.

I step back an' do a little thinkin' because it strikes me as bein' very odd that Juanella should have to be on this Swedish tub-jumper at the same time as I am. An' if you knew Juanella you would understand because this baby is hard to shake an' she once got an idea in her neat little headpiece that she was stuck on Lemmy Caution.

Just at this minute the boat gives a heave. I stick my hand out on to a pile of baggage an' underneath my fingers I feel a ukelele.

I grab it. I don't know if I have ever told you guys that I am a very poetic sorta cuss, and that when I am not rushin' around after some thug I am always thinkin' very beautiful thoughts about dames an' other subject matter.

I grab the uke an' strum a coupla quiet chords. I look around but there ain't anybody near me. I hang over the rail an' start croonin'. I give her this one:

> *If Mister Casanova*
> *Had ever looked you over,*
> *He'd say that you had somethin'*
> *That the other dames have not.*
> *He'd rave about your figure,*
> *He would surely like your figure*
> *But Casanova's dead and I*
> *Do not think you're so hot. . . .*

Juanella takes a peek around. Then she shrugs one shoulder. I go on:

> *Poets may dream of rosebuds,*
> *An' gamblers dream of games,*
> *Drinkin' guys like liquor,*
> *But I'm just nuts on dames.*
> *Sweet neckin' is my hobby,*
> *An' lovin' is my wish.*
> *If curves were served in restaurants*
> *You'd be my favourite dish.*
> *So honeybabe remember,*
> *If you are feelin' blue,*

When all the other dames are dead
I'll get around to you.

Juanella gets up. She walks over an' stands lookin' up at me. She says:

"Say . . . Who do you think you are—Bing Crosby?"

Then she recognises me. She takes a step back as if she was surprised an' hollers:

"Well, for crying out loud. May I be sugared an' iced if it ain't Lemmy Caution. Oh, Lemmy, this is the only good thing about this voyage. Me, I . . ." .

"Pipe down, Juanella," I tell her, "an' if you don't mind just forget that I am Lemmy Caution because right now I am somebody else. I am Mr. Cyrus T. Hickory of the Transcontinental Detective Agency of America."

I go down the steps an' stand beside her.

"Yeah," she says with a cunning little smile. "I bet you are. An' I bet some poor crook who never done anybody any harm so's they'd notice it is dashin' around tryin' to keep all in one piece. Another thing," she goes on, "this is the first time that I ever heard of a 'G' man pretendin' he was a private dick. It must be a tough case."

"Maybe an' maybe not," I tell her. "But at the same time I would like to know what you are doin' on this boat. First of all you know as well as I do that I got your old man Larvey's bank robbin' sentence suspended last year by the Federal Court just because he gave me a hand over that poison gas case, an' you an' he are not supposed to go out of the jurisdiction of the Court, which you are now doin'. Secondly, as a member of the Federal Bureau of Investigation I would like to know what you are proposin' to do in France. These guys have already got one war on their hands without *you* buttin' in. Thirdly, I would like to put on record the fact that when I took a quick look at you just now the idea struck me that you are improvin' with the years; that you are lookin' so swell that if Larvey had guessed what I was thinkin' about you, he woulda socked me with a blackjack."

She smiled an' pushes a curl back into its proper place. Then she comes a little closer to me an' she says sorta winnin':

"Tell me somethin', Lemmy. Do you think it possible that a great big he-man who is also a Federal Agent could just forget himself for a minute an' be sweet an' human? Do you think if a poor little dame like me who has had a vivid past which she regrets all the time an' twice on Sundays was to try very hard to be good, this swell guy would give her a tumble. What I mean is . . ."

"Look, Desdemona," I tell her, usin' great self-control an' a deep knowledge of William Shakespeare, "if all the guys who have fell for that stuff of yours was put in a row they would occupy so much space that they would meet themselves comin' back. Any time you want squeezin' put yourself in the mangle, sweetheart, because so far as I am concerned I am a martyr to adenoids an' duty, an' never try to make a dame on a shelter deck in a squall in case the boat turns over."

"O.K.," she says, "I got it. I suppose there's some other dame. Why is it," she says sorta wistful, "that the only guys except Larvey who falls for me in a big way are palookas that I desire anything else but? Why is it?" she says sorta dramatic. "Must it always be thus?"

She then takes a quick dive at me just as the boat heels over an' before I know where I am this baby has got her arms around my neck an' is kissin' me like it was her last night on earth.

I grab hold of her an' put her on the deck-chair.

"Look, Juanella," I tell her. "That stuff is very nice but it ain't goin' to get you any place."

"Never mind," she says. "I shall always have my memories. One of which will be your sweet visage all mussed up with a nice shade of lipstick."

I am doin' some quick thinkin' because this Juanella is a very smart piece of dresswear, an' I have got an idea in my head that she is putting on this big act to stop me askin' questions. I don't say anything. I take out my handkerchief an' remove the lipstick, which does not taste so hot.

Juanella looks at me an' gives a big smile.

"Look, Lemmy," she says, "you are a great guy for kiddin'. Are you bein' serious about those questions?"

She stands there lookin' at me in a way that would have melted the heart in a brass image.

"You know, Lemmy," she goes on, "I reckon that I don't mind anybody bein' tough except you. I sorta go for you."

"Like hell you do, Juanella," I tell her. "But you come off it, baby, because I am dead serious about those questions. It looks to me like an extraordinary coincidence that you are on the same boat as I am, and I think some explainin' would be in order."

She tosses her head.

"Don't be a sap. Lemmy," she says. "I'm on this boat for the same reason that you are, and that's because there's a war on. If there wasn't I can't imagine the one and only Lemmy Caution—I beg your pardon, Cyrus T. Hickory—travelling on a margarine tub like this.

"Another thing I didn't want Larvey to know where I was going. I think he had an idea that I was goin' to scram outa New York, and when I heard this boat had vacancies for passengers, I made up my mind quick, and scrammed."

"So you're havin' some trouble with Larvey?" I tell her. "What have you been doin', Juanella?"

"Not a thing," she says. "But Larvey got a little bit interested in some blonde, and I thought that when he felt like comin' back to me I wouldn't be there to come back to."

I nod my head, but I do not believe Juanella one little bit, because I know that Larvey Rillwater is so stuck on her that he never looks at any other dame.

Some commotion starts around the decks because we are pullin' inta the harbour. Personally I am very pleased with the idea of walkin' about on some dry land.

"I suppose it would be out of order to ask what Mr. Cyrus T. Hickory is doin' in France," says Juanella.

"It would," I tell her. "Tell me somethin', Juanella, where are you goin' to stay?"

She hesitates a minute. Then she says all brightly:

"I don't know. I'm not quite certain. I think I'll take a look around before I settle anything."

"Well, you'll have to take a quick look," I tell her, "because if you're takin' the train for Paris to-night it won't get you there before twelve o'clock, an' midnight is not a good time to go lookin' around. But you probably know that."

She nods her head.

"I shall stay at Le Havre to-night," she says, "an' go on to-morrow."

"O.K., Juanella," I tell her. "But let me give you a tip off, baby. You know you haven't got any right to go outa the jurisdiction of the Federal Court."

"Oh, no?" she says. "An' how do *you* know I haven't got permission?"

This is a nasty one, because I don't know. So I skip it.

"All right, Juanella," I tell her. "You be a good girl and keep your feet dry."

She smiles an' pulls her fur collar close about her face.

"O.K., big boy," she says. "There's just one little thing. When I fix up where I'm goin' to stay in Paris I'll drop a note to you at the American Express. Maybe you'd like to come around an' drink a cocktail one evening."

"You don't say," I crack back at her, "an' what's Larvey goin' to say about that?"

She raises her eyebrows.

"I ain't goin' to tell him," she says, "so unless he's turned himself inta a thought reader, why worry about that. A girl has gotta have *some* relaxation."

She gives my arm a squeeze, an' I go back to where the steward has put my baggage.

Between you an' me and the door-post, I do not like this business about Juanella. Maybe it is just coincidence, but way back of my head is the fact that both Larvey and this sweet momma of his have been seen around with some very nice guys in New York who have been flirtin' around on the edge of the kidnappin' racket for a considerable time, an' I do not believe that stuff she pulled on me as to why she is on this boat.

By now we have tied up. They have got the gangways out, an' people are beginning to trickle ashore. I get an idea. I grab off one suitcase, find the steward an' give him ten dollars to get the rest of my stuff through the customs and get it put on the train. Then I ease around to Larssen's radio cabin. He is not there, but his assistant is sittin' down smokin' a pipe that smells like Scotch haddocks.

"Look," I ask him, "you might tell me something. There is a lady aboard this boat by the name of Juanella Rillwater. I suppose you wouldn't know if she sent any radiograms off during this trip or whether she received any?"

He says he wouldn't know, but he says that he's got an idea that his boss Larssen—took a radio for somebody just a little while ago, an' he's got an idea that the name was Rillwater. I slip this guy twenty bucks, an' say that I would very much like to have a look at the copy.

He looks through the file an' says that the copy is not there, that he reckons that Larssen has stuck it in his pocket, which is a habit of his, an' will put it on the file later. He says Larssen will be back pretty soon an' why don't I come back an' ask him.

I say O.K. an' scrams because I have an idea that I would like to see what Juanella is up to. I go down the gangway on to the landin' pier which is crowded with a lotta people, an' I take a look around, but I can see nothin' of Juanella. I stick around for a few minutes lookin' for this dame. Then I go back. I go on to Larssen's cabin. He is there. I ask him about the radiogram an' he brings it outa his pocket.

When I look at it I give a big grin. Was I right about Juanella or was I? The radiogram says:

To Mrs. Juanella Rillwater aboard s.s. Fels Ronstrom stop Cyrus T. Hickory Transcontinental Agency is arriving Paris twelve o'clock stop Contact Hickory I am curious stop Good luck stop The Boy Friend stop End

So there you are! An' it looks like somebody has seen my radiogram to Geraldine Perriner an' then told Juanella to sorta keep an eye on me. I thought that baby was up to somethin'.

An' it is also obvious to me that whoever sent this radio does not know that I know Juanella an' that she knows me. So they don't know that Lemmy Caution is aboard. They just think I am Hickory. But Juanella havin' already taken a look at me keeps outa my way. It was a lucky thing maybe that I spotted her.

It is twelve-fifteen when I come out of my hotel an' start walkin' towards Rue des Grecs. I have wired Geraldine Perriner to meet me there because I reckon it is the sorta place where neither of us are goin' to be recognised an' also because I have told Rodney Wilks to meet me there.

Walkin' along I get to thinkin' about this case an' wonderin' just what has happened to Buddy Perriner an' just why this Geraldine dame is behavin' in the way she is. I sorta con over the whole business in my mind an' try an' get some sense out of it.

Here is the set-up: Buddy Perriner is a kid of twenty-one. He is the son of Willis T. Perriner who is the big steel man in Pittsburgh. Geraldine Perriner is his sister. She is five years older than he is.

Both Buddy an' Geraldine are a bit haywire. They have got too much money to spend an' they both play around with the sorta people who like to string along with rich kids. O.K. Well, Geraldine meets up with some Russian guy who calls himself Count Sergius Nakoravo—an' who is probably a phoney anyway. She falls for this guy an' tells her pa that she is goin' to marry him. Old man Perriner then goes up in the air an' says that he will not only stop her dough but will also lock her up as a looney if she don't give the air to this Cossack cream-puff, who is so good-lookin' that he can't bear to use a shavin' mirror.

Buddy Perriner, Geraldine's brother, has also fallen for this Russian bozo. He thinks he is a big guy. Geraldine tells Nakorova bird that if she marries him her old man is goin' to turn the dough off at the main. But Nakorova says he don't care; that even if she worked in a five and ten he would still love her so much that she wouldn't believe it was true. But he also says that she oughta try an' get the old man round to their way of thinkin', an' so they will not get married yet a while but only get engaged.

While all this business is goin' on Buddy Perriner disappears. At first his pa only thinks that he has gone off on one of his usual stunts, but this time he's wrong. That kid just disappears off the face of the earth.

Right then, just to complicate matters, Mister Hitler takes a mean sock at the Poles an' Great Britain proceeds to tell the boyo where he gets off. Directly Nakorova hears about this he starts singin' songs in Russian that sound as if he was drinkin' warm oil, an' tellin' one an' all that Russia is goin' to fight with Britain and France an' that he is goin' to be there. Me . . . I do not believe this guy an' I reckon that the only time he ever got in a fight was when he pushed an old lady off a tram at the Pittsburgh terminus.

Geraldine falls for this line. She thinks that Sergius is the berries. The big mug then fills himself with heroics an' a double shot of vodka an' says that he is goin' to France to join the Foreign Legion. But while he is on the way Joe Stalin, who has been sproutin' about in the undergrowth like a bad-tempered whale, comes up for air an' proclaims to all an' sundry that he does not intend to fight anybody very much an' proceeds to help himself to a large slice of Poland.

Geraldine is now not feelin' so hot. Her Cossack day-dream is in France an' Buddy is still missin'. Old Willis Perriner starts rushin' round in circles an' calls in the Federal Bureau of Investigation to try an' find Buddy an' the Director assigns the case to Rodney Wilks who is a swell guy who knows his stuff backwards.

Before Wilks can do anythin' at all, Geraldine scrams outa New York, an' a week later cables her pa from Paris that she has come over to join Nakorova because she cannot bear to be parted from the guy.

This gives Wilks an idea. He believes that the whole thing is a set-up. He reckons that Buddy has slid off to Paris where he thinks he can have a good time, knowin' that Nakorova an' Geraldine will be comin' over. The idea bein' that old man Perriner will be so goddam het-up about Buddy's disappearance that he will not give two hoots in hell whether Geraldine marries the Russian cake-eater or not an' that he will be so pleased when he hears that the kid is safe that he will consent to anything an' give his blessin' an' a coupla million dollars to the bridal pair.

So there you are. Wilks scrams over to Paris to see if his theory is worth anything. But he don't seem to make out on it an' the next thing is that the Director assigns me to the case an' tells me to contact Wilks in Paris an' take over from him.

Me—I have always believed in a show-down as bein' the best way out of a job. Comin' over on the boat I have made up my mind to have a straight talk with Geraldine an' get her to open up so that I can see if Wilks' idea is O.K.

But I do not propose to be Lemmy Caution of the F.B.I. on this job. No, sir. I have come over as Cyrus T. Hickory of the Transcontinental Detective Agency—a private dick—an' I will tell you why.

If Geraldine an' Sergius an' Buddy are stickin' around in Paris to try an' get old man Perriner to agree to the marriage they are not goin' to open up to a "G" man. They are goin' to get windy if they think that the F.B.I. is on the job. Because they know that you cannot try any funny business with a Department of Justice guy. But if they think I am just a private detective who has been put in by the old boy to find Buddy they may think it worth their while to come across with the truth an' bribe me to keep my mouth shut.

So there you are.

CHAPTER TWO
ANOTHER LITTLE DRINK

IT IS twelve-twenty-five an' I am strollin' down the Rue des Grecs, keepin' my eyes well peeled to stop myself runnin' into the lamp posts. Believe it or not these Parisian black-outs are not so hot.

There is somethin' about Paris that always gets me. Somethin' that I like an' yet it makes me sorta shiver. Me—I am not a guy who suffers from nerves an' you will understand that I do not scare very easy. But at the same time there is a sorta kink in the atmosphere while I am walkin' down that street, with the blued-out lights makin' funny sorta shadows. Well—I told you people that I was a poetic sort of guy, didn't I?

I am a great believer in atmosphere—especially where dames are concerned. Because I have always found that a dame reacts quicker to atmospherics than most guys. Once on a while, while I was on a case down at Agua Caliente—where the warm springs ain't the only things that are hot—I knew some tasty dish who was Spanish an' who didn't care whether it was last Thursday or Christmas. She was just one of them high-pressure forceful babies with a will of her own an' a six-inch knife stuck in her garter just in case she was at a loss for words at any given moment.

Well, this baby thinks that she is stuck on me an' some other doll on whom I have taken a run-out powder the week before tells this Conchita that she has been gettin' the short end of the deal from me. This female scandaleer says that while I have been takin' a tumble with Conchita I have also been givin' a heavy once-over to the girl who does the song an' dance act at the local Follies show.

So Conchita rolls her eyes like a bad-tempered alligator. She is not standin' for any stuff like this. So right then she limbers up an old six-shooter that her pa used in the Spanish war an' goes out lookin' for Lemmy.

Well, just at this minute I am takin' a cold shower around at the Casino an' the massage guy who is partial to me wises me up to the fact that Conchita is runnin' wild with some artillery, that she is lookin' for me, an' that the atmosphere is so electric you could run a cable car on it.

I do a little quiet thinkin' an' I wrap a Mexican blanket around me an' put on the massage guy's sombrero. Then I take my swell check linen suit an' give it to a mean guy who four-flushed me two nights before in a poker game for a present. After which I pull the sombrero over one eye, an' walk out the back way to the depot.

I get the next train out an' the guy I have given my linen suit to gets shot twice in the market place.

All this is due to the massage guy's sense of atmosphere, so you will see there is somethin' very valuable in this atmosphere business to a guy like me. Especially if you are wise to it before it gets around to you.

Walkin' along I get to wonderin' about this dame Geraldine Perriner. I have heard that this baby is a good-looker with a will of her own. If this is right then maybe there will be some fireworks.

When I turn inta Siedler's place, which is down a little courtyard at the end of the street, I see that it ain't changed much since I was here last. Somehow I expected to find the place full of soldiers, but I was wrong. The vestibule—all Turkish with soft red lights—is filled with the usual sorta punks who get around to Seidler's. Most of 'em have got police records and those who haven't are well on the way to gettin' them.

I give my hat an' overcoat to the girl in the cloakroom an' I walk down to the end of the vestibule where there are some Turkish alcoves with tables and chairs inside. In the last one, sittin' back in a chair, is a dame wearin' three gardenias.

So this is Geraldine!

Well, I'm tellin' you that this guy Sergius Nakorova knows his stuff, because she has got *plenty*.

She is of middle height an' wearin' a close-fittin' black dinner frock with a big fur coat flung open over the back of the chair, with the collar sorta framin' her face. She has a skin like pasteurised milk, big eyes, an' the boy who fixed her red hair certainly can swing a mean curlin' tong. I'm tellin' you people if I ever fell down a coal mine with this dame Geraldine I would not even shout when I heard the rescue party comin'. I would just lie doggo.

I walk into the alcove and I say to her:

"Good evenin', I am Cyrus T. Hickory. I'm glad to meet you, Miss Perriner."

She looks at me an' smiles. She has got a slow, wistful sorta smile that would do things to an impressionable guy. When she speaks her voice is very low an' soft, an' she talks sorta slow, pronouncin' her words like the dame on the radio.

"Sit down, Mr. Hickory," she says. "I'm delighted to meet *you*."

I suggest that before we do anything else at all we celebrate the meetin', an' I signal to a waiter an' order myself a shot of Canadian rye an' a clover club cocktail for her.

When this guy has brought the drinks an' scrammed I draw the curtains across the alcove. Then I sit down. I give her a cigarette an' light myself one.

"Look, Miss Perriner," I tell her, "you an' me don't want to waste a lotta time flirtin' around this proposition. Let's get down to cases."

"Of course, Mr. Hickory," she says, "and I think I can save a lot of your time. Believe me. I understand just the way Father is feeling about Sergius and me. He doesn't like Sergius. Why? Just because he is a Russian and a Count. Father is old-fashioned. He doesn't like anybody who isn't American, and he loathes titles. So in his opinion Sergius has to be just an adventurer who is after the Perriner money."

She flicks the ash off her cigarette an' the diamonds in the rings on her fingers twinkle.

"Well, he's wrong," she goes on. "But he's not going to believe me when *I* say he's wrong, and he's certainly not going to believe Sergius." She flashed a smile at me. "But he might believe *you*."

"Oh yes?" I say. "You mean that you want me to meet this Russian guy, to check up on him an' if I think he's O.K. to tell your Pa?"

"That's right," she says. "I think it would be an excellent thing for you to meet soon. I think it would be even better if you investigated his background to the fullest extent. He has nothing to hide."

"That's as may be, Miss Perriner," I tell her. "At the present moment I'm not in a position to argue about that. But aren't you makin' a little bit of a mistake? Have you forgotten about Buddy?"

She looks down. Some tears come into her eyes.

"That's unkind of you, Mr. Hickory," she says. "Naturally I'm terribly worried about Buddy. I'm *very* fond of him, but somehow the idea persists that he's safe. After all this isn't the first time that Buddy has disappeared. He has been off on a dozen adventures and never told anyone where he was going or what he was going to do."

"Maybe that's right," I tell her, "but he's never been on one like this. Even if he has scrammed off before, somebody has known where he was or what he was doin' within a coupla weeks. He has been missin' for over four months. Nobody's heard a word from him. He's just disappeared off the face of the earth."

"I know," she says, "but I was wondering . . ."

I interrupt her.

"What was you wonderin'?" I ask her.

She leans forward.

"You know, Mr. Hickory," she says, "I wouldn't be surprised if Buddy didn't turn up one day in a soldier's uniform."

"O.K.," I say. "You mean you think he wants to do a Kermit Roosevelt act an' go to the war; that he's joined the French or English Army. Well, supposin' he's done that why should he keep so quiet about it?"

She shrugs her shoulders.

"Look, Geraldine," I tell her, "I think the time's come when you an' I oughta talk pretty straight to each other. Your Pa's nearly nutty about Buddy. He's worried about you too, but he reckons the *worst* thing that can happen to you is only to marry this Cossack guy. O.K. But the Buddy thing is different. If you coulda seen what your father was like when I left New York you wouldn't be feelin' so cool about things.

"Another thing, he's got a funny idea in his head an' when I tell you what it is maybe you won't feel so hot about this Sergius guy of yours."

She looks serious. "Tell me, Mr. Hickory," she says.

"Here is the set-up," I tell her. "Your Pa tells me that Buddy was settlin' down to do a decent job of work at the Pittsburgh Works when this Nakorova guy meets you in New York. O.K. Well he falls for you an' you fall for him an' you introduce him to Buddy. The investigations that the Transcontinental have made seem to point out that from that moment this Russian did everything he could to get next to Buddy. He wanted to do all the same things, go to the same places. It has even been suggested that Nakorova spent more time with Buddy than he did with you.

"Well, it is easy to work it out from there, isn't it? Your Pa believes that this love business between you and Nakorova was just a frame-up, that Nakorova was really trying to get next to Buddy so that he could pull this kidnappin' stunt an' hold up old man Perriner for maybe a coupla million dollars."

She shrugs her shoulders.

"Ridiculous," she says. "Mr. Hickory, I tell you that the idea is absolute nonsense. I tell you also that when you have met Sergius you will know that it *is* nonsense."

"O.K.," I tell her. "Maybe we'll find all that out. Now you tell me something. Had Nakorova ever been in America before this last time when he met you?"

"No," she says, "that was his first visit."

"I see." I think for a minute, then I say: "When you got that radiogram to-night—the one I sent to you from the *Fels Ronstrom* tellin' you to meet me here—were you alone?"

"No," she says. She looked surprised. "Sergius was with me. We were dining at my hotel."

"An' you showed him the radiogram?" I say.

"Yes," she says. "I showed it to him. Why not?"

I grin.

"Look," I ask her, "have you ever met a dame called Juanella Rillwater—a very smart, good-lookin' wise baby—with a husband called Larvey Rillwater?"

"No," she says. "I've never met either of them."

"O.K.," I say.

I light another cigarette.

"We won't have to do a lot of worryin' about checkin' up on the Nakorova background," I tell her, "because that's already been done. An operative of the Transcontinental Agency—a side-kicker of mine by the name of Rodney Wilks—has been over here in Paris doin' that very thing. I radioed him to come here to-night too. I expect him any minute. I thought we'd make a complete show-down of this, Miss Perriner. Maybe Wilks can tell us all about your boy friend's background."

She shrugs her shoulders again. She smiles at me. Did I tell you guys this dame was beautiful or did I?

I say excuse me. I get up an' I go out of the alcove. I walk back through the vestibule an' I ask the guy on the door if a short gentleman with a nice round face by the name of Wilks has been along to the Club. He says he don't remember exactly because a lotta people have been in an' out, but he thinks a guy like the one I have described was around about twenty minutes ago.

I go back to the alcove.

"Wilks ain't here," I tell her. "But we'll stick around for a bit. He oughta show up any minute. Maybe he finds it's not easy to get here in the dark.

She nods. She leans back in her chair an' relaxes.

Lookin' at this dame I start wonderin' whether old man Perriner might not be wrong about this set-up. Geraldine Perriner may only be twenty-five years of age, but, believe me, she looks as if she has got plenty sense. She does not look like the sorta dame who would be rushed off her feet by a phoney Russian count.

I throw my cigarette stub in the ash-tray an' put my hand round inta my hip pocket to get my cigarette case out. While I am doin' this my sleeve catches on something that is stuck on the arm of the chair I am sittin' in. I look down an' I get a shock because what my sleeve has caught on is a scarf-pin that I gave to Rodney Wilks four years ago when we were workin' together on the Western Bankers Associated stick-up. This is a tie-pin that he always wears. I don't say anything. I disengage my coat sleeve from the pin. I get out my cigarette case, take out a cigarette.

While I am lightin' it I look down at the scarf-pin. It is stuck in the padded arm of the fauteuil that I have been sittin' on. It is stuck right down with only the head showin'. Whoever has stuck it there has done it deliberately. They meant to do it.

I look at Geraldine. She is still leanin' back in her chair with her eyes half closed. She looks quite happy. I ask her if she would like another little drink. She says no thanks. I say anyway I will have one, an' I get up, pull aside the curtain an' step out just as if I was lookin' for the waiter.

I walk across the vestibule, find the waiter, order the drink an' go into the cloakroom. I start wisecrackin' to the girl behind the counter in bad French, an' while I am doin' it I am lookin' at all the hats that are hangin' up on pegs behind her.

Every guy wears a hat in a different way, an' Rodney has got a fashion of his own. He always wears a slate grey fedora turned up at the front that makes him look more like a kid than ever.

I see it. It is hangin' up at the end of the third row.

So it looks like Rodney Wilks has been in to keep his appointment with me, an' it also looks as if he hasn't gone out again. An' it is stickin' out a mile that it was him that stuck that stick-pin in the arm of the chair so that I should see it an' know he'd been there. An' it rather looks to me as if he did that because he knew he wasn't goin' to get out.

I lean up against the wall, smokin' an' doin' a little quiet thinkin'. Then I go back to Geraldine. I tell her that I will not be a minute, that I think it would be an idea to telephone through to Wilks to see if he has left his flat. She says O.K. I go back to the hat room an' I walk down the little passage opposite it that leads to the men's room. It is dark at the end. I go down some steps and open the door. I close the door behind me an' switch on the light. I am in the usual sorta washroom that these places have. Opposite me is a half open door leading to another little room, where I can see some baskets filled with hand towels that have been used. I go over there and feel for the light switch but there isn't any. I take out my cigarette lighter an' snap on the light.

Rodney is there O.K. He is lyin' over in the corner with his head up against the wall. He's all twisted up like he didn't feel so good. When I look at his lips I see a little brown stain on 'em.

I light myself a cigarette. I reckon that Rodney has done all the investigatin' *he* is ever goin' to do.

I do not like this stuff one little bit because this is what the story writer would call grim. I stand there for a minute or two lookin' at Rodney, who is lyin' there not givin' a goddam about anythin'. By this time I reckon the boy is in the place where "G" men go to after they get bumped an' he is not thinkin' about Geraldine Perriner, which is what I am doin' right now.

I grab hold of the towels basket an' I put 'em so that anybody comin' into the washroom cannot see the body, after which I give myself a wash an' do a little dollin' up which is a process that I am very fond of when I am tryin' to figure somethin' out.

First of all it is a cold hamburger to all the rum in Barbados that Wilks was poisoned in this club. It is also a cinch that nobody knows it except the one who did the poisonin'. An' at the moment it looks to me like Geraldine Perriner is the baby who has slipped Wilks a skinful of morgue-juice while he was sittin' in that chair talkin' to her with the alcove curtains drawn.

Rodney starts to feel queer. Maybe the stuff don't work too quick for him to do a spot of thinkin'. Maybe he thinks that he has only been doped. Anyhow he feels lousy an' wants to get away. But he also wants me to know that he is around, so he pushes his stick-pin inta the arm of the chair hopin' I will see it, an' then staggers along to the washroom.

Nobody is goin' to worry about this, because there are plenty guys who get high in Siedler's an' go rollin
' around the place, but providin' they behave themselves nobody is goin' to take any notice.

O.K. Well, a little reasonin' shows me this: Geraldine Perriner has told me that she was with Nakorova when my radio arrived. She says that Nakorova saw it. So he knew that she was comin' to meet me. Well, why does she have to kill Rodney—supposin' that she is the one who killed him?

The obvious reason for her wantin' to bump him seems to be that he has got next to Nakorova, that she knows that he has got the works on the Cossack an' that when he sees me he is goin' to wise me up. She makes up her mind that she is goin' through with this marriage an' she knows that if Rodney says his piece old man Perriner will cut off the dough like he says, so she thinks that she will bump Rodney before he has a chance to talk to me.

How does that sound to you? To me it sounds lousy. First of all this Geraldine is takin' a helluva chance when she sticks whatever it was that killed Rodney into his drink. Supposin' that he'd passed out then an' there? Another thing how did she know who Rodney was? How did she know that he was an F.B.I. man? Rodney would never have spoken to that dame before I got along. He would have hung about an' stalled around until he saw me blow in.

So she had to speak to him first. She had to tell him some sorta phoney story that would get him sittin' in that chair, opposite her, in the alcove with the curtains drawn so that she could give him the works. Maybe she knew that the stuff she was goin' to give him would make him feel lousy enough *before it killed him* to wanta get out into the air some place.

But when I start tryin' to kid myself that I am gettin' somewhere near what happened I look at myself in the mirror an' say this is all bull because hasn't the dame just told me that Nakorova is a good guy; that she don't mind any investigation into what she calls his "background." She knows good and well that if Rodney is dead I am goin' to be even more interested in Nakorova's background than if my old side-kicker was still with us. So she wouldn't have done herself any good that way.

No. Rodney was bumped because he *had to be bumped quick.* He had to be put out of the way, whatever the risk, *before I got round,* an' the reason for that would be that Rodney was wise to somethin' that would have made things plenty hot for Geraldine an' Nakorova if he had got the chance to spill it to me. Whatever the risk was Rodney had to be got outa the way.

There is a slim chance that somebody else bumped Rodney before Geraldine got to Siedler's; but it is so slim that it don't matter. The guy on the door says that he sorta remembers Rodney comin' in, an' not so long ago. Just long enough for Geraldine to spot him, get into conversation with him, get him inta that alcove an' give him the works.

Me—I am gettin' a very funny sort of idea into my head—an idea that—if it was right—would sorta match things up.

Maybe old man Perriner wasn't so wrong after all! Just for a minute look at it this way: Supposin' Nakorova contacts Geraldine originally because he reckons that he can make a play for her, knock her off her feet an' marry her. He knows that she is a spoiled kid, that her father eats outa her hand, an' he thinks that the old man will say yes to everything.

But he finds that he was wrong. He finds that Pa Perriner ain't havin' any. But he don't mind because he has a second string to his bow. He reckons that if somebody snatches Buddy Perriner he will have the old man where he wants him anyway. If Pa Perriner consents to the marriage everything will be O.K. If he don't he will presently get a little ransom note asking for a coupla million dollars. But this note will not come from Nakorova. Some other guy will be put in to do that so that he can still be the big-hearted Cossack hero.

An' wouldn't it be a funny thing if the guys who was put in to do the snatchin' an' send the note was Juanella an' Larvey Rillwater.

It would be right up their alley an' if this guess is right then that would account for Juanella bein' on the *Fels Ronstrom* an' comin' over here, an' that would also account for her gettin' that radio askin' about me an' signed "the Boy Friend."

Geraldine said that she showed that radio to Nakorova. I reckon that the radio that Juanella got was from him.

O.K. Well, supposin' for the sake of argument that somethin' had happened to Buddy. Maybe Geraldine didn't know about the original kidnap plan. Maybe she didn't know that Buddy had been snatched as an alternative scheme. Then, at the crucial moment Nakorova discovers that Wilks is hangin' around an' knows the whole works.

Well . . . what a set-up for Geraldine! Nakorova is in a jam. He knows durn well that the Federal punishment for kidnappin' an' takin' over a state line is a life sentence at Alcatraz. An' the only person who can give Nakorova away—except Buddy who is safely on ice somewhere an' can't talk—is Rodney Wilks.

I reckon that if Geraldine was keen enough on Nakorova she coulda killed Wilks to save the Russian from a life sentence. I know enough about dames to know that when they get well an' truly stuck on a guy they will do any durn thing to keep him around.

I go back to the alcove. She is still sittin' there with the same quiet an' charmin' smile on her pan.

My second drink is waitin' on the table but I give it a miss. I say to her:

"I can't get this stuff about Wilks. I just telephoned his flat an' one or two other places where he might be but he ain't there. I reckon it ain't any good waitin' around for him."

She pulls her cloak around her.

"Well," she says, "Mr. Hickory, what would you like to do now?"

I grin at her.

"It's a bit late," I tell her. "But I'm sorta keen to get this business over an' get back to New York before Hitler runs out of submarines. Would it be O.K. for us to go along an' see this fiancé of yours. I reckon after what you've told me about him that I would like to meet the guy who is lucky enough to give *you* blood-pressure—even if he is a Russian Count."

She laughs.

"Why not?" she says. "Let us go around to Sergius' flat. He will be glad to know you. I will telephone him."

I tell her that will be fine. She gets up an' we walk over to the telephone booth on the other side of the vestibule. This booth is in an alcove. When I open the door for her I see that it is not a coin-box instrument.

I close the door an' streak over to the waiter. I show him a fifty-dollar bill.

"If there's an extension on that booth line," I tell him, "an' you put me on to it you get fifty dollars."

He grins.

"This way, M'sieu," he says. "I also am sometimes curious about what the ladies are saying."

He takes me across the vestibule an' into an empty office in the passage beyond. He points to a telephone on the table. I give him the fifty bucks an' he scrams.

I grab off the receiver. I listen for just five seconds an' then I get it. I don't wait to hear anythin' much at all, I just streak back to the vestibule an' wait for her to finish phonin'.

After a bit she comes out. I'm tellin' you that she looks so lovely that you'd think that butter wouldn't melt in her mouth.

"Sergius will be delighted to see us," she says. "He is waiting for us."

I tell her that this is swell. I order a taxi an' we wait outside for it. When it comes I put her inside an' get in myself.

It is as dark as hell. After a bit I reckon that we are goin' somewhere near the Place de l'Opera. She pulls her cloak closer about her an' moves a little bit towards me. When she does this her knee touches mine an' I can smell the perfume she is wearin'. It is one of them quiet an' subtle scents that make you wonder what you are gettin' het up about an' why.

This dame has got plenty. She has got everything it takes an' then a packet. To look at she is the doctor's favourite treatment, an' she has also got brains.

In the darkness I can sorta feel her smilin'.

She says: "Being a private detective must be a wonderful life. I expect you get a lot of thrills, Mr. Hickory?"

I grin. I tell her yes. I tell her that sometimes I get one too many. She moves a little bit closer. I can hear her breathin' softly.

I just don't do a thing. Me—I have had my moments with dames an' I hope there's some more comin', but kissin' this baby would be like makin' love to a green snake.

I think she is just poison.

CHAPTER THREE
FIREWORKS

IT IS about half-past one when we pull up outside some swell apartment block. I pay off the cab while she opens the main door. We go up in an electric lift to the second floor an' walk along a passage an' she rings the bell on the end door.

This place is class. There are thick carpets an' the passage furnishin's are swell. I reckon that this Sergius guy has either got some dough or he is gettin' some nice credit.

She rings two or three times but nothin' happens. Then she turns an' looks at me with a little smile an' shrugs her shoulders.

"Sergius is funny," she says. "When I telephoned through he said he would be delighted if we would come round. Now it seems he is out. I expect he will be back in a little while."

She gets a key out of her handbag an' opens the door. She walks in an' switches on the hall-light. I close the door behind me an' go after her.

We go into a long, swell room with a low ceilin'. The place is furnished so that it looks like Sam Goldwyn has been doin' his best with the Arabian Nights scene. Everything is expensive an' colourful. The floor is varnished black an' the middle is covered with a thick white rug about fifteen feet square. When I walk on it is like trudgin' through snow.

There is a big fire goin' an' the gold curtains are pulled close. On each side of the fire is a big white an' gold armchair an' in front of the fire is a white an' gold lounge settee that is so big that if Hitler hadda seen it he woulda wanted to occupy that too. All over the place are cushions an' things in colours that have been picked by somebody who knows their onions in the furnishin' line, an' there is a sorta heavy sweet perfume hangin' around the place that makes me feel like Ali Baba workin' up a little atmosphere before ringin' for two tons of sherbert an' the harem dancin' girls.

I take off my coat an' put it on a chair. She goes over to the big table that is covered with drinks an' glasses an' pours me out a four-finger whisky. She gives herself some vodka in a little glass. Then she throws off her fur coat an' comes over to me where I am standin' with my back to the fire.

She hands me the drink. She looks at me under her eyelids.

"Here's to Mr. Hickory!" she says.

I grin.

"I think that's sweet of you, lady," I say. I look at her an' take a drink. "At the same time," I go on, "I wish this Sergius guy was here. Why does he have to take a powder on us just when I wanta talk to him?"

She drops on her knees an' starts pokin' up the big fire. The way she is I can see that she has got everything in the way of shape an' that her calves are as good as her ankles. She says, lookin' round at me:

"Sergius is temperamental. That is why I adore him. Temperamental men drive me mad. They affect me. It's an odd thing but there it is."

She puts the poker down an' stands lookin' at me with a funny sorta smile playin' about her mouth. All of a sudden it hits me like a ton of bricks that this dame is a dope.

"Are *you* temperamental, Mr. Hickory?" she says.

I grin.

"No, lady," I tell her. "I am anythin' else but. But it looks as if you thought that Rodney Wilks was! Maybe you thought he was gettin' a bit *too* temperamental for you an' your boyfriend . . . hey?"

She takes a step back an' sits down on the settee. She is still smilin'. The smile is sorta fixed like the smile on a doll's face.

"And what the hell do you mean by that?" she says.

I take out my case an' light a cigarette. I stand there lookin' down on her. I am still grinnin'.

"First of all," I tell her, "if you are Geraldine Perriner then I'm Mussolini's girl friend. You put on a very sweet act to-night down at Siedler's place, but it didn't work. The second thing is you killed Rodney Wilks down there to-night. I found him in the washroom lyin' around with the dirty towels. He crawled in there to pass out after you slipped some stagger-juice inta his drink. But he managed to put one over on you first. He left a little message for me."

"Did he?" she says sorta sweet. "What did he say?"

"He didn't say anythin'," I tell her. "This is the message he left. He stuck his scarf-pin in the arm of the chair I was sittin' in. I gave him that pin. He reckoned that if I saw it I would get wise."

I take the pin outa my coat pocket an' show it to her.

She shrugs her shoulders. Then she gets up an' walks over to the table where the drinks are. I am watchin' her like a cat. She opens a box an' takes out a cigarette an' lights it. She turns about an' leans back against the table, smokin' an' looking at me. She is as cool as a couple of Esquimaux in the snowball season.

"You interest me," she says. "You seem to have an intelligence not always associated with private detectives."

She draws a mouthful of smoke down into her lungs and sends it out of her nostrils. They quiver when she does it. Everything about this dame, her face, her walk, the way she smokes, *everything,* is sorta cool and calm an' decided, but underneath I reckon she is a tiger.

She moves away from the table an' she walks towards me. She stops right in the middle of the white rug an' she stands there with the cigarette held up in front of her. She looks marvellous.

"Why do you say that I am not Geraldine Perriner?" she says.

"That was easy," I tell her. "When you went into the 'phone booth I saw it wasn't a coin-box booth. I gave a waiter fifty bucks to put me on the main line. I heard you talkin'. You were talkin' Russian. Maybe you are a Russian. Maybe that's why you speak so slow. So that you don't make any mistakes."

"*Au contraire,*" she says. "I am not Russian. I should not like to be a Russian. I am French. I am very proud of the fact."

"O.K.," I say. "Well, I hope it's goin' to do you a lotta good. I'd like to be there when you try an' get the judge to believe that bumpin' Rodney Wilks was a *crime passionel.* You'll get life. Even a dame as pretty as you gets life for premeditated murder—even in France. Maybe they'll cut your pretty head off."

"Perhaps," she says.

She begins to move. She walks around the end of the settee and comes up to the fireplace. She throws her cigarette into the fire. She stands there with her white hands restin' on the mantelpiece lookin' down into the flames. She is considerin' somethin'. I watch her—sideways.

She stays there lookin' down for a coupla minutes. It seems like years. This dame is beginnin' to give me the jitters. She is too goddam beautiful and she is too sure of herself.

She steps back from the fire. She takes a step sideways that brings her dead in front of me. She stands there lookin' at my eyes. She is so near that I can almost hear her breathin' an' I can smell that perfume she is wearin'. I don't sorta go for that perfume. It gets you. I reckon if a guy smelt a lot of that stuff when she was wearin' it he might qualify for a nut-house before he knew which way he was pointin'.

She starts talkin'. Her voice is low an' soft an' there is an odd sort of vibrancy in the way she speaks.

She says: "There is something about you that I find extremely attractive. You have intelligence and a very quick brain. Because I am a little afraid of you and what you may do, you become even more interesting to me each moment."

I give a little grin.

"So we're talkin' business," I say. "Well . . . I'm still listenin'."

She turns away an' she walks back to the table—slowly. She takes a fresh glass an' pours out some rye. She squirts a little soda into the glass an' brings it back to me. She hands me the glass in an odd sorta way that makes me begin to feel that she is givin' me the crown jewels or somethin'. That is the effect this dame has.

"You need not be afraid of the drink. There is nothing harmful in *that* glass."

She smiles. She has got herself back to where she was before, standin' right in front of me, watchin' my eyes.

"Yes, my friend," she says. "We are talking business as you so aptly put it. I will tell you what I have to offer. And you need not be afraid that we shall be interrupted. Sergius will not return here to-night. At least I do not expect him."

I swallow the liquor.

"That's a pity," I tell her. "If he was here we could have a really nice party, couldn't we?"

She says:

"I wish to be serious. I wish to tell you that I have a great deal of money here, in this place, which is at your disposal. I wish also to tell you that *I* am at your disposal. I include myself only because of the rather peculiar attraction that I find in you. I did not think that any man would be able to make me feel as you do."

I do not say a word. I am beginnin' to get a little hot around the collar. I am trying to work out whether this dame is schemin' for time, whether she expects the Nakorova guy to come back an' do a rescue act, whether she is playin' me for a sucker, or whether she is speakin' the truth. Because this dame is so goddam hypnotic that she would make George Washington's ghost believe that he was President Roosevelt an' like it.

I give her a sweet smile.

"Lady," I tell her, "you might as well give up. Because I am a very funny guy about seein' a job through to its logical conclusion. Dames have tried to make me before. But I am not a guy who is made durin' business hours—well, not much. Maybe if you hadn't mixed that hell broth for Rodney Wilks I might get myself so bull-dozed lookin' at you an' listenin' to you talkin' that I would even fall for that swell line you are puttin' over an' go haywire. Maybe I would strip an' run up the wall, or bite the necks off bottles or do some of the other funny things that I reckon you have got guys doin' for you. But not this time, baby. Didn't they tell you the F.B.I. was tough?"

She nods her head.

"The F.B.I.," she whispers. "That would be the Federal Bureau of Investigation. That was what Sergius was afraid of. He was afraid that this would be important enough for the F.B.I. He was right. So you are a 'G' man."

"This time you're right," I tell her.

She says sorta simply:

"You would not like to reconsider my offer?"

"Nothin' doin' sweetheart," I tell her. "Let's get goin...'."

"Very well," she says smilin' sweetly. "And where do we go to?"

"We're goin' to take a little cab ride to the Sûreté Nationale," I tell her. "I want to introduce you to a coupla policemen I know. They're nice guys an' they tell me that the cells have improved a lot over here."

She throws a little smile at me an' she goes over to where her fur coat is an' slips it on. She looks down at her foot an' raises her dress a little an' she says:

"How fearful. I have a ladder in my stocking. It is impossible to be arrested with a run in one's stocking. May I change my stockings, M'sieu?"

So she is goin' to try that one!

"Lady," I tell her, "you can change nothin'. If your brassiere was in tatters an' you'd put your camiknicks on backwards you would still not get out of this room without me. Besides, I don't suppose they'll look at your stockings where we're goin'."

She says: "You are sweet but you do not understand that it is impossible to do anything with a ladder in one's stocking. However . . . if you force me to be a little indelicate . . ."

She wets her finger like I have seen a dame do when she has a run in her stockin'. Then she half turns away an' raises her frock. I am just thinkin' that this dame has a leg that wouldda won a Ziegfeld competition when I get it. Stuck in the top of her stockin', underneath her suspender, is a .22 automatic.

I jump to it. I have told you guys that the varnished floor is covered with a big white rug. Well, I have noticed that the rug is loose on the floor. As she goes for the gun I jump for the edge of the rug, duck down, get hold of it an' give it a helluva pull.

Her feet go from under her but as she falls she lets me have it. She gets me somewhere at the top of the left arm an' although it is only a .22 gun it knocks me over. I mighta known that that baby would use high velocity ammunition.

Before I can get up she is by the door. Then the lights go out. I am in a spot because I can't see her but she has got me where she wants me. The fire is behind me. I jump for the settee. I hear her talkin'.

"*Au revoir* . . ." she says. "My dear one . . ."

She fires three more rounds at the settee an' I hear a couple of slugs smash inta the fireplace. Then the door bangs. From the hallway I can hear the lift goin' down. The hell-cat has made it.

I switch on the lights an' give myself a drink. I take off my coat an' have a look. She has got me through the top of the left arm, just missin' the artery, an' havin' regard to the fact that she was nearly upside down when she started shootin' you will admit that she knows how to use a hand-gun.

I tie up my arm with my handkerchief an' while I am doin' so I ask myself one question. Am I the sonofabitch or am I?

I put on my coat an' I give myself another shot of rye. I reckon I might as well have *somethin'* off this dame.

Then I go over to the telephone an' get through to Erouard at the Sûreté Nationale.

He says he will come around.

Then I sit in front of the fire an' try an' think up some new names for this hell-cat.

Has that dame got somethin' or has she?

It is round about three o'clock when Erouard an' I go round to Siedler's Club in the police car. This guy Erouard is a nice guy. He is a Chief Inspector at the Sûreté Nationale, with a sense of humour, an' he has already told me that this business is a nice change from chasin' spies which is what he has been doin' since this war started.

We have already been to the U.S. Embassy, where I have got myself identified and an official request to the French police to let me play this thing my own way. I have done this because any stuff in the papers about Rodney Wilks gettin' bumped off is not goin' to help.

Erouard has also been through to the Records Department at the Sûreté and is askin' them to check up on this dame who took shots at me. He reckons this won't be very difficult because the French are keepin' a very close eye on foreigners. They would have checked very carefully on Nakorova when he arrived in Paris because he was a Russian. Anyway the local precinct section would have kept an eye on him an' the people who went in an' out of his apartment generally. These French cops have got medals for that sorta thing. So Erouard reckons that with a bit of luck he will be able to identify this dame.

He is plenty surprised when I tell him that even if they *do* identify her, and even if they find out where she is, I do not want her picked up, and you will see my reason for this. If this dame is tied up in some way with Nakorova an' the police pick her up, that boy is goin' to get plenty scared an' scram. The whole of the set-up that we are tryin' to work on will be all upset. Geraldine Perriner—the real one— will start rushin' around in circles an' we shan't know where we are.

Erouard agrees with me that the only thing to do is to leave the job where it is an' let this dame think she has got away with it.

My arm is hurtin' like hell, but the doctor who has taken a look at it says it ain't so bad an' it oughta heal pretty quick. But I am not feelin' so good-tempered when we get to Siedler's.

A police van is down there an' they have already put a cop on the door of the linen room where Rodney was. Erouard reckons that they'll get the body out in one of the dirty linen baskets so as not to cause too much excitement.

When we get in there the place is still goin' strong. From the restaurant on the other side of the vestibule I can hear a band playin'. We have a few words with Siedler an' tell him what we wanta do. Then I go back with Erouard an' have a talk with the girl in the cloakroom.

Erouard does a little cross-examination. He points to Rodney Wilks' hat which is still hangin' on the peg. He asks the hat doll if she remembers Rodney comin' in. He describes him, stressin' the fact that he is a guy who wears his soft hat with the brim turned up in front, which is a thing that very few people do. Well, we are lucky. She remembers Rodney. She remembers him because she thought his hat looked funny and because it made his face look round an' childish.

An' she remembers him because he gave her a twenty-five franc tip. When Erouard asks her why, she says because she got a telephone number for him. She says she reckons he came into the club about ten past twelve, an' that when he checked in his hat he asked her to get a call through to the Hotel Dieudonne and not to make too much noise about it. She says she sorta got the idea that he didn't want anybody to hear what he was talkin' about. She says he took the call on the 'phone that is on the counter that is in front of her.

I wonder why Rodney did this. I wonder why if he wanted that call kept quiet he didn't go through to the booth in the vestibule—the one that my girl-friend 'phoned from. Then I get it. Rodney didn't want to leave the hallway. He wanted to be there in case that dame came in. He wanted to see her. If he'd been in the call booth in the vestibule she mighta got in without him noticin'.

Erouard asks the hat girl if she heard anything at all of the call that Rodney made. She says she did. She heard just a little bit. He was tellin' somebody not to come around as arranged. He said he'd explain later.

O.K. Well, there you are. Now you will get it. Rodney knew that this hell-cat who shot at me was comin' to the Club at half-past twelve. He wanted to stop Geraldine Perriner comin' round an' he must have had a helluva reason to do that.

So he arrives at Siedler's Club early, an' he 'phones through to Geraldine Perriner from the hallway so that he can notice if the dame he is expectin' comes in. Now why would he do this? Why would he stop Geraldine Perriner comin' around, knowin' that I wanta see her an' knowin' that I am arrivin' myself at twelve-thirty? Well, that is easy. It looks to me as if Rodney had found out something about the dame who killed him. Maybe she told him she'd got some important information on the business we're workin' on. Rodney thinks I'd better hear this before contactin' Geraldine Perriner. So he rings up Geraldine Perriner an' he tells her not to come round, that he will ring her later.

O.K. By this time the dame arrives. She gets there early an' she is wearin' three gardenias. She is wearin' three gardenias because when she gets there she has planned to fix Rodney, to get him outa the way, an' then wait for me, an' make out that she is Geraldine Perriner. She gets Rodney into that alcove, knowin' that she's got to fix him before I arrive, before he gets a chance to talk to me.

She slips some stuff into his liquor knowin' that it'll make him feel lousy, knowin' that he'll want to get away some place. Well it comes off. Rodney gets as far as the washroom an' passes out, an' she waits for me because I am the second on her list.

I have a drink with Erouard an' I scram. I have fixed with him that he will send me a police identification pass round to my hotel next morning. He thinks it may be useful. I go outside an' I get into a cab. I tell the guy to go to the Hotel Dieudonne.

On the way round I start thinkin' about Geraldine Perriner again. But believe it or not my experiences this evening have sorta shaken me up as regards dames. I am not quite certain of anybody now, but I make up my mind about one thing. Until I have got this case sewn up an' in the bag I am not trustin' any dame who blows along, even if she is wearin' angels' wings an' is carryin' a gold framed certificate of merit from the Y.W.C.A. slung round her neck.

I have always found that things go in threes, an' I am tellin' you that Geraldine Perriner is no exception to the rule. To-night I have come up against three dames—Juanella Rillwater, who as I have told you guys is a brunette honey; the other dame who took a shot at me round at Nakorova's apartment who was a lovely with red hair, an' now here is Geraldine. This dame is tall an' slim an' willowy. She is a swell blonde with a complexion like peaches. She is still a little bit sleepy an' a bit surprised like you would be if you were yanked outa bed in the middle of the night.

She is standin' in front of the fire in her sittin'-room at the Hotel Dieudonne. I have parked myself in the arm-chair an' am smokin' a cigarette. I have explained away the fact that my left arm is in a sling by tellin' her that I got a mean sock from a piece of luggage on the boat. I am bein' very careful with this dame. I tell her nothing about what has happened earlier that night. But I do tell her that I got through to Rodney Wilks—an associate of mine—an' told him to 'phone through to her an' tell her not to keep the appointment at Siedler's.

I ask her if she has ever come across Mr. Wilks. She says no, she'd never even heard of him.

Then I start talkin' around this proposition. I tell her very much the same story as I told the other dame earlier in the evening, an' I still make out that I am Cyrus T. Hickory of the Transcontinental Agency who has been put in by her father to try an' clean up this job. I tell her that the old man is very worried an' I tell her that maybe there is some connection between this Nakorova guy, an' the disappearance of her brother—Buddy Perriner.

When I've finished talkin' she don't say anything for a minute. She goes over to the table an' gets a box of cigarettes. She gives me one an' lights one herself. Then she sits down in the chair opposite me an' looks at me. The way she is sittin' I can see that she also has got a very swell pair of ankles, but before I can think anything else about this my left arm gives a twinge an' I get the idea in my head that it is a good thing to be a bit scared of dames with sweet ankles. All the dames I am meetin' to-night have got the swellest sorta legs, an' the idea flashes across my brain that it would be a real treat to meet a woman with legs like stove-pipes just for a change.

She starts talkin' an' when she talks she speaks sorta slow as if she was weighin' up every word, as if she was bein' very careful not to say anything that she don't actually mean.

She says: "Mr. Hickory, I think that my father has got this business all wrong. Don't think that I don't understand his point of view. I do. But of one thing I am certain. He is wrong about Sergius."

I think to myself like hell he is. I think to myself that if I was to tell this dame about the other lovely who has got a key to the Nakorova guy's apartment she might not be feelin' so good.

"What you mean is," I tell her, "you don't think there is any connection between the fact that this Russian wants to marry you an' the disappearance of your brother?"

She nods her head.

"That is what I mean," she says. "I don't think that there is the slightest connection. Don't you think," she goes on, "that you're basing that idea merely on the fact that Buddy was rather fond of Sergius. I think that's rather a point in my fiancé's favour."

She knocks the ash off her cigarette, an' a little smile comes round her mouth.

"You know, Mr. Hickory," she goes on, "whenever an American girl who has money, or expects to have money, becomes engaged to a foreigner, it is almost a national habit to think that the man must be an adventurer."

"That's so," I tell her. "We are a bit like that. But if Nakorova isn't an adventurer it ought to be pretty easy for him to prove it. Any man who is on the up-an'-up has the sorta background that proclaims it. He has a family, relatives, business, banking accounts."

She raises her eyebrows.

"Well," she says, "Sergius has all those things. You know, Mr. Hickory," she goes on, "I think you'll alter your opinion when you have met Sergius." She smiles again. "And you'll certainly alter your opinion when you've met his sister."

My brain clicks.

"Oh yes?" I say. "An' what is his sister like?"

"She's one of the loveliest things you've ever seen, Mr. Hickory," she says. "Of course, every woman wants different coloured hair. I suppose that's natural. But I would give anything to have hair like Edvanne Nakorova. It is the most beautiful titian red hair you have ever seen, Mr. Hickory, and her nature is just as beautiful."

I think Jeez! For crying out loud! So this dame with the artillery—the dame who has already bumped off Rodney Wilks an' who opens up the cannonade on me round at the Nakorova flat—is his sister Edvanne, an' she's got lovely hair an' a lovely face an' a lovely nature!

Well, all I gotta say is if this dame has a lovely nature any time I get myself married I'm goin' to tie myself up in wedlock with a couple of steamed-up gorillas because I think they would be more charmin' in the long run.

I say to her: "That's as maybe, Miss Perriner, but the fact that this Sergius has got a good-lookin' sister don't mean a thing. I have known plenty of racketin' guys with good-lookin' sisters. What about it?"

She smiles at me.

"Sergius is not rich," she says, "but he certainly is not poor, an' I tell you quite candidly, Mr. Hickory, that if my father will not consent to our marriage an' if he likes to cut me off from my allowance, that would not affect Sergius very much. We shall simply have to live on his income."

I nod my head.

"Well, the thing is, you're not married yet," I tell her. "An' I can take it that you are not goin' to get married to this guy right away?"

"I wouldn't say that," she says. "We're both very keen to be married."

"Well, anyhow," I tell her, "I take it that you're not goin' to do anything in a hurry until you've given me a chance to make a few inquiries."

I take a pull at myself and remember that I am supposed to be Hickory—a private dick.

"You see, Miss Perriner," I go on, "my Agency have received specific instructions from your father. I think you oughta give us a chance to do our job. If I can put an O.K. report in on your boy friend, I'll be the first person to want to do it."

She smiles.

"I'm quite certain that you'd be quite fair, Mr. Hickory," she says. She gets up. "I'm not a good hostess," she says. "I forgot to ask if you'd like a drink. Would you?"

I tell her yes. She goes over to a sideboard an' mixes me a whisky an' soda. She brings it over.

"I'd like to ask you something, Miss Perriner," I tell her. "When you got my radio to-night—the one I sent you off the *Fels Ronstrom* askin' you to meet me at Siedler's Club at twelve-thirty—did you show that to anybody?"

Her eyes widen a little.

"Of course," she says. "I showed it to Sergius. He dined with me here and it came after dinner."

That tells me what I wanta know. It tells me that the radio that Juanella Rillwater got aboard the *Fels Ronstrom* was sent to her by Nakorova after Geraldine had showed him my radio. He wanted to know what sort of guy I was. The devil of it is if I can't get my hooks on Juanella Rillwater before she contacts him she will blow the works and tell this Russian tea-cake that I am not Cyrus T. Hickory at all, but Lemmy Caution of the F.B.I., which is a thing I wanta keep to myself right now.

I finish my whisky an' give myself another cigarette.

"Forgive me askin' you a lot of questions, Miss Perriner," I say, "but there are one or two points I wanta straighten out in my mind."

"Ask anything you like," she says, "I'll give you all the help I can."

"Did you ever meet a dame called Mrs. Rillwater?" I ask her. "Or maybe if you did meet her she mighta been callin' herself something else."

I give her a description of Juanella.

"No," she says, "I've never met a woman like that."

I look at her. She's lookin' me straight in the eye. I believe she's speakin' the truth. I get up.

"O.K., Miss Perriner," I say. "I guess I'll be gettin' along. This arm is hurtin' me a little bit, an' I've got to get myself fixed up at some hotel." I look at her. "Look," I tell her, "let you an' me make a bargain. Don't let's go behind each other's backs. Let's be straight with each other."

While I am sayin' this I am thinkin' what a goddam liar I am, because if I was to be straight with this baby, I reckon she'd have half a dozen fits one after the other.

She gets up. She is wearin' some lacy sorta negligée. I'm tellin' you that this Geraldine is a tasty dish.

She says to me: "I intend to be as frank as possible with you all the time, Mr. Hickory. All I want to do is to get this business settled, to marry Sergius and not to offend my father. Of course I'm terribly worried about Buddy, but I feel somehow that he'll be all right, that he'll turn up."

I tell her that I hope so too. I pick up my hat.

She says: "You've asked me one or two questions, Mr. Hickory. Would you be offended if I ask you a personal question?"

I say no. I wonder what is comin'.

"Are you married?" she says.

She stands there lookin' at me. Now here is a nice one. Why should this dame wanta know if I am married or not. I think I will lead her up the garden path.

"Yeah," I tell her. "I got a sweet wife and seven kids. They're livin' on a chicken farm in Milwaukee."

"How interesting," she says. "Does your wife like you being away so much? It must be very trying for her and your family."

I shrug my shoulders.

"I don't know," I say. "I'm a private dick an' I have to do my job."

I wonder what the hell all this is about.

She says:

"Do you like being a private detective, Mr. Hickory?"

I grin at her.

"I don't really know," I tell her. "I never thought about it. It's the way I make my livin' so I just do it."

She nods.

"Is it a good living?" she asks.

I shrug my shoulders again.

"So-so," I tell her. "Why?"

She gives me a sweet smile.

"You and I must have a talk some time, Mr. Hickory," she says. "I think we could be of great help to each other. I would hate to offend you, but I have the idea in my head that your Agency are not paying you as much as you deserve."

The little smile is still playin' around her mouth. Here we go. In a minute this dame is goin' to slip me a thousand dollar bill if I will play ball an' do what she wants me to do.

"I think you're very sweet, Miss Perriner," I tell her, "and very considerate. But we won't talk about that sorta stuff to-night. Maybe I will come round an' see you some time to-morrow."

"Please do, Mr. Hickory," she says. "Come and see me here. I shall be glad to see you, and Sergius—he will be glad to meet you too. I want you to meet him. When you meet him you'll know he's wonderful."

I say goodnight an' I scram. I get a cab outside an' tell the driver to take me to the Grand Hotel on the Boulevarde Montmartre, which is a nice little dump where they don't know Mr. Lemmy Caution.

As we go crawlin' along through the darkness I get to thinkin' about this Nakorova guy—the guy who has got a lovely sister—who has got this Geraldine so steamed up about him that she don't know which way she is pointin'.

I reckon this guy Nakorova must have something too. I reckon it must run in the Nakorova family.

They got oomph!

Chapter Four
PALM OIL

It is twelve o'clock an' the sun is shinin' when I wake up. My left arm is hurtin' like hell, but it could be worse an' I reckon the tough treatment the doctor handed out last night has kept the wound clean an' that with a bit of luck I'm not goin' to have too much trouble with it.

I sit up in bed an' ring for some coffee and start a little deep consideration. Up to the minute I do not reckon that I am doin' so well.

The score is not goin' my way. Rodney Wilks who knew somethin' about this set-up has been bumped an' is no more use to anybody. Edvanne Nakorova has also got away with it.

Here is a dame that has already bumped one guy an' also tried to iron me out, lurkin' somewhere around Paris waitin' for me, with her tongue hangin' out an' a gun all loaded up for yours truly stuck in the top of her fully-fashioned reinforced silk stockin' top. Well, all I can say is I hope it scratches her when she walks.

Maybe you will think that I was a fool to fix with Erouard to lay off tryin' to find this dame but it looks to me that this is the only way we can play it.

Here is a dame who is goin' to stick at nothin'. She first of all gets Rodney outa the way, after which she proceeds to lay for me. A little thing like a coupla murders in one night is just nothin' to that honey-pie.

Well, what is the big idea?

One thing is stickin' out a mile an' that is that there is somethin' very screwy goin' on around here. Work it out for yourself. Supposin' Sergius Nakorova is a big-time racketeer who is out for the Perriner dough; supposin' that our idea that he had Buddy Perriner snatched as a second string in his scheme is right. Well . . . so what?

Look—Nakorova knows, and that hell-cat sister of his, Edvanne, knows—an' I am supposin' that she is in it with him right up to the top of the bottle—that Geraldine Perriner is nutty about Nakorova. *I know it because she told me so herself.* Then why have these guys got to go about killin' people?

Geraldine says that anyway she is goin' to marry Nakorova. O.K. Well, if she don't know that Nakorova's pals have snatched Buddy an' got him hidden away some place, they are still pretty safe.

All they have got to do is to get the marriage through as quick as they can. That ties everybody's hands. Directly Buddy knows that his sister has married Sergius he's goin' to keep his mouth shut, ain't he. He is not goin' around savin' that he was snatched by his own brother-in-law. So all Nakorova has got to do when he is married is to tip off his pals to let Buddy go, an' when the kid turns up the Russian says that he didn't know a thing about it.

Supposin' that Rodney Wilks had actually found out that Nakorova was responsible for the Buddy kidnap. Supposin' he could prove it. Well, the case is still the same. Sergius has only got to say that he was so goddam desperate to get married to Geraldine that he lost his head an' was prepared to stick at nothin'. Well, bein' a woman in love she's goin' to forgive him an' she's goin' to talk Buddy into keepin' his trap shut too.

So why did Edvanne have to kill Rodney? I am still lookin' for the answer to that one.

Here's another thing. You remember when I was havin' that show-down with Edvanne—just before she started the artillery practice on me, when I told her the F.B.I. was tough. She said: *"The F.B.I.! That would be the Federal Bureau of Investigation. That was what Sergius was afraid of. He was afraid that this would be important enough for the F.B.I. He was right. . . ."*

That's what she said. An' she wasn't worryin' about bein' careful, because when she was sayin' it, she had already made up her mind to pull that I've-got-a-run-in-stockin' act an' start a little target practice on Lemmy. She thought she was goin' to get me too!

What is the answer to that one? Why was Nakorova afraid because this was an F.B.I. job. I bet he knew durn well from the start that kidnappin' over a state line is always an F.B.I. job. It's a Federal offence.

The one thing it does show is that Nakorova was afraid of this thing bein' handled by the Federal Bureau of Investigation. An' it looks as if he an' Edvanne might have been wise to the fact that Rodney was a Federal dick. But it still don't make sense because the suggestion that they wouldn't have bumped Rodney and wouldn't have tried to bump me if we had been just ordinary private dicks workin' on this case sounds goddam silly to me!

What the hell!

Another thing—what about the Juanella Rillwater angle? Here is another dame who is gettin' in my hair. Where does Juanella come into the set-up?

Work it out: Nobody except old Willis Perriner and the F.B.I. know that I am comin' over here on the *Fels Ronstrom* as Cyrus T. Hickory. O.K. Well I send that radio off the boat to Geraldine an' I send one to Rodney Wilks at the Hotel Rondeau where he is stayin'. Juanella is aboard too an' she may have recognised me, but she hadn't sent any radios off about the fact otherwise Larssen would have told me. Yet within a coupla hours of my radio goin' off somebody signin' himself "The Boy Friend" radios Juanella an' tells her to contact me because they are curious about me. An' where do we go from there!

If this ain't a screwy case, then I am William the Conqueror's aunt.

The only possible explanation is that "The Boy Friend" is Nako-rova, an' that when Geraldine told him about my radio he immediately sent off that message to Juanella. But even if this is right what good would that do him. If he an' Edvanne had already arranged to bump Rodney an' me off why the hell should he worry to tell Juanella to contact me because he is curious about me?

I reckon that when I get my hooks on Juanella I am goin' to have a little talk with that dame that she will remember—*plenty*!

I am just gettin' myself outa bed when there is a knock at the door an' Erouard comes in. If you took a quick look at this guy an' remembered that he was a policeman you would think that you was dreamin' an' that he is anythin' else but. He is thin an' wears glasses an' has a little beard that sorta sticks out, but he is a good guy an' knows his stuff.

I worked with Erouard one time on a counterfeitin' case with a Paris angle an' we got on swell because he is a guy with imagination an' if you've got that you've got everythin'.

He sits down an' I ring for another cup an' give him some coffee an' a cigarette. He puts his head on one side an' starts talkin'.

"Mon vieux," he says, "I have had a long talk this mornin' with the Prefect of Police, and he is prepared to do what you want. Of course he was not particularly pleased at the idea of allowing the Nakorova woman to remain at large, but I was able to persuade him that the process was necessary for your plan."

"That's swell," I tell him. "So the set-up is like we arranged."

"Precisely," he says. "To-day, in the quietest possible manner I shall endeavour to make the fullest investigations into the French backgrounds of Sergius and Edvanne Nakorova. I have already given instructions that a discreet operative of the Sûreté shall endeavour to find out where Juanella Rillwater is staying and to keep observation on her. Any information that comes to me I shall immediately send to you."

I say thanks a lot. He has another cigarette an' a drink an' he scrams.

I go over an' look outa the window. Outside I can see the sun shinin' an' one or two nice-lookin' dames walkin' on the other side of the road. I wonder why it is that dames always look so much better when there's a war on. I suppose there must be a reason for it. One day when I get some time I will try an' figure it out.

Lookin' outa the window I reckon it is a bad thing for any guy to be kickin' around in a hotel bedroom at this time of the day. It is one of them nice snappy days when a guy oughta be out an' his brain workin'. That is what I think.

So havin' thought this I then go back to bed.

I get up at half-past three, give myself a shower an' stick around till the doctor comes to take a look at my arm. He says that everything is doin' swell an' that he reckons that in a day or two I will be able to do without the sling.

Just after he has gone the telephone bell rings. It is Erouard.

Erouard says that his guy has picked up Juanella Rillwater. This baby is livin' at a very nice hotel—the Hotel St. Anne on the Rue St. Anne. An' he also tells me that although she checked in herself at eleven o'clock this morning, the hotel sent down to the station for her luggage the night before. So this shows me that the story Juanella told me about staying in Le Havre last night was just hooey. It looks like she came on the train that arrived half an hour after mine, bringin' her luggage with her, went off somewhere else for the night an' checked in at the Hotel St. Anne this mornin'. I know this is a fact because there was no early train from Le Havre this mornin', an' if she'd come up by car the night before she'd have taken her luggage to the hotel with her. I get the idea inta my head that I will have a few words with Juanella.

I finish dressin' an' give myself a shot of brandy, after which I grab a cab an' I go round to the Hotel St. Anne. I tell the reception that I am Mr. Cyrus T. Hickory an' that I would like to see Mrs. Juanella Rillwater. They ring through to her on the telephone an' she says go right up. I go up in the lift to the first floor. We go along the passage an' a page opens the door for me. I go in.

Juanella is certainly doin' herself very nicely. She has got a big sittin'-room with a connectin' door that looks as if it leads to her bedroom an' bath. She is standin' in front of the window an' she is dressed like she always dresses when she is out to make a killin'. She is wearin' a very well-tailored blue suit that looks as if it had been stuck on to her with a paste pot, a big double fox fur an' a little tailored hat over one eye.

Her eyes are bright an' sparkling an' she looks a hundred per cent. She gives me a big grin.

"How's Mr. Hickory?" she says. She walks over to me. "Would you like a little drink, Lemmy?"

I put my hat on the chair.

"Now listen to me, baby," I tell her. "First of all I want to tell you that I do not want any funny stuff from you. Secondly, I would like to point out to you that just because you an' that husband of yours—Larvey—gave me a hand last year over that poison-gas case, an' have behaved yourselves more or less decently ever since *so far as I know,* does not alter the fact that you two are a couple of big-time crooks. Another thing is, who told you you could call me Lemmy, an' lastly I will have that drink you was talkin' about, an' make it rye."

"O.K.," she says. "You know I'd do anything you tell me any time, sweetie-pie, because I go for you like hell, an' because when you are around there is no other man in the world for me, an' if you don't want me to call you Lemmy I won't. Is that O.K., Lemmy?"

She goes over to the sideboard an' opens it. Inside I can see two or three bottles of brandy, some gin an' a lot of rye. It looks as if Juanella has laid in stores for a long siege. She makes the drinks an' brings mine over to me. Then she sticks a cigarette in her mouth an' lights it. She gives it to me. This is the sorta fresh thing that this dame does an' she does it in such a sweet sorta way that you can't even do anything about it. She throws off her furs, takes her hat off an' stands in front of the big mirror pattin' her hair.

"O.K.," I tell her. "You don't have to do that. I knew you had a nice figure without you havin' to go through all them contortions. Another thing," I go on, "I think it is time that you and I had a show-down."

She turns around.

"O.K.," she says. "I'm for that. An' I would like to tell you this here an' now, Mr. Hickory, so far as I am concerned, you have got to be one of two people an' I don't mind which. If you are being Cyrus T. Hickory of the Transcontinental Detective Agency, then so far as I am concerned you got to be very polite because I do not like private dicks very much."

She sits down an' shoots me a little grin.

"If you are being Lemmy," she says—"the big-hearted 'G' man who has got something—I *might* talk turkey with you."

"Oh, you might, might you?" I tell her. "Juanella, I reckon you've got enough nerve to run a mental home."

"That's as maybe," she says, "but that's how it is."

"All right," I say. "First of all I wanta know what you are doin' over here."

She looks at me. She has got a sorta innocent look on her face which is almost heart-breakin'.

"I'll tell you something, Lemmy," she says. "Between you an' me and the doorpost I do not know why I'm over here. I would like to know myself. But," she says, an' her smile sorta deepens, "I'd like to take you up on a crack you made last night. You said I hadn't got any right to be over here, that I had no right to be outa the jurisdiction of the Federal Court because I was an accessory to that job of Larvey's, an' because we are both under suspended sentences. Well, you're wrong, I got permission. See?"

"Oh, yes?" I tell her. "I bet you have. Me—I would like to be able to tell lies like you do."

You guys will realise that I find it very difficult to believe that Juanella has got this permission, because anybody who is under a suspended sentence is not supposed to go out of the jurisdiction of the Federal Court without permission, an' do not get that permission, unless they have got some very big guy rootin' for 'em, an' unless there is a very big reason for it.

"Who is the guy who got you permission, Juanella?" I ask her.

"Wouldn't you like to know?" she says. "An' I tell you this here an' now—that I'm not tellin' you. I will also tell you something else," she says. "I would like to point out to you that *you* are also out of the jurisdiction of the Federal Government. This is Paris, France, sweetheart. My passport's in order an' I am entitled to be here, an' I don't have to sit around in my own sittin'-room being cross-examined by a big flat-foot like you, an' how do you like them apples?"

Me—I am beginnin' to get very annoyed because it looks like this dame is takin' me for a ride. At the same time she is right. If I want to put the screws on Juanella I have got to get the French police to help me, an' I have got to have a very good an' sufficient reason, because this dame is not the sorta baby who will take anything lyin' down. On the slightest provocation she will start shoutin' the odds which is a thing I do not want. I think maybe I'd better try an' play this quietly.

"Look, honey," I tell her, "I think you are a great dame. You're the sort of dame that if I was a guy who went for women I would go for you so hard that you would think there was a *blitzkrieg* on. But I am not like that. I do not go for dames."

She tosses her head.

"Hear me laugh," she says. "So you don't go for dames. Well, if you don't, then Romeo was a sissy. What about that dame Georgette last year? An' what about . . . ?"

"Now lay off, honey," I tell her. "That was business. When I am makin' an investigation it is sometimes part of my job to give the impression that I am a bit stuck on a dame. After all that's bein' an investigator."

"Like hell it is," she says. "Because if that is so I would like to know when you are goin' to get around to doin' a little investigation on me. Up to now I personally have not noticed any of this love stuff from you. I would also like to know what any other dame that you have ever met up with has got that I have not got plenty of."

"Look, Juanella," I tell her, "what are you gettin' so steamed up about? You got everything. You know it. An' your husband is very fond of you."

"O.K.," she says. "So where does that get me? Can't a girl have a little change? I read in some book that every woman has to relax *sometimes*."

I have already got wise to the fact that Juanella has taken the conversation right out of my hands an' is stringin' me along. I can see that this dame is tryin' to get me off askin' questions.

"Look, Juanella," I tell her, "let you an' me get down to cases. I do not want to have any trouble with you, but you know me. I'm a tough guy when I am on a job an' I am on one right now." I stub out my cigarette. "If I want to make trouble for you over here I can do it, an' you know it. If I like to go to the French police an' tell them that you are Juanella Rillwater with a record very nearly as long as my arm, the fact that you are a sweet-lookin' dame who looks as if butter wouldn't melt in her mouth is not goin' to help you very much. I reckon these French dicks would hold you for extradition if I asked them to."

"Oh yeah!" she says. "An' what would the charge be?" She grins. "I'd have a lovely story for 'em," she says. "I'd tell 'em that you came around here an' tried to make me, but I fought for my honour because I loved Larvey. So you got nasty an' tried to turn me in. An' how do you like *them* apples?"

I give a big sigh because I'm tellin' you guys that she would do it just as soon as take a look at you.

"All right," I tell her. "Let you an' I stop threatenin' each other for a minute an' try an' get on with this business. There is one question I would like to ask you, an' if you answer it the right way I'm prepared to lay off an' not worry you at all."

"The question bein' what?" she says.

"Look," I tell her, "last night I sent two radios off from the *Fels Ronstrom*—two radios to Paris—one of 'em to one person sayin' I would be in a certain place at twelve-thirty, the other to a guy tellin' him to be there. Well, before we docked you got a radio. That radio was sent by somebody who knew that I was aboard the *Fels Ronstrom,* somebody who said they was curious about me, somebody who asked you to contact me. Well, you didn't contact me, the reason bein' that after you got the radio you went diggin' around to find who Mr. Cyrus T. Hickory was, an' the first thing you know is that he is Lemmy Caution. This gives you a little bit of a surprise, so you kept outa my way, an' if I hadn't come along an' done that big croonin' act you woulda kept outa my way.

"Now here are the questions. First of all who was it sent you that radio, an' secondly what did you do when you got here last night? Did you go along an' meet up with that guy an' tell him what you knew. Did you tell him that Cyrus T. Hickory was an F.B.I. operative named Lemmy Caution?"

She gets up. She walks over to the sideboard an' she gives herself a shot of rye an' a cigarette. She lights the cigarette sorta slow. She is doin' some heavy thinkin'.

"Look, Lemmy," she says, "I'm not talkin'. But I will tell you this much. I was plenty surprised to get that radio on the *Fels Ronstrom* myself. I don't say that I am gonna do anything about it, an' I don't say that I'm not. Up to the moment since I been here I haven't seen the guy who sent that radio or anybody else except the hotel people here an' you, an' I have not told anybody you are a 'G' man. Beyond that I'm not sayin' a goddam word an' you can do what you like. See, honeybunch?"

She comes over an' stands in front of me lookin' down on me. Then she starts smilin'. She looks as pretty as paint. She is a saucy dish.

"Look, big-boy," she says, "you can do what you like, any time you like, but I'm still not talkin'! Also," she goes on, plantin' herself on my knee an' puttin' one arm round my neck, "I'd like to tell you this one, an' for once in your life you can believe what I say. If you start musclin' in tryin' to get next to what I am at an' generally tryin' clever stuff you'll be sorry. See?"

She puts her other arm around my neck an' gives me a kiss that hits me right outa the field for a home run. Then she gets up an' goes over to the window an' stands there lookin' at me lookin' like the cat who has just swallowed a coupla canaries.

What is a guy to do with this dame?

I get up.

"O.K., Juanella," I tell her. "So you are bein' tough. You better look out for yourself, honey. You're takin' chances an' if you ain't careful you'll get your feet wet."

She says: "Me . . . I do not like bein' careful. Also I am fulla sex antagonism about you because I am nutty about you, Mr. Caution—like I always have been. But I am not goin' to talk to you—well, not yet. How come," she goes on, "that I should be butchered to make a Roman holiday?"

"All right," I tell her. "Have it your own way, but if you cut across what I am doin' you will not only be butchered to make a Roman holiday but I will also take a size nine slipper to you where you will feel it plenty. I would go so far as to say that when I get through with you you would be forced to maintain the perpendicular position for about a fortnight."

She starts comin' over to me. Her eyes are blazin'.

"I see," she says, sorta ominous. "So you're goin' to get rough with me. You'd even go so far as to give me a good smackin'!"

The angry look fades off her face an' she starts smilin'. She looks sorta dreamy.

"Oh boy," she says, "would I love it or would I? Any time you feel that way, Lemmy, just call through!"

She takes a coupla steps towards me an' I pick up my hat an' make for the door.

I give up.

Well, I reckon that I have not done so well with Juanella. I am intrigued with that dame's attitude because the way she is behavin' gives me the idea that she thinks she has got a trump card somewhere that she can use if I try to force her hand. Juanella has got her nerve all right but she knows just as well as I do that she cannot afford to get funny with me, that I can make things good an' hot for her an' her husband when she gets back to the United States—unless she has got somethin' in the bag.

An' I have got to get next to that somethin'.

It is a swell day an' I go walkin' along, lookin' at the dames an' thinkin' that life would be very swell if I was not always chasin' around tryin' to find somebody who is up to their neck in crime, mayhem an' what-have-you-got. I suppose this is sorta natural just as every guy always wishes that he was doin' anythin' else except his own job.

Me—I am just a little bit worried about this case. Because I reckon that I don't know anythin' about it at all. I know just about as much as I did when I was on the *Fels Ronstrom,* an' exceptin' for the fact that Rodney Wilks is laid out down in the Montmartre morgue an' that sweet baby Edvanne has took a poke at me I might just as well be sittin' back in the old homestead smokin' Lucky Stripes an' playin' sweet hotcha on the uke. That bein' a habit of mine when there is nothin' doin'.

I stroll along lookin' in the store windows but I am not seein' anythin' much. I have got an idea that I will have to start somethin' in this case because it has always been a habit of mine to start somethin' goin' whenever it looks like I am stuck.

I get around to thinkin' about Geraldine Perriner. Here is a honey-lamb who might be anythin' you like. Is she on the up-an'-up? Is she really so nutty about this Nakorova guy that she will do any goddam thing to get him an' try an' keep him? Or is she playin' his hand against her old man's and ours? I would give somethin' to know whether she is wise to what has happened to Buddy or not.

I get a flash. Maybe this idea will show me somethin'! I grab myself a cab an' I go around to the American Express. I show the Manager my badge an' send a cable in code. Here it is:

Director Federal Bureau of Investigation
Department of Justice Washington U.S.A.

Request rush me following information what is financial standing of Geraldine Perriner in Paris stop What money or credits had she when she left New York stop Is Larvey Rillwater in New York stop Why did Passport Office issue passport for France to Juanella Rillwater now under Federal Court suspended sentence stop Situation

*here vague stop Rodney Wilks permanently laid off stop Cooper-
ation of French police secured through U.S. Embassy stop Request
further instructions stop Caution F.B.I. Identification B47 stop End.*

The Manager is a good guy. He tells me that he will telephone
this cable an' will rush a reply around to my hotel.

I start strollin' again. I light a cigarette an' feel better because
anyhow I am gettin' some sorta action. I now think that I will start
work on the second idea I have got in my head. I stop a cab an' tell
the guy to take me around to the Hotel Dieudonne.

I reckon I am goin' to pull a fast one on Geraldine!

Me—I always seem to be sittin' down lookin' at some dame.

I am sorta balanced on the edge of a chair in Geraldine's suite
at the Hotel Dieudonne. I am tryin' very hard to look like Cyrus T.
Hickory an' I have got the sorta expression on my face that I reckon
he would have if he was tryin' for a touch.

It is gettin' dark. Geraldine is drawin' the curtains in front of
the big windows. She looks swell. I like the way she moves an' I
am stuck on the clothes she is wearin'. She has got on a black sorta
afternoon frock, very plain an' close fittin' with beige stockin's an'
black georgette shoes with four-inch heels. It is a funny thing but it
is marvellous what a pretty foot an' a high heel will do for a dame.

But the best thing about her is her hair. She is a true blonde an'
the colour of her hair never come out of any bottle. She has got it
dressed up high in the front an' fallin' over her shoulders at the back
caught up in a black ribbon. I'm tellin' you guys that there are plenty
of fellas I know woulda paid fifty cents just to take a look at her.

Me . . . I am lookin' sorta diffident an' nervous. This is not easy
but I am doin' the best I can. Also I am thinkin' very hard about
that screwy story I told this dame yesterday about havin' a wife in
Milwaukee an' seven kids. I hope that she has fallen for this one, an'
I am trying goddam hard to look like the sorta guy who has a wife in
Milwaukee an' seven kids, which is a difficult thing because I have
never seen a guy like this so far as I know.

I am holdin' my hat in my hands an' I begin to twist it like I have
seen nervous guys do.

I say: "I reckon I was pretty pleased at you sorta bein' interested in my wife an' kids, Miss Perriner. I didn't want to talk about 'em last night because I was a bit tired. You sayin' that I didn't get a proper deal from the Transcontinental Agency sorta got me thinkin'."

She turns around from the window. She stands there with the beige-coloured curtain draped behind her. She is smilin' an' there is a nice expression in her eyes.

"Just because I want so badly to be married myself, Mr. Hickory," she says, "I feel for anyone who *is* married. Your wife must feel your absence a lot."

I nod.

"I suppose she does," I say. "But there it is. We're sorta used to bein' separated."

She didn't say anything for a minute. Then:

"I imagine if you had your way—if it were possible—you'd like to give up this private detective business and go back home," she says.

I nod my head again.

"You're tellin' me," I say. "There is a corner drug store in my home town that I could buy—if I had the jack. Gee . . . would I like to settle down there an' operate it. You can have all your detective business. Me—I would sooner be sellin' aspirin an' fixin' sodas."

She leans forward. Her eyes are shinin'.

"Look, Mr. Hickory," she says. "I don't see any reason why you shouldn't have your drug store. Why not?"

I grin.

"Why not!" I say. "Where does a guy like me get ten thousand dollars from?"

She gets up. She goes over an' stands in front of the fire with her hands held behind her. She looks as sweet as sugar.

"You get it from me," she says.

She waits a minute to let that sink inta Mr. Cyrus T. Hickory's head, an' then she goes on:

"Mr. Hickory. Let you and me play ball. I have a suggestion to make. I have already told you that I am perfectly satisfied with Sergius: that I am certain about his character, his morals and his background. I am also certain that he is sufficiently well-off to look after me if my father should cut off my allowance. Well . . . here is my proposition:

"I propose to hand you now the sum of fifty thousand francs. To-night I will make arrangements for you to meet Sergius. You will meet him and you will form your own opinion of him. I know that opinion will be a good one. You will then return immediately to New York and report that I am determined to marry Sergius. You will also tell my father that in your opinion Sergius is a man of good character who is likely to make me a good husband. Well . . . is that a deal?"

I get up.

I say: "Is it a deal? It's swell business. When can I touch for the dough?"

She smiles at me. She is lookin' pleased but it sorta seems to me that the pleased look is artificial. That underneath maybe she is a bit worried.

She says: "I have the money here. I'll get it for you. Please wait a minute."

She goes out of the room. I light myself a cigarette. It looks like bein' Mr. Cyrus T. Hickory would be a profitable business. I mean if I *was* that guy.

After a bit she comes back. She hands me a packet of French dough. I am very glad to see that the notes are new. She gives me fifty one-thousand franc notes.

"Nice work, Miss Perriner," I tell her. "For dough like this I would report anything you like on anybody you like. But just to make the book right I would like to take one little peek at your boy friend. Just so's I can tell your Pa that I've actually contacted him and talked to him."

"Of course," she says. "Tell me where I can get in touch with you and I will arrange that you meet him to-night."

I give her my address an' she writes it down.

Then she puts out her hand.

"Goodbye for the present," she says. "I feel certain that I can rely on you."

"Absolutely," I tell her. "I'm carryin' out my part of the bargain as sure as my name's Hickory."

We shake hands and I scram.

Outside I do a big grin. So it came off. I grab myself a cab an' I shoot round to the Sûreté Nationale. I send in my name an' go up to

Erouard's office. He is sittin' behind his desk lookin' like a college professor with his little beard stickin' out an' a smile on his pan.

I put my hand in my pocket an' I pull out the fifty one-thousand franc notes that Geraldine has just given me.

"Look, Erouard," I tell him. "I just got these notes from Geraldine Perriner. They're dead new. They just come outa some bank. O.K. Well, you tell me where she got 'em from."

He rings a bell.

"Mon vieux," he says. "*That* is very simple."

So that's that.

CHAPTER FIVE
TEA FOR THREE

AFTER I have left Erouard I take a walk an' go into some café bar an' give myself a vermouth-cassis. It is by now six o'clock. Then I grab a cab an' drive around to the Hotel Rondeau—the place where Rodney Wilks was stayin'.

This dump is on the Boulevard St. Michel. It is a quiet sorta family pension that nobody wouldn't notice much.

I go in and ask for the proprietor. After a minute some plump dame comes out an' asks me what I want. I show her the police pass that Erouard has given me an' I say that I have come to collect Mr. Wilks' things an' to pay his bill, because he will not be comin' back there.

She says this suits her all right an' she takes me upstairs an' opens the door of a room on the second floor. I see Wilks' suitcase standin' in a corner an' I grab it an' put it on the bed and start takin' his things outa the wardrobe. She watches me for a minute, then she gives me a grin an' says that she is busy an' that I can see her later in the office when I am through. Then she scrams.

I stop doin' the packin' act an' take a look round. I open a coupla drawers an' by the look of this room it is as plain as peanuts that somebody has been here before me an' given the place the once-over. Rodney was the tidiest guy that ever happened. He was so goddam tidy that he got on your nerves. He was the sorta guy who usta go around stubbin' out cigarette ends an' puttin' 'em in the ash-trays just because he was like that.

But all his drawers are in disorder. Things are chucked all over the place. In the wardrobe there are a coupla suits with the sleeves turned inside out an' the linin' edgin's slit where somebody has been tryin' to see if Rodney had got somethin' hidden up between the cloth and the linin'.

Over in one corner is a little writin' table. I go over an' take a peek an' I can see where some guy has torn off the top sheet of blottin'-paper off the blotter. I suppose they wanted to see if they could read what Rodney had been writin'. I reckon they will be unlucky.

So it looks to me more than ever that Rodney had got wise to somethin', an' it is also pretty clear that some other guys was wise to the fact that he had. I reckon this business is gettin' to be more like a Chinese puzzle every minute.

Hangin' on the wall over the mantelpiece is a sort of carved bracket for puttin' papers in. I go over an' I see stuck in this bracket two or three letters in envelopes addressed to Rodney at the Rondeau. One is a bill from the cleaners, an' there is a letter from some library on the Rue Clichy an' some odd papers he has stuck there an' which the guys who have been searchin' around have not worried about. I take out these envelopes an' things an' I switch on the electric light over the writin' table an' sit down an' take a close look at 'em. Written on the back of one of the envelopes in Rodney's handwritin' are some words that I cannot get:

"Before seven. Will you have it straight? And how much?"

Now I wonder what the hell this is supposed to mean—that is if it means anything. Because Rodney is not the sorta guy who wastes time writin' things on the back of envelopes just to pass the time away.

I stick this envelope in my pocket an' I put the rest of the papers back where they were. I reckon that there is no good my searchin' around here because if there was anything interestin' in this dump the other guys will have got it first.

I take Rodney's clothes and stuff an' pack 'em up in the suitcase. I take it downstairs an' pay the fat dame off an' tell her that I will send somebody around to pick up the suitcase. After which she asks me if I think America is comin' inta the War an' I tell her that I have not yet decided but when I have I will write her about it.

She tells me I am a fathead, an' I crack back at her that if her head was the only fat thing about her she would maybe have somethin' on Mae West.

I start walkin' back towards my hotel an' I am wonderin' what the devil Rodney meant by writin' those words on the back of that envelope. You can bet your life that he did not write those words down for the purpose of rememberin' them because he has a memory like an elephant. So he wrote 'em down because he wanted somebody to see 'em, an' they must have meant somethin'. I would like to know why he did this because when I think about the words: *"Before seven—will you have it straight? And how much?"* they don't seem to make a lotta sense. Except for the remarks about the time, the other things are the things you say if you are askin' a guy to have a drink.

When I get back to the hotel one of Erouard's guys is waitin' for me with a packet. Inside the packet are the fifty 1,000-franc notes with Erouard an' a note which says:

My dear Lemmy—We have traced these notes very easily. They were drawn this morning from the Credit Lyonnais on the Rue Henri Martin. The account is that of Colonel Sergius Nakorova and it was his cheque which was cashed.

I am at your disposal—Sincerely,

Felix Erouard.

So there you are. Now we know which way we're pointin'. It is stickin' out a foot that first thing this mornin' Geraldine Perriner has got in touch with Nakorova an' told him that she reckons I am a guy who can be grafted, that she's gotta have some dough. An' he cashes in with the 50,000 francs. But whether this dough is his, or whether it is money which she has given him which he had paid inta his bankin' account, I shall not know until I have received a reply from Washington.

Anyway Geraldine an' Sergius have got to be pretty thick with each other for her to be able to touch him for 50,000 francs. So it looks to me as if she is playin' along with this guy. It looks at if he has got her so bull-dozed that she will stick at nothing. This does not surprise me a great deal because I have already told you guys that when a woman is really stuck on a man there are not many things she won't do for him.

I go up to my room an' give myself four fingers of rye an' lie down on the bed. My arm is achin' a little bit an' anyway it looks as if I will not be wastin' my time in doin' a little quiet thinkin'. Also it looks as if it is not goin' to be very much good lettin' the grass grow under my feet. I have gotta do something.

It is stickin' outa mile that if I go on bein' Mr. Cyrus T. Hickory Geraldine will expect me to have one meetin' with the Nakorova bird an' then scram off to New York, that being the arrangement we made. In other words if I don't come out inta the open, then that baby will believe that I am not keepin' the arrangement an' will get suspicious. If she gets suspicious it is a cinch that she will tell the Russian an' they will probably scram off some place, leavin' me up in the air. So I gotta do something. I reckon I will do it.

I get up an' start puttin' on my overcoat. I am just goin' to the door when the telephone rings. The desk downstairs tells me that Colonel Sergius Nakorova is on the telephone. I say O.K., that I will take the call. I hang on, waitin'. After a minute a big boomin' voice comes through the 'phone. It is one of them rich an' fruity sorta voices that are hearty an' good-tempered an' strong, the sorta voice that you'd expect to hear from a sporty sorta guy. Standin' there I can imagine this boyo openin' his mouth very wide every time he says a word an' rollin' it round his tongue before he shoots it out.

"That is Mr. Hickory?" he says. "Very well, I wish to present myself. I am Colonel Count Sergius Alexandrieff Nakorova—at your service!!"

I can almost hear him clickin' his heels.

He goes on that he wishes to apologise for telephonin' me, that he would have liked to have called round at my hotel personally, but that he is on his way out to Auteuil and will not be back until to-night.

"Well, Colonel," I say, "I reckon that by now you know what I am over here for."

He says yes he knows what I'm over here for. He says he welcomes me bein' over here. He says that the fact that Willis Perriner—his fiancée's father—is suspicious of him is causin' him the greatest pain. He says he desires nothing so much as for me to be able to assure Willis Perriner that everything is on order, an' that nothing but good can result from the marriage which he hopes will shortly take place.

I say that's fine, but I am thinkin' that the probability is that Geraldine has already been on to this guy an' told him that I have taken the dough an' that I am playin' ball, so he is not worryin' very much. He is just puttin' on this act so as to keep everything nice and sweet.

Then he says: "Mr. Hickory, to-night I desire to give a party in your honour. It will also give you an opportunity of talking to me and finding out what you desire about me and my associates. I do not think that you will have an uninteresting evening. There will be some charming women there who I am sure will be delighted to meet you."

I say that is swell, that I would like nothing better than that, an' he asks me to be at the Café Cossack near the Place Pigalle at eleven o'clock to-night. That he has got a private room an' a special supper ordered, that he is lookin' forward to seein' me there. He says that he hopes that this won't be too late for me, but that he reckons he won't be back from Auteuil till then.

I say that's O.K., thanks a lot, an' hang up.

I give myself a cigarette an' indulge in a little thought. If this guy is telling me the truth, an' I don't see why he should be lyin'—an' is goin' out to Auteuil an' not comin' back until this supper date we have got, then unless Geraldine is goin' out there with him it looks as if he might be able to have a little talk with this dame before he can get at her.

I go downstairs an' order a taxi. When it comes I drive round to the Hotel Dieudonne. When I get there I ask the guy in the reception if Miss Perriner is in. He says he'll ring through an' find out. I pull out my police pass an' say that that's just what I don't want him to do, that I want to know if she is in or not. He says she is in, that she rang down a few minutes ago for some tea. I say all right, I will go up, but I do not want to be announced.

I go up in the lift and walk along the corridor. When I get to the door of Geraldine's sittin'-room, I listen. There is some talk goin' on inside. I can just hear the voices. I grin to myself because I recognise one of 'em as being Juanella's. I open the door an' I step inta the room.

"Well, honeylambs!" I tell 'em. "How's it goin'?"

Geraldine an' Juanella are sittin' down one on each side of a tea table. Geraldine is pourin' out some tea. She looks so goddam surprised when she sees me that she nearly drops the teapot.

"Mr. Hickory," she says, "I'm delighted to see you, but how strange that they didn't call through and tell me you were on your way up."

I put my hat down on a chair an' light a cigarette. I grin at her.

"I didn't want to be announced, Miss Perriner," I tell her, "an' I am very glad I wasn't. I reckon if I had been Mrs. Rillwater would have slipped out the back way.

"An' by the way," I go on, "I thought you told me that you didn't know this dame, that you'd never met her."

"That was perfectly true, Mr. Hickory," she says. "I *had* never met her. I have only just met her. Incidentally," she says, "aren't you being a bit odd about this? I thought you and I understood each other. I thought we were going to deal with this matter in a friendly spirit."

"Like hell," I tell her. "That's what *you* thought."

I sit down.

"Look, Geraldine," I go on, "it looks to me like you thought a lotta things an' most of 'em are wrong. An' also I'd like to tell you that the deal you made with Mr. Cyrus T. Hickory of the Transcontinental Agency of America is off. He can't keep to that deal because he's dead."

"Dead!" she says. "What is this? Is this a joke?"

I look at Juanella. She is sittin' there smokin' a cigarette with her legs crossed. She looks quite happy. It looks like Juanella does not give one hoot about anything.

"No, it's no joke," I tell Geraldine. "You see, the point is there never was a Mr. Cyrus Hickory. Juanella here knows me. My name's Lemmy Caution. I'm a 'G' man, an operative of the Federal Bureau of Investigation, an' how do you like that, lady?"

She goes as white as death. She looks at Juanella with her mouth open. Juanella shrugs her shoulders. I put my hand in my pocket an' I bring out the fifty 1,000-franc notes. I put 'em on the table.

"There you are, Geraldine," I tell her. "There's your dough. I took it because I wanted to find out where it came from. Well, I have found out. That dough was drawn this morning outa your boy friend Nakorova's bankin' account, an' it looks to me like first thing this mornin' you rang him up, told him that Cyrus T. Hickory was easy, that if he had a little palm grease he'd do anything he was told. He sent you round that jack an' you both thought that everything was hunky dory."

Geraldine looks straight in front of her.

She says: "I see . . . I see . . ."

"Honey," I tell her, "you take a tip from me an' get yourself some sense. Me—I reckon I can understand almost anything, an' I can certainly understand you bein' so stuck on this Russian guy that you don't know what you're doin'. But after this bribery business it looks to me as if Willis T. Perriner might not be so far wrong when he believed that there was some connection between your marriage with Nakorova an' Buddy's disappearin'. Maybe you don't know anything about that. Maybe if somebody was to tell you you wouldn't believe them, because you're so stuck on this Russian guy. But you gotta watch your step, an' I want you to get this inside that pretty little head of yours. You're not goin' to marry that Russian guy until I am satisfied with the job an' it won't be Mr. Hickory who is bein' satisfied either, it will be Mr. Caution, an' Mr. Caution is a tough guy."

She tosses her head.

"Not only a tough guy," she says, "but it seems a rather uncouth one."

She turns round to me an' her eyes are blazin'.

"I would like you to know, Mr. Caution," she says, "that I am free, white and over twenty-one. I'm entitled to do what I like. I'm going to marry Sergius Nakorova, and nothing you, the Federal Bureau of Investigation or my father, can do will stop me."

I'm tellin' you this dame Geraldine is angry an' when she looks angry she looks swell. It's a funny thing but I always go for dames when they are gettin' steamed up about something. It sorta gives 'em character plus.

I take a look at Juanella. She is still sittin' back in her chair smokin' a cigarette. She looks as if she's a bit amused at all this. I think I would like to know what that baby has got up her sleeve.

I stub out my cigarette end. I go over to the table.

"Look, Geraldine," I say, "let me tell you something. Don't you get the idea into your head that you're marryin' Nakorova because you're not. You say that none of us can stop you doin' it. You're wrong, I can. I'm goin' to."

"How interesting," she says sorta icy. "And may I ask how you're going to do that?"

"Just a little thing called international police courtesy," I tell her. "If I go an' have ten minutes at the Sûreté Nationale, there is nobody in Paris would marry you. They'd put the bar up."

She shrugs her shoulders.

"I see," she said. "So you'd go as far as that. Well, even if you succeeded—and I don't believe you'd be successful, Mr. Caution—although you might stop me marrying Sergius, you certainly *will not* stop me joining him. In any event I shall do that."

"I certainly would stop you joinin' him," I tell her, "because even if I have to stick that Russian teacake inta the local clink on a framed charge to stop you gettin' next to him I'm goin' to do it, an' how do you like that?"

She sits down in her chair again. Her shoulders are sorta droopin'. She looks at Juanella.

"This is terrible," she says. "What are we going to do?"

Juanella looks at her. She gives a little grin, a comfortin' sorta grin. Then she stubs out her cigarette end in the ash-tray. She gets up, picks up her gloves an' handbag off the chair beside her, an' says:

"I don't see you can do anything, Geraldine. This guy's tough."

She opens her handbag an' takes out her lipstick. Then she says to me:

"But maybe I can do something."

She puts the lipstick back in the bag an' when her hand comes out she's got a gun in it, an' the barrel is pointin' at my stomach.

"Look, Lemmy," says Juanella, "you know me. I'm nice with a gun. Take your weight off your feet, big boy, an' sit down, because you're goin' to do what you're told."

I sit down in the chair that is close up to the table between these two dames an' I look at 'em. Geraldine is sittin' lookin' at Juanella with a sorta hopeful look on her pan. When I look at Juanella I can see she is smilin' but I don't reckon that this means very much because I have known dames who could squeeze a mean trigger even if they was laughin' out loud.

I take a cigarette outa the box on the tea-table an' I light it.

Juanella says: "Look, Lemmy, even if you don't like this you gotta play this thing our way. Believe it or not it's not possible for you to go around makin' any excitements for just a little bit. An' it won't be healthy for you."

I give her a big grin.

"Listen, Juanella," I tell her. "Why don't you put that shootin' iron away an' be your age. I have already promised you a good smackin' an' it looks as if it's comin' nearer to you every minute. Get wise, baby. Another thing," I go on. "What is all this stuff? Have you two dames gone nutty or what?"

"Not so nutty as that," says Juanella. "The point is we want a little peace an' quiet for a coupla days, an' we're goin' to get it one way or the other. I reckon that if we have about forty-eight hours without you kickin' around we can maybe do what we want to do."

"Which is to get this dame married to Nakorova," I say. "All right, Juanella, but you remember that one of these fine days you are goin' back to New York an' when you do am I goin' to stick you right in the cooler or am I?"

She says: "Nuts to you, you big gorilla. Button up your trap for a minute while I do a little thinkin'."

I stay quiet. It looks to me as if Geraldine is worried sick about not marryin' this Cossack, but at the same time I do not see why Juanella should have to pull a gun on me just because it looks as if I am goin' to stop this marriage.

Juanella gets herself a fresh cigarette with her free hand. She lights it an' blows a coupla smoke rings an' then she says:

"I reckon that we oughta be tough with you, Lemmy. You pulled a fast one on Geraldine here when she trusted you. You told her you was Hickory an' also a lotta punk stuff about bein' a married guy with seven kids in Milwaukee. You gave her the idea that she could slip you a little dough an' that you would behave yourself an' go back to New York an' keep Willis Perriner quiet. Instead of which what do you do? You come bustin' in here pullin' a threatenin' act like you was a coupla dictators with enlarged livers."

I shrug my shoulders.

"The trouble with you dames is," I say, "that you will not play ball. What the hell is all this mystery about? Why don't you put your cards on the table? First of all I wanta know what you are doin' in this set-up, Juanella, an' if you don't like to tell me I'll find out some other way. The second this is why Geraldine here tries to bribe me to get out when she thought I was Hickory. Is she so struck on that Russian guy that she has to sorta employ you as a muscle-man? Me—I think you two dames are screwy."

"Yeah?" says Juanella. "Well, maybe we are but just for the minute we are gonna stay that way."

"O.K.," I tell her. "That's all right with me." I stub out my ciga-rette. "Now," I go on, "I want you two dames to listen to what I've gotta say. You're both playin' a mug's game. Last night I pulled into this town to do a little investigatin' inta this Nakorova boyo. Well, I'm still goin' to do it. An' I'm goin' to do it in my own way. The second thing is that there is a whole lot of funny business goin' on that I cannot get next to. An' it is also quite obvious to me that I cannot trust either of you dames any more. So I am not goin' to."

"Oh no?" says Juanella. "Well, right now what are you gonna do, handsome?"

I don't say anythin' for a minute because I have already made up my mind what I'm goin' to do. I am sittin' up close to the tea-table which is one of them light, three-legged things. On the table is a big silver tray with a silver hot-water kettle an' a spirit flame burnin' under it.

I also begin to think of Edvanne Nakorova an' that ladder-in-the-stockin' act. I grin.

"The position is like this," I tell 'em. "Not so long ago I had a little talk with Sergius. Sergius sounds a nice sorta guy to me. He has got a big, boomin' voice an' I bet he has his initials worked on his crepe-de-chine shirts. O.K. Well, this boyo has been on the telephone an' asked me to attend a little supper party to-night for the purpose of meetin' up with him an' doin' a little checkin' up.

"It is as plain to me as a dead whale on the seashore that for some reason best known to yourselves you two honeys are goin' to try an' stop this meetin'. Well, I reckon that I know why. I reckon that Geraldine has found out that our idea about Buddy is right. I reckon she knows that Nakorova has had Buddy snatched an' that she is tryin' to get the business straightened out an' maybe to fix it so that Buddy keeps quiet about it so's she can still marry the Russian guy. An' I bet I ain't far wrong in my guess."

Juanella says: "It's your guess an' you can keep it. An' what else have you been thinkin', Sherlock?"

"Nothin' much," I say. Then I take a quick peek at Juanella's legs an' I say: "Kid, you got a ladder in your stockin'!"

It works.

She takes a look down at her leg an' right then I kick the tea-table over. The silver kettle full of hot water shoots over Juanella's skirts an' she lets go a howl like a coyote. At the same moment I jump across an' grab the gun.

She sits there wrigglin' like a Hula girl.

"You lousy moron," she says. "Ain't you got one instinct of a gentleman? One of these days I am gonna take a poke at you that you will remember."

She looks at Geraldine.

"I'm sorry, kid," she says. "I thought it might have worked. But I know this guy. You can't pull much over on him. He's as hard-boiled as a knuckle of ham. The big stiff!"

I get up. I take the ammunition clip out of Juanella's gun an' throw it back to her.

"There you are, honey," I tell her. "Now you can play Wild West in peace an' quiet. Also I notice that you are wrigglin' a bit more than usual, an' I suggest that you apply a little carron oil to the affected part as per the label on the bottle. An' even if you do have a little trouble when you sit down, don't worry—just smile an' think of Lemmy!"

She says a rude word at me.

"O.K., you tub of lard," she says. "I'll even up with you for this if it's the last thing I do."

I pick up my hat.

"Listen to me, you two," I tell 'em, "an' remember that I am dead serious. To-night, after I have had this meetin' with Nakorova, I am goin' to have a showdown. Too many little things have been happenin' since I got into this city for my likin'. I want to know about 'em, see?"

"I see," says Juanella. "So you're issuin' ultimatums, hey?" She looks at Geraldine. "What did I tell you, honey?" she says.

Geraldine shrugs her shoulders.

"You're dead right," I say to Juanella. "I am issuin' an ultimatum. After this supper party is over to-night I am gonna hold a little investigation. I am gonna have all of you there. I will probably also have a coupla French cops around too just in case somebody tries to start a little shootin'. And you'll either talk about something I want to know or else . . ."

I go over to the door.

"So long, you two sweethearts," I say.

I give 'em a big grin.

"I wish it was goodbye for ever," says Juanella. "You get outa here an' I hope you fall down the lift-well an' break both legs. You give me a pain!"

"I have already noticed that, Tutz," I tell her. "I have given you a hot water pain an' if an' when you see the doctor about it you ought to tell him that it is in the region of the lower lumbar muscles because that is more delicate an' I know that you are a delicate dame."

I get outa the door just before she throws the sugar-bowl at me.

I go back to my hotel an' relax. My arm feels a bit easier an' I am takin' a more cheerful outlook on things.

An' the main reason for this is that I have got a ghost of an idea in my head. An' even if it is only a ghost it is better than nothin'.

Get this: Geraldine has told me that Edvanne Nakorova—the red-haired honeybelle who tried to iron me out—is Sergius's sister. Well, that's interestin' because you guys will remember that when this Edvanne dame an' myself was havin' that little talk around in Sergius's flat last night an' I said I'd heard her talkin' on the 'phone in Russian an' said she probably was a Russian, she said she wasn't. She said she was French!

Right then she wasn't thinking that I was ever goin' to get out of that apartment. She thought that she was goin' to give me the works an' send me along to join Rodney Wilks. That bein' so there is no reason why she should tell a lie.

So all right. If she is French, how in heck can she be Nakorova's sister? Have you got me?

I have also pulled a fast one on Geraldine an' Juanella. I have told 'em that I am goin' to have a showdown after the supper party to-night an' that I will probably have a couple of French cops around. Well, I don't intend to do anythin' of the kind because I do not want any official trouble at this moment when I know nothin' about anythin'.

But if Geraldine and Juanella have been up to somethin' tough; if they are tied in somehow with the Nakorova crowd they are goin' to get scared. An' when people get scared they always do somethin' that they didn't intend to do. They give themselves away.

Which is what I want.

I am interrupted in these ruminations by the arrival of a bellhop with an envelope. He says that it was left down at the desk for me by a messenger about half an hour ago an' that there ain't any reply.

I open it up. Inside there is a plain sheet of quarto notepaper an' typed on it is:

Dear Mr. Caution—In your enthusiasm you have probably over-looked the fact that sticking one's nose into other people's business is a process that may be fraught with a little danger to yourself.

Realise the possibility please. Realise that you are neither popular nor wanted in Paris. You may even become a definite nuisance.

I suggest that you return to U.S.A. as soon as possible. The suggestion is made for your own good.

If not I feel that you will be fished out of the Seine one morning.

As you would say get wise to yourself and get out. I mean business.

I put the note in my pocket an' light a cigarette.

It looks like somebody don't like me!

Chapter Six
COSSACK CAFÉ

AT A quarter-past ten I get up an' get myself into a very swell tuxedo that I have got. I also pack my Luger pistol in a shoulder holster just in case somebody decides to start some funny business to-night.

While I am dressin' I am thinkin' about this note, but I am not worryin' very much about it. If I was to take notice of all the threatenin' notes I receive in my life I would be in a nuthouse.

But I am wonderin' who sent this note. It was not Juanella, because she would not write a note in that language, an' I am pretty certain that it was not Geraldine. That baby was lookin' pretty scared at that little tea-party this afternoon. I do not think she'd have done it. O.K. Well, it might be Nakorova but that is not my guess. My guess is that that note was sent round here by that red-haired cat Edvanne, because she thinks maybe that havin' very nearly laid me out once before I will get a bit scared if I think somebody else is comin' gunnin' for me.

At a quarter to eleven I take a cab an' go round to this Café Cossack. This dump is the usual sorta good-class near-Russian Café that you meet up with around the Place Pigalle.

I go inside an' ask for Colonel Count Nakorova, an' they take me upstairs. When I go in I reckon that Nakorova is certainly throwin' a nice party. The room I am in is big an' well-furnished. At the door end is a bar with some guy in a white jacket servin' cocktails. At the other end of the room is a table laid for supper with flowers an' everything you can think of, an' in the corner I can see a dozen bottles of champagne in an ice pail so it looks like this is goin' to be a bean-feast.

Directly I get my foot inside the door Nakorova sails over to me an' I'm tellin' you guys that this fella has certainly got some looks. He is a tall, slim fella of about six feet two. His hair is black an' he has a dude moustache. He is smilin' an' I can see his teeth are big an' white an' regular. He is wearin' full evening dress an' it fits him like he was poured inta it. Takin' a quick look at him I come to the conclusion that this Nakorova is goin' to be a big problem in my life. He looks tough *and* clever.

By this time I have been able to take a look around the room an' I nearly get heart disease, because at the other end of the bar havin' a nice easy an' polite conversation I can see Juanella, Geraldine an', believe it or not, Edvanne! I have to take a pull on myself when I think of the nerve of this dame bein' around here.

Nakorova says: "Mr. Hickory, I am honoured to meet you."

He clicks his heels an' gives me a little bow from the waist an' puts his hand out. When I take it I feel that his fingers are long an' very strong. This guy has got a grip like a steel band. I think I might as well start somethin'.

"I am glad to know you, Colonel," I tell him, "but there is just one little point that I think I oughta put right away. My name is not Hickory an' I am not a private detective.

"I am Lemuel H. Caution of the Federal Bureau of Investigation of the U.S. Department of Justice. I thought I'd better let you know I was a Government man."

He smiles. He shows his big teeth.

"But excellent," he says. "That is better still. I have always been very interested in the 'G' men. I have a great admiration for those such splendid fellows."

I think like hell you have. I also think that by the time I am through with this mug all the admiration that he will have for me he could stick in his eye an' not notice.

He takes me over to the bar an' he introduces me to everybody. I think this is funny—everybody keepin' up this sort of appearance of not knowin' anybody, when as far as I can see we all know plenty about each other.

First of all he presents me to Geraldine. She takes my hand an' she looks at me as if she didn't quite know which way to look. After that I meet Mrs. Juanella Rillwater. She flashes me a charmin' smile an' says she is always very glad to meet an American in Paris. I say that I am tickled silly to meet anybody anywhere who looks like her. I ask her if she had a good passage over an' if she's fond of bein' on the water. I am thinkin' of the tea-kettle. I grin at her an' she gets it. She says she is not very fond of water. She gives me a dirty look an' goes back to the double martini that she is dealin' with.

After this Nakorova takes Edvanne by the arm an' says that this is his sister an' he hopes we will all be great friends. I am tellin' you guys that I have got an admiration for this red-haired dame. She puts out her hand an' takes mine an' gives it a little squeeze. She looks at me with a pair of soft an' pleadin' eyes as if her middle name was innocence. Edvanne has got her nerve all right.

Just at this minute the door opens an' some guy comes in. He is a short thin guy of about fifty. He has got a thin face with a big sharp nose stickin' out of it. Nakorova calls him over an' tells me that this is his Agent, Alphonse Zeldar, who looks after his business affairs. I shake hands with this guy, who asks me how I am in very good English.

So that is the set-up, an' I reckon this Zeldar has been brought along to show me that Nakorova has really got some income or some business or something.

I have a little rye an' we all start talkin'. Everything is very nice an' easy an' pleasant, but underneath it all I can feel the sorta atmosphere that you can cut with a knife.

After a bit we go over an' sit down to supper, an' believe me this Nakorova guy knows how to order eats.

It is a swell meal an' there is a lotta talk. Juanella is tellin' Edvanne all about life in New York. Geraldine an' Nakorova are lookin' at each other like a pair of sick love-birds, while this guy Zeldar tells me how

Nakorova is the proprietor of an importin' an' export business, an' how he proposes to show me last year's balance sheet some time or other, so that I can really assure myself that his boss is a guy of substance.

I keep on sayin' yes, but I am not listenin' very hard, because first of all I know it is very easy to get out facts an' figures with nothin' behind 'em, an' secondly, I am not particularly interested in whether Nakorova has got any business or not. I would not care if he was a multi-millionaire. What I am thinkin' of is the fact that within the next half an hour or so I am goin' to start doin' a little heavy talkin' to these guys an' we will get down to hard tacks. In the meantime the champagne is very good.

After a bit when supper is over, Geraldine takes a look around the table, an' the women get up to go an' powder their noses. Nakorova rushes over to open the door for 'em an' Zeldar starts to walk towards the bar.

From where I am standin' at the top of the table, the three dames have to go past me. Geraldine goes past lookin' straight in front of her. After her comes Juanella, who slips me another very dirty look, an' last of all, Edvanne.

She has got her napkin in her hand an' just when she gets opposite me she drops it on the floor. I stoop down an' pick it up an' as I give it to her she slips a piece of folded paper inta my hand. Then she goes outa the room.

Nakorova an' Zeldar go over to the bar an' start talkin'. On a chair up against the wall I can see a folded newspaper. I go over, pick it up, open the note that Edvanne has given me inside it, an' read it. It says:

I ask you to believe this. Whatever has happened and whatever I may seem to have been, I implore you to believe that I now ask nothing better than to assist you.

Please do not create any scene at this party. Instead I suggest that you make an excuse to leave at half-past twelve and that you go straight to my apartment at 772 Place Claremont. The key is with this note. I shall join you there before one o'clock. I shall not only be able to tell you what you want to know but I shall be able to help you. I desire . . .

The note finishes off there an' it looks like she was interrupted while she was writin' it.

I think here is a nice one an' what am I goin' to do about this? But while I am thinkin' it I *know* what I am goin' to do.

Me—I am a guy who has always followed his nose an' I have always found that when you try an' work anything out without having the proper facts to go on, in nine cases outa ten you come to the wrong conclusion.

First of all I reckon there is something to this note that Edvanne has sent me, an' I do not mind meetin' up with her again one bit, because this dame knows that she's got no chance of pullin' any more funny business.

The second thing is that if I have a showdown with the lot of 'em like I said I was goin' to have, well maybe I won't get anything from that, because if they all keep their traps shut an' say nothin', where do I go from there?

Maybe this dame Edvanne has really got something to spill to me. Maybe after takin' those shots at me she's good an' scared of what I may do. Maybe she thinks I am goin' to have her pinched. Maybe she's scared of the whole business an' wants to get out of it, in which case she might give me a lot of information that I want.

But even supposin' she don't, supposin' she tells me some phoney story. Well, I reckon that even a phoney story sometimes tells you something you wanta know. It's better than nothin'.

I slip the note back inta my pocket an' put the newspaper down on the chair. I go over to the bar an' pour myself out a shot of rye. I say to Nakorova:

"Look, Colonel, I reckon that you an' me have got to have a little straight talk about all this business an' maybe we oughta have Mr. Zeldar there so that he can tell me all about this import business you got in Switzerland. I sorta want to get the facts right, but I don't think this is the time or place to do it."

He says he agrees with that. I then suggest that he an' Zeldar show up at the Grand Hotel at eleven o'clock next mornin' an' we will have a little drink an' a heart to heart talk, an' I will there an' then get out my report on this business.

Nakorova says that will be fine, but he says he cannot understand one thing, and that is why the Federal Bureau should be sufficiently interested in the proposed marriage between himself an' Gerald-ine to put a "G" man on this business. He said he could understand

Willis Perriner sendin' a private detective over here but why a "G" man. He looks at Zeldar who looks back at him. They both grin an' shrug their shoulders.

"I can explain that," I tell 'em. "The point is that it is not just a schmozzle about Geraldine's marriage."

I tell 'em about the disappearance of Buddy Perriner. I tell 'em that Willis Perriner thinks that the two things have been in some way connected. I say I do not think there is much in the idea myself, but there it is. I have been given the job an' I've got to see it through.

Nakorova laughs. He says he thinks that Pa Perriner must be sufferin' from hallucinations, but that anyhow he will bring Zeldar along at eleven o'clock next mornin' an' we'll thrash the whole thing out.

Just then the women come back. I have a few more drinks an' I look at my watch. It is twenty minutes after twelve. I say to Nakorova that I must be gettin' along, that I got one or two things to do. I also say thank you for a very nice evening. I give a big grin at everybody else an' I go over to the door.

Nakorova comes over with me. Just when I am goin' out I say to him sorta quiet:

"Oh, by the way, Colonel, when you come along to-morrow morning with that agent guy of yours you might bring your bank passbook. You've got an account at the Credit Lyonnais on the Rue Henri Martin, haven't you?"

He looks a bit surprised. He says yes he has. He will bring the passbook with him. He puts his hand out. He gives me a cheerful smile an' says goodnight.

Outside I get into a cab an' tell the guy to drive me to the Place Claremont. I am sorta lookin' forward to that date with Edvanne.

When I get to the Place Claremont I start lookin' around the street for Edvanne's apartment block. It is so goddam dark that it ain't so easy but I finally find this dump.

The main door is open an' on the other side of the hallway is an electric lift with the light on inside. On the wall is an indicator that says: "Nakorova—2ième étage."

I go up in the lift an' find the apartment doorway along the corridor. I let myself in an' switch on the hall light.

I park my hat and coat on the hallstand an' go across an' into the room opposite. It is a big room with good furnishin's. The lights are switched on an' there is a big fire burnin' in the grate. I see that the lights have all got funny sorta pink shades an' are arranged in a cunnin' sort of way so as to give a soft an' mysterious light. This does not surprise me because I have already told you guys that I have come to the conclusion that Edvanne Nakorova is a dope. An' dopes always go for soft lights because an ordinary bright sorta light gets their eyes any time they are comin' out of a jag.

There is a sideboard against one wall with a lotta bottles an' glasses on it. The place is O.K. an' smells sorta nice, but there is something screwy about the atmosphere—if you know what I mean.

I take a walk around. There are a coupla swell bedrooms with very heavy furnishin's in white an' blue, servants' rooms, pantries an' a dinky bathroom in green tiles. The place is as quiet as an empty morgue.

I go back into the sittin'-room an' grab myself a drink off the table, flop down in one of the big armchairs an' light a cigarette.

I sit there smokin' an' tryin' to get a line on this thing, but the more I think about it the less I know.

I am wonderin' what new idea this Edvanne baby is goin' to pull on me. First of all it is a cinch that she knows that I am not goin' to be an easy case. After my last experience with her I am goin' to watch things very closely. At the same time there is always the chance that she is goin' to come across with somethin' that matters.

I have always discovered that when guys are workin' together on some crooked business they are liable to get bad-tempered with each other. An' when they get bad-tempered they get suspicious. An' the next thing is one of 'em squeals. I reckon that nine outa ten successful police jobs are pulled off because some underworld rat opens his trap an' squawks just because he thinks that if he don't do it one of the other boys will get in first.

An' a doll is always inclined to talk quicker than a man. She's got more to get annoyed about. A dame will play around with a guy for a long time an' while she thinks that he is givin' her a square shootin' match she will be as close as an oyster; but directly she gets the idea into her little head that the boyfriend is castin' a mean eye over some other dame she will rush round to the nearest copper an' squawk so loud that you can hear her over in Japan.

I remember one time when I had a baby on ice in the local cooler down in Denver City. I was holdin' this honeypot as a material witness officially but in reality I was tryin' to make her talk about her boy-friend who was the counterfeitin' guy that I was after.

Was that doll loyal or was she? I worked on her for four days. I tried everythin' I knew. I tried pleadin' an' threatenin' but it was no good. She just wasn't talkin'.

So I got a big idea. I got a picture of her boy-friend outa the police records. This picture showed him sittin' on a chair. Then I got another picture of a good-lookin' dame, an' photographed the two pictures together. Eventually we got a print of the dame sittin' on the boy-friend's knee. I then take this print along an' show it to the dame with the tight mouth. She takes one look at it, lets go a holler that shook the roof off, an' then proceeds to come across with every durn thing she ever knew about him an' a lot that she made up on the spot.

All of which will prove to you mugs that a dame is swell so long as she ain't jealous; but if she gets good an' jealous you would be better off tryin' to tickle a bad-tempered alligator with a rusty nail.

Right in the middle of these deep thoughts I hear somebody at the door. I turn around an' look round the edge of the chair-back an' I stick my hand on the Luger under my coat because I have already come to the conclusion that if anybody else starts any shootin' I am goin' to be there first.

Edvanne comes in. She stands in the doorway an' she sees me peekin' around the chair. She throws a quick little smile at me. Then she shuts the door behind her, throws off her cloak an' walks over to the fire. She stands there lookin' at me with the slow sorta smile that she uses just like she was considerin' whether she should give you a hug or a double dose of poison an' she ain't quite certain which.

I throw my cigarette-end in the fire an' take out my case. I offer her a cigarette an' get up an' light it.

Then I go back to my chair.

"Well," I say, "an' how is Mrs. Sergius Nakorova?"

She gives a little shrug.

"How did you know?" she asks. "*Did* you know or were you just guessing?"

"Work it out," I tell her. "First of all you told me that you are a French dame an' not a Russian when we were round at Nakorova's apartment. An' after that Geraldine Perriner tells me that Nakorova has got a lovely sister with lovely red hair an' a lovely nature. Right then I reckoned that you was his wife. Call it a guess if you like but it's a good guess."

She don't say anythin'.

"In the second place," I go on, "I have never durin' a long an' arduous experience spent in chasin' one hundred different assortments of thugs around generally, come across a brother who would put his sister in to do a killin' for him—especially a killin' where somebody has got to be poisoned; but I have known plenty of guys who would put their wives in to do a thing like that because a wife is always a sorta partner an' a sister seldom is. You get me, Edvanne?"

She says yes, she gets me. She strolls over to the sideboard an' gets herself a shot of vodka. She turns around suddenly an' she says:

"It is true that I killed your friend Wilks."

"That's old news," I tell her. "But what I want to know is why? Why did you have to slip that coffin-juice into Rodney? What the hell had that boy done to you? You tell me that one."

She makes a face.

"I propose to tell you many things," she says.

She sits down in the chair opposite me with the little vodka glass poised in her hand. She is cool an' casual. I think it would take a helluva lot to get this dame really steamed up—except maybe love. I think she could get very steamed up about a guy.

She says: "I am of course very sorry about Mr. Wilks; but I am a woman who is not inclined to regard human life as being so very valuable—especially when it is the life of someone else."

I nod my head.

"That is swell, Edvanne," I tell her, "an' I reckon that if Rodney Wilks could hear that he would be very pleased to know that you ain't worryin'."

I get up an' put my glass back on the sideboard. I light a fresh cigarette an' stand there lookin' at her.

"So you've got wise to Sergius, hey?" I tell her. "The boyo has annoyed you. Maybe I can make a guess about that too . . ."

"Please tell me," she says. "I am interested in your guesses."

"O.K.," I tell her. "Well, my guess is this. I reckon that you an' Sergius have been interested in the Perriner family from just one angle an' that was the snatchin' of Buddy Perriner. Sergius went off to New York to arrange that business. When he gets there he meets Geraldine an' she promptly falls for him like a sack of coke. This is O.K. by him because its gonna help him in his scheme.

"Well, he is lucky. Buddy Perriner likes him too. They get around together. Sergius lets everybody think that he wants to marry Geraldine an' that that is the reason for his stickin' around.

"The next thing is the snatch comes off, an' Sergius' pals grab Buddy. Nobody takes very much notice of this because Buddy has done a disappearin' act before. Everybody thinks he will turn up in a few weeks or so.

"So Sergius waits around for a month or so, an' then scrams over here to Paris. He probably writes to Geraldine an' says that he is nutty about her, but that he wants to get her father to consent to the marriage. He thinks that by carryin' on with the love stuff nobody is goin' to suspect him of havin' anything to do with the Buddy snatch.

"But what he don't reckon with is Geraldine. That baby has got a will of her own an' she is not inclined to stick around in New York. So she comes chasin' over here to Paris after Sergius. She thinks that by doin' this she will probably force old man Perriner's hand an' that he will consent because he don't want any sorta scandal."

She nods her head.

"You are really doing very vell," she says.

"Thanks a lot," I grin at her. "Well—in the meantime Pa Perriner has got a bit suspicious of Sergius. An' he is beginnin' to be worried about Buddy. He starts connectin' Sergius with Buddy's disappearance. He goes to the Department of Justice an' they instruct Rodney Wilks to keep an eye on the Sergius-Geraldine set-up an' find out what he can about things. He don't seem to be doin' so well an' so they decide to send me over.

"The first thing that Geraldine wants to do is to graft me to lay off the job. She thinks I am Hickory, a private detective, an' that I will take a little dough an' say anything she wants. She gets the dough from Sergius—at least it comes outa his bankin' account—but the next thing she finds out is that I am a 'G' man an' that the bribin' business is not comin' off.

"But anyway she still believes in Sergius. She don't believe that he has got anythin' to do with Buddy's disappearance.

"O.K. I tell her that I am goin' to take steps to stop her marryin' Sergius. She then says she don't give a hoot, that if I stop her marryin' him she will join him here an' stick around with him.

"Well, Edvanne, I reckon that is what got your goat. You didn't mind this phoney love business when it was just a part of the kidnappin' idea. You were out one hundred per cent. to help Sergius over that. But maybe you don't feel so good now. Here is Geraldine offerin' herself on a plate to Sergius an' I reckon that guy has begun to get ideas in his head about that dame. While it was a question of his marryin' her you didn't give a hoot in hell because you knew he couldn't because he was already married to you . . . but when it comes to a little love stuff without any marriage ceremony you start gettin' jealous. So you tell Sergius that unless he lays off the Geraldine dame an' sticks to the business in hand you are goin' to get difficult.

"Sergius tells you to go fry an egg so you think you will have a few words with Mr. Caution an' put the screws on him. Well . . . how's that?"

"Perhaps not too bad," she says. "My friend, you certainly have imagination. . . ."

"Maybe," I tell her, "but there's some things I don't imagine. Some of 'em I know. An' one of them things is that Wilks is dead. If you want to talk start right in. Why did you kill Rodney?"

She says sorta simply:

"I'm a little sorry about that. You see, I didn't know!"

Here is a nice one! I ask you guys! *She didn't know!*

"That's just too bad," I say. "But it looks to me as if the result was just the same for Wilks as if you hadda known. But I reckon we will come back to this business in a minute. Right now I would like to ask you a question."

"Ask on," she says. "I am at your service, my delightful Lemmy."

"This evenin'," I tell her, "just before I came around to the Cossack I got a note. It was left around at my hotel. It was a helluva note. In this note some guy tells me that I am stickin' my nose inta somebody else's business an' that I had better watch out. The suggestion is made that if I am a wise guy I will get outa here while the goin' is good an' that if I don't I shall probably be fished out of the Seine one mornin'."

She is lookin' at me sorta surprised.

"How unkind!" she says.

"Thanks for the sympathy," I say. "Well, you wouldn't know about that note, would you? I was thinkin' that maybe you sent it."

She spread out her hands.

"Why should I send you such a note?" she says. "Why should I? Does it seem sensible that I should at one moment write a note like that and then seek *this* interview? Ask yourself, dear Lemmy."

"I see," I say. "So it was Sergius."

She smiles.

"I really don't know," she says. "I think you will have to ask him. He is sometimes quite untruthful."

She takes a long draw on her cigarette. Then she says:

"I wonder if I can trust you."

I nearly have a fit. The nerve of this dame is about the sweetest thing I have ever struck.

"I wouldn't know," I tell her. "But up to the moment, I am not the one who has been pullin' tough acts. Was it you or me who pulled that I-have-got-a-run-in-my-stockin' act? If anybody's doin' the distrustin' it's me, an' my advice to you is to talk an' talk plenty."

"I wonder," she says. "I wonder . . ."

She starts lookin' at the ceilin' again with that sweet an' innocent look on her pan.

I just stick around and wait. I have got plenty of time. Because one thing is obvious to me.

This dame is goin' to try an' do a deal.

CHAPTER SEVEN
ORCHIDS FOR EDVANNE

AFTER a bit she slings me one of them demure look-me-over-kid-I'm-hard-to-get glances an' she says:

"Dear Lemmy, life can be so difficult for me. I would like to be with you forever. I would like to go with you to the very ends of the earth. I would like to stand by your side and support you. You are a delightful animal. You enchant me."

"Oh yeah?" I tell her. "Well, that's swell but I'm tellin' you, baby, that if I was with you at the end of the earth I reckon you wouldn't be standin' by my side supportin' me. No, Sir! I got an idea you would be standin' behind me waitin' for a good chance to push me over the edge."

"I despair," she says. "I cannot make you believe me. That is because of the unfortunate Wilks episode. But of that I was quite guiltless. I have told you I didn't know."

"I see," I tell her. "So you didn't know you was killin' Rodney. You just sorta killed him by accident?"

She nods.

"That is true," she said. "I killed him but I didn't know."

"That's fine," I say. "Well, it looks to me, Edvanne, as if you got me round here to-night for the purpose of makin' a deal. If you wanta make a deal you are in a tough spot. There's been a killin' in this job—the Wilks killin'—an' that don't make it so easy for you. So I am goin' to suggest that before we do anything else you wise me up about what happened to Wilks. You say you didn't know that you were goin' to kill him. What does that mean?"

"I'll tell you," she says. "You will remember that you sent a radiogram to Geraldine Perriner when you were aboard the *Fels Ronstrom*. You told her that you wanted to see her at Siedler's Club at twelve-thirty. You said that you were Hickory—a private detective.

"Geraldine showed that radiogram to Sergius. Then he came to me. He told me that he was expecting some interference with his plans, that that interference would come from an individual by the name of Wilks He said that he was certain that Wilks would be present at the interview between Geraldine and yourself.

"Sergius said that it was essential that we should gain some time. He said that it was also essential that Geraldine should not meet you as arranged. He gave me some instructions and I obeyed them. I obeyed them because I have always done my best to help Sergius. I was, as you say, one hundred per cent. for him.

"Sergius told me to get into touch with Rodney Wilks. He told me to telephone him at the Hotel Rondeau, to tell him that I had some very important information for him about the Perriner business generally. I was to say that it was essential that I talked with him and Mr. Hickory, who would arrive in Paris that night, before

Geraldine Perriner met Hickory. I was to arrange to meet Wilks at Siedler's Club at twelve-fifteen and I was to wear three gardenias.

"Sergius said that whatever happened Wilks was not to meet you. He gave me a perfume flask. He said that if Wilks agreed to meet me at Siedler's Club I was to take the opportunity of putting the contents of the flask into his drink. Sergius said it would make him feel ill, that he would have to leave and that I could tell him before he went that the information I had I would give to you when you arrived. Sergius said that Wilks would then leave the Club—he would *have* to do so because he would be feeling *so* very ill; that I was to wait there and meet you, pretending to be Geraldine Perriner; that I was to tell you that I was perfectly satisfied that Buddy had not been kidnapped; that in any event I should marry Sergius.

"Sergius believed that you would then insist on meeting him as you did. I was to take you to his apartment and he was to be awaiting us there. I was to leave you two together." She smiles sorta cynically. "I don't know what Sergius had planned for you," she says.

"You don't?" I tell her. "Well, I reckon it was something as interestin' as what you tried to pull round here. What you're sayin' in fact is this," I go on. "That you gave somethin' to Rodney Wilks that you thought was just a Mickey Finn, somethin' that would make the guy feel lousy an' doped an' have to get out. Then you were to pretend to be Geraldine Perriner, meet me an' get me around the Sergius' place so that he could fix me. An' I suppose you're goin' to tell me that the reason you took those shots at me round there was because I discovered that Wilks was dead in the wash-room at Siedler's. So then you knew that you were goin' to be suspected of deliberately killin' Rodney Wilks. You thought I was goin' to take you round to the police, so you lost your head. Is that it?"

She nods.

"It is fairly correct," she says, "except that I didn't lose my head. But I thought that as I was going to be accused of one murder I might as well commit another and escape."

"Hooey," I tell her. "You didn't even *try* to escape. You just stuck around in Paris. Another thing," I go on, "when I went round to Sergius' apartment with you, you were all ready for me. You had that gun stuck in your stockin' top. Do you always carry a gun like that?"

She nods her head.

"Most of the time," she says. "It's a habit of mine."

"I don't like your habits, Edvanne," I tell her. "An' your story don't sound so good to me. But I reckon I know why you're puttin' it that way."

"Why?" she asks.

"You think that if I believed you knew you killed Rodney Wilks deliberately I would not make a deal with you," I tell her. "But if I thought that there was a chance that you killed him by accident I might."

She says: "Are you going to make a deal?"

"I'm not makin' any sorta deal with you," I tell her. "But I tell you what I might do. If I can find some sorta corroboration of that story of yours that you didn't know you were givin' Wilks poison, that you thought you were only goin' to dope the guy an' get him outa the way; if you like to come across an' tell me something that looks like the truth about all this business, I might try an' make things a bit easier for you, that's all I'm sayin'. That's plain enough, ain't it?"

She throws me a little smile.

"You are never ambiguous, my sweet," she says. "Do you mind if I think for a moment?"

"You can think all night if you want to, honey," I tell her.

She leans back in the chair an' puts her arms behind her head. She is lookin' up at the ceilin'. I go over to the sideboard an' give myself another drink. I light a cigarette an' turn around an' take a look at her. She is still doin' the big thinkin' act.

I get the idea in my head that this dame is in a jam, that she's wonderin' just how much she can tell an' just how much she has to keep back in order to look after herself. It looks like she is plannin' to take a run-out powder on Sergius. An' why not?

After a bit she says: "Lemmy, supposin' for the sake of argument that the ideas which you have put up to me here this evening were more or less correct . . . you will realise that I am saying *supposing* they were correct. . . ."

"O.K.," I tell her. "Well, only *supposin'* they were, so what?"

"Supposing for the sake of argument," she says, "that Sergius had contacted Geraldine Perriner because the real idea was to kidnap her brother. Supposing the kidnapping plot carried out by Sergius' associates had been successful, but for reasons of my own, which I need not explain at the moment, I had become rather tired of all this business; that I had begun to think that possibly Sergius and I were getting in deeper than we thought. Supposing I could persuade Sergius to arrange that Buddy Perriner was able to return home immediately, and that I was to successfully scotch the idea of Geraldine Perriner marrying Sergius by divulging to her the fact that I am his wife? I imagine that this would clear up the situation very successfully from your point of view, dear one."

I shrug my shoulders.

"It would clean up one bit of the situation," I tell her, "but not the other. It would clean up the Sergius-Geraldine marriage situation an' it would clean up the Buddy Perriner kidnappin' situation. But what about the Wilks killin'?"

She says: "I have already told you that was an accident."

"Fine," I tell her. "So that was an accident? Well, maybe it was an accident on your part, but was it an accident on Sergius' part? Maybe you didn't know what was in that bottle. Maybe you didn't know what the stuff was that you put inta Rodney's drink, but what about Sergius? Didn't he know?"

"Possibly not," she says. "That is a matter which you can take up with Sergius."

"I see," I tell her. "So you don't mind Sergius takin' the rap for murder so long as you get out of it?"

She says: "Do you know, my dear Lemmy, I am really becomin' a little bored with Sergius. I used to think that he was a very clever man. I am thinking now that he is not so clever. And may I have a cigarette, please?"

I give her a cigarette.

"Well," she says, "do we do this deal?"

"You got your nerve, Edvanne," I tell her. "Do you think you can sit down an' do a deal like that with me? What do you think I am? I'm not makin' any sorta deals now. I'll talk cold turkey with you when I've had the whole inside dope on this story, and I wanta have it from Sergius too."

She nods her head.

"I thought you would," she says. "Let me tell you what I have arranged. Sergius of course does not know of this interview. I propose to tell him about it. I propose to tell him about it *now* and I am also going to give him some advice. It will be good advice. I am going to advise him to put his cards on the table, to rely on the hope of making a deal with you. I think that would be the simplest way out of it for both of us."

"That sounds like sense to me," I tell her.

I take a look at her, because you will realise as well as I do that all this stuff sounds very screwy, but I think maybe I will give this dame her head for a bit. That way we'll find out something.

"So where do we go from here?" I ask her.

"I go," she says with a little smile. "You do not. You stay here." She looks at the little jewelled watch on her wrist. "It is half-past one now," she goes on. "I'm going directly to Sergius' apartment. I'm going to have what you would call a heart-to-heart talk with him. I am going to try to persuade him to do what I think would be best for us all. I want to give myself a clear hour."

She gets up.

"Will you join me at Sergius' apartment—the scene of our last meeting—at half-past two? It is not very far from here. I expect it will take me an hour to drum some common-sense into Sergius' obstinate head, and I want you to arrive soon after I have talked to him. If we wait until to-morrow he may change his mind."

I think for a minute.

"That's O.K. by me," I tell her, "but there's just one little point. . . ." I tap the shoulder holster under my coat—"I would like you to know, sweetheart," I tell her, "that this time I am carryin' a gun; that I am supposed to be very nice with guns. If you or Sergius try any funny business round at his place there'll be plenty trouble an' you will, both of you, finish up either in the morgue or in the local cooler. You got that?"

"Yes," she says. "As you say, I've got it. May I have my cloak please?"

I get her cloak an' I help her on with it. She walks over to the doorway. When she gets there she turns around an' says:

"*Au revoir,* my beloved bear. Wish me good luck!"

She goes out. After a minute I hear the main door close behind her. I go over an' sit down in front of the fire. I am thinking that this is the most haywire case I have ever met in my life. It is stickin' outa foot to me that something has happened that has scared Edvanne good an' plenty, an' you will realise that that dame does not scare easily.

Here is a dame who is tough enough to go about puttin' sleep juice in guys' drinks, who is tough enough to take three shots at me after I told her she'd killed Rodney an' who is now gettin' an attack of nerves. I reckon it would take something pretty tough to frighten Edvanne.

I get to thinkin' about the story she has told me. I wonder if that bit about her not knowin' what the stuff was she gave Rodney was true. Maybe yes, because you will realise that if my idea about this case is right then Sergius an' Edvanne are a pair of kidnappers who were out to make some dough over snatchin' Buddy, an' as they hadn't yet asked for any ransom money it is a bit odd that they should indulge in a little killin'. They would know that that would upset their apple-cart. So it looks to me as if there is just a chance that what she says about not knowin' that the stuff in the bottle was poison might be true. An' if she didn't know, did Sergius know or did somebody make a mistake when they was mixin' this stuff?

I look at the clock on the mantelpiece. It is just after one-thirty. I think I will take a little sleep which is a very good thing to do any time you are undecided about anything.

I wake up on the dot. It is half-past two an' the fire is very nearly out. Also it is plenty cold. I get up, give myself one for the journey out of the rye bottle on the sideboard, put on my hat an' coat an' go downstairs. I stick around for ten minutes waitin' for a cab, then I get one. I tell the driver to drop me at the Place de l'Opéra.

When I get there it is ten to three. I pay off the cab an' walk around to the apartment. The main door on the street level is open. I go in an' go up in the lift. I walk along to Sergius' apartment an' I ring the bell. I keep on ringin'. Nothing happens.

Standin' there the idea strikes me that Edvanne an' Sergius have taken a run-out powder on me, but after a minute I know that this idea is not right. If they wanted to scram they had plenty of time to-day to do it. They didn't have to wait until to-night an' Edvanne didn't have to come an' tell me all that stuff first.

I try the door of the flat. The lock is good, but it looks a bit old-fashioned to me. I try it with my shoulder. It looks as if I go for it it might give. I park myself against the wall on the other side of the corridor an' take a dive at the door with my good shoulder. The lock bursts. I go in.

The light is on in the hallway an' the door opposite leadin' to the big sittin'-room is half open. I stand there for a minute listenin'. The place is all quiet. I walk across the hallway an' kick the sittin'-room door wide open. I go in.

Oh boy!

The first thing I see is Edvanne. She is lyin' straight out on the white an' gold settee in front of the fire. Facin' me, slumped forward in the big arm-chair, is Sergius. He is sittin' there with his head hangin' over to one side. Down one side of his mouth is a brown stain—the same sorta stain that was round Rodney's mouth. His face is twisted up as if he didn't feel so good when he passed out. His right hand is hangin' over the side of the chair an' just below it, showin' up on the white rug, a gun is lyin' where it has dropped out of his hand.

I walk over an' stand in front of the fire. I look at 'em. They are both as dead as last week's cold cuts. On the left hand side of Sergius' chair is a broken glass. I reckon this fell outa his hand. There is another glass by the side of the settee that Edvanne is lyin' on. This glass ain't broken. I go over to her an' pull her lower lip down. It is stained like Sergius'.

I get up an' light myself a cigarette. Here is some sweet business! It looks to me as if Edvanne's persuadin' act didn't come off. It looks to me as if these two guys talked this matter over an' then decided to take a quick way out of it. I think about this for a minute, an' I think this ideas is nuts. Because why has Sergius had a gun in his hand? I go over an' pick up the gun with my handkerchief. I take out the ammunition clip an' smell the breach. The shells in the clip are intact and the gun has not been fired. So what!

It is four o'clock when I get back to my hotel. I am feelin' so tired that I could go to sleep standin' up like a horse, an' I am also beginnin' to feel that so far as this job is concerned I might as well be one. Because right now it looks as if all the evidence has died on me.

When I get in the night porter gives me a code telephone message that has come through the U.S. Embassy from Washington in answer to my cable to them. It says:

Financial standing of Geraldine Perriner in Paris is nil stop She had approximately six thousand dollars when she left New York stop She is entirely dependent on allowance from Willis Perriner stop Larvey Rillwater is in New York and is apparently unaware of whereabouts of his wife stop Passport Office issued passport to Juanella Rillwater at request and on recommendation of Willis Perriner stop Permission accorded to Juanella Rillwater to leave jurisdiction of Federal Court although under suspended sentence at request and on responsibility of Maul, Garraway and Laners Attorneys representing Perriner interests stop Continue investigations stop Funds and cooperation U.S. Embassy at your disposal stop Good luck stop Director F.B.I. Washington.

So that's that an' as far as I can see the information is not very much good to me except for the fact that it tells me that Geraldine has got very little dough, that the fifty thousand francs that she wanted to use to graft me with was Sergius' dough an' that the money she has with her is not likely to keep her going for very long.

It also looks like Larvey Rillwater does not know that Juanella is rushin' about the world.

But the thing that gets me is the fact that it was Willis Perriner who got Juanella's passport through, an' it was his attorneys who got permission for her to leave America. Here is a nice one an' I would very much like to know what all these guys are playin' at.

Maybe Willis Perriner told the Federal authorities that he reckoned Juanella might be good company for his daughter while she was away!

This idea gives me a thought. Maybe I got something here. An' what do you guys think?

Here is Willis Perriner worryin' his head off about Buddy an' the next thing is that Geraldine scrams off an' goes to Paris chasin' after Sergius who is the guy that Perriner has begun to associate with his son's kidnappin'.

O.K. Well, he wouldn't be so pleased at Geraldine bein' around in France with Sergius, would he? But until he can prove somethin' he can't stop her. So the next thing he thinks about is protectin' her.

Somehow or other he hears about Juanella. He hears that she is a tough baby an' afraid of nothin' so he gives her a job to come over here to Paris an' stick around with Geraldine.

Maybe this is the slant on Juanella, although why she shoulda scrammed outa New York without sayin' anything to Larvey I do not know. An' why should she be so goddam close with me about everything?

I give myself a warm shower an' go to bed. I lay there with the light on lookin' up at the ceilin', tryin' to puzzle this thing out.

First of all I get to thinkin' about Sergius an' Edvanne. Here is a funny set-up. It don't make sense to me an' I am not inclined to agree with what Erouard thought about it after I had got him round to take a look at those two stiffs. His idea was that it was suicide; that those two guys had got themselves in good an' deep over this job an' thought they would take the easiest way out. When I told him that if this was so what is Sergius doin' with a gun, Erouard says that anyway Sergius did not fire the gun, an' that maybe the first idea was that he should bump off Edvanne and then kill himself, but this does not go so well with me because I have got my own theory about this business.

When I found those two guys, Sergius was sittin' up in the chair with the gun fallen outa his hand on the floor on the right hand side of the chair. The broken glass—the one that he drunk the poison out of—was on the floor at the left of the chair. But Edvanne is lyin' out nice an' straight on the settee. The glass that she drank out of is put on the floor by the side of the settee nice an' tidy, an' she looked as if she'd sorta composed herself to pass out.

My theory is that Edvanne tried to talk Sergius into comin' across an' tellin' the truth when I got around there at two-thirty. But Sergius wasn't bavin' this, so Edvanne got tough. She told him that if he didn't spill the beans she would. Sergius gets nasty. He pulls a gun on her. He says that if she's goin' to talk that way hell let her have it.

So then Edvanne pulls a fast one on him. She says O.K. she'll play ball, she'll do what he wants. Then maybe she suggests that they have a little drink. Maybe she has got some of the stuff she gave Rodney Wilks in a bottle in her handbag, or maybe the bottle that it came out of is somewhere around Sergius' apartment an' she knows where it is. So she goes over to the table, mixes a coupla drinks an' puts the stuff in 'em. She takes the glass over to Sergius an' gives it to him. He drinks it, an' before he can do anything the stuff gets him. The gun drops outa his hand on one side an' the glass falls on the other an' breaks. Havin' done this Edvanne lays herself out nice an' neat on the settee an' drinks the rest of the stuff.

Anyway this business does not matter a lot. The only thing is, it looks to me like we have lost the villain an' villainess of this case before we got started on it, which is not a nice thing to happen to any guy.

One thing is stickin' out a foot an' that is that Edvanne Nakorova, who as I have told you before was not a scared dame—not by a long chalk, was gettin' pretty nervy about something. That baby was not the sorta dame to throw her hand in an' try an' make a deal with me unless she was scared. If my idea about her killin' Sergius an' then bumpin' herself is right, then she musta been scared. Guys don't kill themselves except when they are very scared or very angry or very hopeless about something. An' if my idea is right then Sergius was not scared, because he was the guy who was *not* goin' to make a deal with me. So it looks as if whatever it was between those two was something that did not scare Sergius but did scare Edvanne.

All of which is a great help if I only knew what it meant. Lyin' there, blowin' smoke rings an' wishin' that my left arm would stop achin', I get to thinkin' about all the screwy bits in this case; questions that I would like to answer an' for which I can't find any answers.

I get outa bed an' go over to the table an' I get myself a piece of writin' paper an' I write 'em down. Here they are:

1) Why does Edvanne suddenly get scared an' wanta make a deal with me?

2) If it is good enough for her to make a deal why is it not good enough for Sergius? These two have both got nerve enough to go through with the kidnappin' deal; they have got nerve enough to try and dope or kill Rodney Wilks, and I reckon that Sergius knew that stuff was going to kill him.

Edvanne has got nerve enough to take three shots at me when she thinks I am going to take her in and hand her over to the French police. So we know that they are both guys who are not easily scared; yet something scares Edvanne but it don't scare Sergius.

3) What was the meaning of those words that Rodney Wilks wrote on the back of the envelope:

"Before seven. Will you have it straight? And how much?"

4) Why does Juanella Rillwater scram out of New York without saying anything to her husband or tellin' him where she is going, come over to France and join up with Geraldine?

5) Why do the Perriner attorneys, after Willis Perriner suspects that Sergius Nakorova has got something to do with the disappearance of Buddy, get permission from the Federal Court for Juanella Rillwater—whose husband is one of the swellest counterfeiters in the U.S.—to go over to France; and Willis Perriner fix her passport? Maybe we have got an answer to this one. May be it is what I said before, that Willis Perriner has put her in, knowing she is a tough baby, to look after Geraldine.

6) If this is so, why is it all kept so secret, and why does Perriner say nothing to the F.B.I. or me about it? He knows where I am in Paris and I have not heard one word from that guy.

7) If Nakorova or his associates are responsible for kidnappin' Buddy Perriner, why haven't they already asked for some ransom money?

The next thing I get to thinkin' about is this guy Zeldar. You will remember that Sergius an' Zeldar were supposed to come round to see me at my hotel at eleven o'clock in the mornin'. Zeldar was supposed to bring the papers an' things which were goin' to prove that Nakorova had got some business or other. Well, it will be interestin' to see if this bozo turns up. Erouard has arranged to' keep the deaths of Sergius an' Edvanne quiet, so Zeldar should not know anything about them. That bein' so he oughta get in touch with me at eleven as arranged. Maybe I can find out something when I tell him that Sergius is dead, that is if he turns up.

I reckon I could stay here all night lookin' at the ceilin' an' askin' myself questions that I can't answer, so I give it up. I switch off the light an' I go to sleep.

They call me at nine o'clock an' I get up. I go over to the window an' look out. It is a lousy sorta day with a wind blowin' an' the rain tryin' to come down. I give myself some breakfast, after which I take a cab an' go to the Hotel Dieudonne, because I have an idea in my head to ask Geraldine what happened at the party last night after I left.

When I give my name to the guy in the reception I get a big surprise. He tells me she has gone. He says that Miss Perriner left the hotel at half-past three this mornin'. He says that she hired a car an' went off with all her luggage aboard. He's got an idea she went to Le Bourget, but he ain't certain. I ask him if anybody was with her—Mrs. Rillwater for instance—an' he says no, she went off on her own. I say thanks a lot an' I scram.

I go round to a little café that is nearby an' I give myself some coffee. This case gets sweeter every minute, because it looks like I have now lost Geraldine, although I reckon it will not be very diffi-cult to find out where this baby has gone. The fact that she has gone to Le Bourget looks as if she is goin' to fly somewhere. Well, there ain't many places she can fly to these days, an' my guess is that she's either taken a trip to somewhere else in France, or else she's gone to England.

When I have finished my coffee I ring through to the Hotel St. Anne an' ask if Mrs. Rillwater is there. They say yes but she has given orders that she is not to be disturbed till noon, because she was very late last night. I say thanks a lot, an' that I will not disturb her. I am very glad to hear that Juanella is still here because I have an idea in my head that she will know where Geraldine has gone, an' I have got another idea that I am goin' to stick so tight to this Juanella baby that even if she turns herself into a rabbit she will not give me a miss.

I have already arranged with Erouard to put a very quiet guy doin' observation on Sergius Nakorova's apartment so's we can see who goes round there, because work it out for yourself, if Zeldar doesn't know Sergius is dead he will go round there to pick him up. If he *does* know then we will want to know why.

I ring through to Erouard an' I tell him about Geraldine. I say I will be very much obliged to him if he will send someone out to Le Bourget to see just where this dame has gone to, whether she was on her own an' anything else that there is to be found out. He says O.K.

I then ask him to do somethin' else for me. I tell him that I want him to stick a guy around at the Hotel St. Annie to keep an eye on Juanella an' that if she goes outa the place this guy is to keep on her tail an' let me know what she's at. He says that he will also do this, an' it looks to him as if this is goin' to be a very interestin' case before it is through. I say this is maybe right but up to the moment it don't look as if it matters very much as all the bad guys in this case seem to be executin' themselves. He said *mais oui* but that this makes it a lot simpler for him.

By which you will see that this bozo Erouard has gotta sense of humour.

He goes on to say that if I want anythin' else I am to let him know because the Prefect has already had a message from the U.S. Embassy askin' him to give me co-operation as required, an' the Prefect is all for a clean-up as soon as possible. He also tells me that the guy he is goin' to put on to Juanella is a guy by the name of Briquet an' very smart at that, an' that this Briquet will contact me direct.

The reason that I am puttin' a tail on Juanella is because at the back of my head I have got an idea that somehow or other the solution of all this business is with Juanella an' that if I could make that baby talk I might get a spot to kick off from.

I go back to the hotel. I reckon I will get ready for this Zeldar interview. When I get inta the reception they give me a cable that has come round from the American Express. I open it. It is from Willis Perriner. It says:

Reference your investigation in Paris stop Regret trouble to you and F.B.I. Am now perfectly satisfied with marriage between Sergius and Geraldine stop Buddy situation is O.K. stop Have heard from him he is well and returning shortly stop Please inform your head-quarters of these facts stop Willis T. Perriner stop. End.

Now laugh that one off!

CHAPTER EIGHT
MISTER BORG COMES THROUGH

I GO up to my room an' I read the cable from Perriner again. I think I am gettin' wise to this guy.

I call through to the American Express an' I send a cable, to go off to him right away. I say that I have got his cable, an' I am very glad to hear all the good news, that I am layin' off the case an' that I will get in touch with F.B.I. headquarters at Washington an' let 'em know.

I then get through to the American Embassy an' ask 'em to get a telephone call through to Washington tellin' the Director about the wire I have just got from Perriner, sayin' that it looks to me like a lotta hooey, an' that I am keeping on with the job here.

Maybe you guys would think I would be surprised at gettin' a wire like that from Perriner but I am not surprised at all, because the technique of a kidnappin' case is always the same. Somebody gets snatched an' the relatives go rushin' around to police headquarters or the F.B.I. an' try to get 'em back. Then before the law officers have got a chance to do anything at all the guys who have pulled the kidnap stick in their ransom note an' in it they always say that in the event of there bein' any trouble with the police they will bump off the guy they have kidnapped pronto. So it looks to me as if Perriner has got the ransom note, has been told that two F.B.I. operatives—Wilks an' myself—are playin' around tryin' to get next to this job, an' that if he wants to see Buddy Perriner back again he'd better get us to lay off.

Perriner then gets plenty scared an' sends that cable off to me right away. So I reckon he musta got the ransom note a coupla days ago—in other words it was goin' off to him just about the time I arrived in Paris.

I reckon this is an interestin' situation because if the demand for the ransom was sent off by the Nakorova guys, an' if Nakorova was supposed to finally receive the dough if an' when it was paid, then they will be in a little bit of a spot because at the present moment Nakorova is not interested in ransoms.

I give myself a cigarette an' four fingers of rye. I am feelin' a little bit better because I have got an idea in the back of my head that things will start movin' in a minute.

Just then my telephone rings. It is the desk downstairs an' they say that Mr. Alphonse Zeldar is around here to see me. I tell 'em to send him up.

A coupla minutes after he blows in. His nose looks sharper than ever, but he is cheerful an' smilin' as if he was glad to see me. Under his arm he has got a big document case that looks as if it is pretty full.

"You're on time, Zeldar," I tell him. "But where's Nakorova? I thought he was comin' round with you."

He puts his case down an' takes off his overcoat. He shrugs his shoulders.

"I do not know what has happened to Sergius," he says. "I called at his apartment on my way round. I rang the bell for a long time but nothing happened. I thought possibly I should find him here."

"Well, he ain't here," I say. "Listen, Zeldar," I go on, "I don't see why you an' me shouldn't talk straight to each other because I'd hate you to do anything that was goin' to get *you* into a jam, but the fact of the matter is that I am not very pleased with this Sergius Nakorova. I'm beginnin' to think he is very bad medicine. That bein' so I'm inclined to cast a suspicious eye on his pals, an' I take it that you're one of 'em. I ain't tryin' to be rude," I go on. "I'm just tryin' to show you how my mind's workin', see?"

I give him a cigarette. He lights it an' sits down. He spreads his hands.

"You must realise, Mr. Caution," he says, "that all this business is to me very mysterious. I have known Sergius Nakorova for a considerable period and to tell you the truth I know nothing about him which does not reflect to his credit. I hoped that this morning, by the time that he and I had finished with this interview, I should have been able to prove to you that he is an essentially honest man of business, and that there was no possible reason for him being implicated in the startling kidnap plot of which you spoke last night."

"That's swell, Zeldar," I tell him, "and it sounds marvellous. Now you tell me something. What do you think of Edvanne Nakorova?"

He gives another little shrug.

"You mean Sergius' sister?" he said. "I think she is a very charming woman—a little temperamental possibly, and inclined to be always falling in love with some man or another—otherwise a charming woman."

I grin.

"So you're tellin' me that you didn't know Edvanne Nakorova was his wife?" I tell him.

He raised his eyebrows.

"But I always thought she was his sister!" he says.

"Not on your life," I tell him. "She ain't even Russian, although she speaks the language pretty well. She's French. The other thing is what would be your position if Nakorova wasn't here?"

"I'm afraid I don't quite understand you," he says. "What do you mean?"

I grin at him.

"Nothin' very much," I tell him, "except that Nakorova ain't here. He's dead. Last night he got himself poisoned somehow. Maybe you can tell me where we go from there."

He looks at me with his mouth open.

"That's the reason," I go on, "that you couldn't get inta the flat this mornin'."

He looks sorta blank. Then he picks up the document case an' snaps it open. While I'm lookin' at it I see that some of the fingers on his left hand are stiff an' he can't bend 'em. He keeps 'em straight all the time. I get the idea in my head that at some time or other maybe this guy has had a bullet through the wrist an' the finger nerves are bust.

After a bit he says: "Well it looks as if there is not much use in continuing with this conversation, Mr. Caution."

I come to the conclusion that this guy is not puttin' on an act. He looks to me as if he is really dumbfounded. He also looks as if he's doin' some very quick thinkin', tryin' to work out what actually happened about this Nakorova killin'.

"Just a minute," I tell him. "If you don't mind I think we'll go head with this investigation into the Nakorova business just the same as if he was here. So far as I was concerned, an' certainly as far as the French police are concerned, Nakorova was a suspect, but he had other people workin' for him. The fact that he an' Edvanne are dead don't mean that we are givin' up. So maybe you'd like to let me know something about Nakorova's background that you an' he was so proud of."

"With pleasure," he says. "Incidentally, Mr. Caution," he goes on, "I would like to tell you that so far as I am concerned I welcome an investigation into any of the facts which I disclose to you this morning. First of all I would like you to look through these documents."

He pulls a bunch of papers outa the document case an' puts 'em on the table. I start to look through 'em. He stands by my side an' starts explainin' what they are.

To cut a long story short there is a perfectly good certificate of registration of the firm of Gloydas, Nakorova & Haal with registered offices in Zurich, Switzerland. This firm, according to the certificate, was registered two years ago. It has got a capital in Swiss money which is equivalent to about 200,000 dollars American. There is another

Dutch registration certificate showin' the registration of a subsidiary office of the same firm in Delfzyl, Holland. There are attached to both these certificates the tradin' reports of the businesses over the last eighteen months, an' it looks as if they have handled considerable import an' export business.

There are statements from the Rotterdamsche Bank an' the Swiss Bank, showin' balances an' bankin' transactions carried on on behalf of the two corporations for a considerable period, an' it looks to me as if this business is on the up-an'-up. If it is, it certainly proves that Nakorova was a guy of some sorta substance, although the fact that he is a member of a firm that is doin' fairly big business is no reason why he shouldn't have tried to screw a coupla million dollars outa old Willis Perriner on the side.

I get my notebook an' I make some notes about this business, after which I tell Zeldar that so far as I am concerned it is O.K.

He says: "You will of course check on these documents, Mr. Caution. You can do that quite easily through the French or American Consuls in both places. I have nothing to hide and"—he drops his voice—"I am certain that my poor friend and principal, Sergius, had nothing to hide."

I say that is O.K. so far as I am concerned, that I am sorry I've given him a lotta trouble.

He gets up an' holds out his hand.

"Goodbye for the present, Mr. Caution," he says. "Possibly we shall meet again."

"Maybe," I tell him. "In the meantime do you mind my askin' you a personal question. I'm sorta interested, see? I was lookin' at the fingers of your left hand. They look stiff to me. Was that a bullet?"

He smiles.

"Yes," he says. "It was an accident on a rifle range two years ago. One of the nerves was affected and I have lost the use of those fingers. I manage very well without them," he goes on.

I say that is too bad. Then I put on a very friendly look an' I say:

"Listen, Mr. Zeldar, I do not want to make a lot of trouble for you an' I reckon that the best thing I can do is to send you around to see my pal Felix Erouard at the Sûreté Nationale. I want you to give him the names an' addresses of the two Nakorova organisations in Switzerland an' Holland because he can check on 'em easier than I can. Then if they're O.K. with him I shall know that so far as you are concerned you are personally all right in this business."

He says that he reckons that this is very kind of me an' that he will call around an' see Erouard first thing next mornin'. He says thank you again an' he scrams.

The guy has just closed the door behind him when my phone bell goes, an' Erouard's guy Briquet comes through. He introduces himself an' then says that Juanella left the Hotel St. Anne about a quarter of an hour ago an' that she is now havin' her hair done an' a facial at some dump on the Rue de la Paix.

I say thanks a lot an' I tell this guy Briquet to stick close to Juanella, to keep on her all day an' to let me know just what she does an' where she gets around to.

I then smoke a cigarette an' do a little quiet thinkin'. I am not feelin' so good about Geraldine. I would like some idea as to where that dame is. Somehow I am sorta worried about that baby.

After a bit I get my hat, go downstairs, take a cab an' drive around to the Hotel St. Anne. I show the Manager my police pass an' tell him I would like to take a look around Mrs. Rillwater's apartment while she is out. He says O.K. an' gives me the key. I go up in the lift, open the door an' go inta Juanella's sittin'-room. I look around because I have an idea that maybe Geraldine might have sent her a note before she scrammed, but I can't see anythin' at all, not that I really expected to because I reckon Juanella is too cute to leave anything that matters lyin' around.

I walk across the sittin'-room an' stand in the doorway leadin' to the bedroom. I look around at the dressin' table an' on the writin' table but I cannot see anythin' there. The room is nice an' tidy. I am just steppin' back inta the sittin'-room when I hear a noise from the bathroom on the other side of the bedroom. The bathroom door is open an' for a minute I get the idea that maybe one of the chambermaids is cleanin' up in there.

I ease quietly across the bedroom, around the bottom of the bed, an' look through a crack in the bathroom door. Through this crack I can see the other end of the bathroom. There is a sorta white medicine cupboard fixed on to the wall. Standin' in front of this cupboard, goin' through the bottles, is a dame.

She has got her back to me so I cannot see what her face is like, but I am tellin' you that she has got a honey of a figure. She is about five feet seven inches high an' is wearin' a very well-fittin' suit that looks as if it come from a good tailor.

An' she is goin' through the bottles an' boxes in the cupboard as if it was somethin' important. She is takin' 'em out, puttin' 'em on the floor, searchin' around generally, as if she expected to find something hidden behind or under one of the bottles. After a bit she gives it up an' starts puttin' the bottles back in the cupboard.

When she does this she turns around an' I can see her face matches up with the rest of her figure. Her hair is black, an' she has a pretty little nose an' a mouth that shows what they call character. I think she is a nice dame, an' I think it would be a pity to disturb her now that I know what she looks like.

I step back quietly, turn around, ease outa the bedroom, across the sittin'-room an' scram downstairs.

I see the manager an' I ask him if anybody else has been around in Mrs. Rillwater's suite this mornin'. He says no, which tells me somethin', because as Juanella's door was locked when I got up there it looks as if this doll I have seen upstairs is just another mystery dame who has got herself a key to Juanella's room.

I go back to my hotel an' give myself a little drink. I reckon this case is gettin' thicker every minute. Whichever way a guy turns some fresh dame pops up.

An' I would not mind if some of 'em was ugly. An ugly dame would be a nice change. There are too many good-lookin' babies stickin' around in this Perriner business an' I do not like this very much because I have always found that even one good-lookin' dame spells plenty trouble an' when you get a lot of 'em there is goin' to be a riot.

At seven-thirty I am havin' dinner when Erouard's man Briquet comes in. First of all he tells me that Erouard has got the lowdown on Geraldine. Geraldine went out to Le Bourget aerodrome. She hired a private plane for England. Where she was goin' to when she gets there nobody knows. So that's that. Here is one dame who anyway for the moment is outa the picture.

Briquet then tells me about Juanella. After this baby has her hair done she drives around and does some shoppin', after which she gets along to Montmartre to a place called the Hotel Mouton. This Hotel Mouton is a third-rate sorta dump which the French cops have had an eye on for some time. It is one of them places where the funny guys hang out. Briquet sees Juanella go in there an' sticks around until she comes out. He then goes in an' flashes his police card at the proprietor, who is a guy who has already done one stretch for receivin', an' asks him to talk. The guy decides to do so. He tells Briquet that Juanella has been enquirin' about some bozo who has been stayin' at the Hotel Mouton for some time—an American by the name of Borg an' it looks like Juanella wants to see this guy Borg plenty bad. Borg ain't in, but the proprietor says he will be around at half-past eleven that night, an' has told Juanella that if she will come around at that time she will probably catch him, to which she says she will be there.

Briquet then tells the proprietor that it will be healthy for him to keep his mouth shut about this little conversation an' not to let Borg know anything about it. The proprietor says this is O.K. by him, that he will stay as close as a clam.

I reckon this is good work, because I think that if I can find out what Juanella wants with this Borg we might get some place. I ask Briquet to tell Erouard somethin' from me. You remember when I was seein' this guy Zeldar I told him to go an' see Erouard, that Erouard would check up on the businesses that Nakorova was interested in in Holland an' Switzerland? Now the only way that Erouard can check up is through the consular offices in those places, an' as I reckon that this business is a legitimate one, the consular reports will be O.K. for the very simple reason that if there is any funny business goin' on it will be well under the surface, an' the consular guys will know nothin' about it.

If this guy Zeldar is crooked an' if he takes me for a mug he will think that I will be satisfied with those reports, which is where he is makin' a big mistake, because all I am trying to do is to keep this guy's mind at rest while I get on with a little investigation on my own.

So I tell Briquet that it will be a good thing if Erouard does not really make any enquiries at all, that the thing for him to do is to *say* he is goin' to make the enquiries an' to tell Zeldar to come back in a coupla days, an' when he comes back to say that everything is hunky dory, that the French Consuls in both places have reported that the businesses are legitimate an' everything is swell.

You get the idea? If Zeldar is tryin' to pull somethin' on me he will think that he has got away with it an' that I believe everything he has said about the Nakorova business, which is a thing I would like him to believe because I have got an idea that I am goin' to take a look at things myself.

I give Briquet a big drink an' he scrams off to report to Erouard. I then stick around in the reception tellin' some funny stories that I know to the blonde in the office. She is a nice doll, an' even if she don't see the point all the time she has got a nice line in hips.

It is a quarter past eleven when I stop my cab at the end of the street an' ease along to the Hotel Mouton.

This place gives me the jitters. It is as dark as hell, an' smells like the Romans under Julius Cæsar had been cookin' fish around there an' forget to take 'em away with 'em.

I go across the hallways an' into a passage on the other side. Halfway down is a sorta reception office. There is a fat guy inside smokin' a rattail cheroot, an' wearin' a beret.

I show him my police pass an' remind him about Briquet seein' him that mornin'. He remembers an' says what do I want. I tell him that I reckon that the dame who wanted to see Borg will be comin' along an' that I would like to stick around some place where I can see this guy Borg without him seein' me.

He says that is O.K. by him because he reckons that Borg will see the lady in his room an' that there is a coupla holes in the wall between Borg's room an' the next one, an' when I ask him how he gets these holes in the walls he shrugs his shoulders an' says that times are very hard an' he has gotta make a livin' somehow. He then takes me upstairs an' along a passage an' into a room that smells like a garlic factory. He shows me where the hole is an' scrams.

I sit down in the dark an' smoke a cigarette. I get to thinkin' that maybe one of these days I will get myself a really nice case to work on where all the dames are beautiful an' good instead of bein' beautiful an' screwy, an' where rooms do not smell like somebody had left a lot of dead bodies around for about twenty years, an' where I can use the better part of my nature which is sorta poetic, instead of havin' to be tough all the time an' slammin' guys around.

Right in the middle of these thoughts I hear a noise next door. I stick my eyes to the hole in the wall just as the guy turns the light on, an' believe it or not I nearly let go a yelp.

Because this is Borg all right. This is Freddy Borg the one an' only—the guy who snatched the Fremer kid back in '32 with Johnny Landera. I give a big sigh because I think that now maybe somethin' might happen.

I watch him lightin' a cigarette an' while he does it I think that I have maybe got this set-up. I reckon that Nakorova used Borg to snatch Buddy Perriner, an' that Borg has come over to Paris as arranged to contact Sergius an' tell him that the job is O.K. Maybe he has already done this an' that is why Willis Perriner has got the ransom note that has made him send me that cable tellin' me to lay off.

Well if this is so what is Juanella doin' around here? What does this dame want with Borg?

Right then the door opens an' the proprietor comes in an' says something to Borg. Borg nods his head an' a coupla minutes later Juanella shows up.

She shuts the door behind her an' Borg sits down on one side of the bed lookin' like a good-natured gorilla. I can see him grinnin' at her an' makin' some crack.

Then Juanella starts in. She starts talkin'. I am cussin' like hell because I cannot hear one word that anybody is sayin' but I can see by the way that Juanella is carryin' on that she is handin' out some very rough stuff to this mug.

An' he don't like it. He gets off the bed an' starts wavin' his arms about an' talkin' back at her. After a minute Juanella tries somethin' else. She starts smilin' at him an' puttin' on a sweet act. She opens up her handbag an' pulls out a big packet of dough. Borg's eyes pop when he sees this. He starts amblin' across the room towards her. I grin to myself because I am thinkin' that if Borg thinks he is goin' to pull a fast one on Juanella he had better think some more. An' I am dead right because just when the mug gets over to Juanella she pulls a nice little .32 outa her handbag an' sits on the bed.

Juanella gets a cigarette outa her handbag an' lights it. I can see she is sorta arguin' with him, but he only grins an' argues back.

After a bit she gives up. I can see by the look on her face that she is beat. She puts the dough back in her handbag, goes over to the door, opens it, turns around an' says somethin'. He shakes his head. She shrugs her shoulders sorta hopelessly and goes out. I ease over to the doorway an' listen to her walkin' along the passage an' goin' down the stairs.

I give a grin an' go back to the hole in the wall. Borg is lyin' on the bed smokin' a cigarette.

I sit down on the chair an' do a little thinkin'. It looks to me like Juanella has come along here for the purpose of gettin' this guy to do somethin' for her. Either she wants him to do somethin' or to tell her somethin'. She offers him dough to come across but he is not havin' any. First of all he tries to grab off the dough an' then when that don't work he just says no.

O.K. Well I reckon if it was good enough for Juanella who I think is a very smart dame then it is good enough for me.

I get up. I creep along the passage very quietly until I come to the door. I push it open an' step in. Borg slides off the bed sideways an' sees me.

"Jeez!" he says. "Caution!"

He starts grinnin' at me.

I sit down on the chair.

"Look, Freddy," I tell him. "You an' me have met before an' are sorta old pals. I got a little bedtime story I want to tell you. This is the story about two frogs. One of these frogs wanted the other frog to talk an' the other frog wasn't havin' any so the first frog got tough."

I grin at him.

"Maybe you know the rest of the story?"

He lays himself down on the bed again. You gotta realise that this guy Borg is very tough indeed.

"Can it," he says. "This ain't America, an' I don't scare easy. Scram, copper. I got nothin' to say to you. You ain't got anythin' on me. Go fry an egg, flatfoot!"

"O.K., mug," I tell him. "We'll get goin'. There's a French police wagon waitin' downstairs for you. An' how will you have it? Are you goin' quietly or do I have to get 'em to come up for you?"

His eyes pop.

"Say, what is this?" he says. "This is a frame-up. . . ."

"Listen, Borg," I say. "You tell that story around at the police dump here. Get goin'."

He tells me just what I am. Then he gets up an' starts walkin' towards the door. I open it for him. Just when he is opposite me I catch him a smack across the side of the neck that woulda killed an ox. He goes down but he is up before you can say go an' takes a slam at me that woulda put paid to me if it had contacted.

I side-step, pick up the chair an' let him have it. I hit him across the dome with it but it only makes him pause. He just gathers himself together an' comes for me. It looks like he is goin' to be difficult.

I stick up my knee at the right moment an' it takes him on the jaw. He gives a yelp an' tries to jump back. I walk in an' slam one right on his nose an' finish with a very subtle right hook in the stomach. He tries one final kick but misses again. I then bust him a smack on the kisser that they coulda heard in Spain. He goes over an' I go on top of him.

Everything is now very nice except I wish that this guy had not been eatin' onions. I pick up his head an' I bang it on the floor so hard that I am afraid of goin' through to the next floor. He does not react at all well to this. He gives me a mean kick in the stomach. I then let him have a haymaker right between the eyes, after which I drag him up against the wall an' start practisin' gymnasium short-arm jabs on his gold-fillin's. I am now very annoyed with him.

His head starts to drop back. I think that he has had enough an' I ease up. He brings up his knee an' gives me a push in the waistline that woulda sunk a battleship. I go over backwards with a nasty sinkin' feelin'. He gets up to his feet an' fetches a kick at my face that woulda made a coupla mommas I knew sorry for me but he misses because he cannot see very well. While I am tryin' to get up he goes over to the washstand an' comes back at me with a filled water bottle. If he hits me with this I think I will have white violets on my grave. I let him think that I am worse than I am. I stagger towards him sorta dizzy.

As he swings the bottle I fall back on the floor, get a Japanese scissor lock on his legs an' twist. He goes over.

By now I am very angry with this guy. I get to work on him properly.

I give him the elbow. I do not hit him with my fist. When he tries to get up I bring my elbow up under his jaw. I give him two of these. I then get up an' pull him up to his feet. He stands there lookin' dreamy. I take a step back, give myself a very nice stance an' let him have one very sweet and very beautiful sleepin' draught. I hit this guy so hard that I nearly knock his block right off.

He goes out.

I sit down on what is left of the chair an' give myself a breather. Right then there is a knock on the door an' when I say come in the door opens and the fat proprietor guy comes in. He is smilin'.

He looks at Borg an' he says: "Did you ring? I thought you might want something?"

"No," I tell him. "My pal an' me have just been practisin' a new dance, but you might bring along a bottle of brandy an' two glasses an' some cigarettes."

He says but yes certainly an' goes off.

I pour the water bottle over Borg. He opens his eyes an' looks at me. Then he starts feelin' his jaw.

"O.K., pal," I tell him. "Now let you an' me do a little talkin'. An' any time you wanta start somethin' go right ahead."

"That suits me," he says. "But I wanna tell you somethin'. One of these times I'm gonna get at you. I'm gonna do somethin' to you. . . ."

He tells me what he is goin' to do to me one of these times an' I'm tellin' you guys that it is not very nice at all. An' he has got a sorta descriptive way of tellin' it that makes it worse.

I go over to him an' yank him up. I stick him up on the bed an' I smack him a nice one on the beezer.

"Take it easy," I tell him. "Because you are goin' to talk an' talk plenty. If you talk you get a drink, a cigarette an' no coppers. If you don't I am goin' to start a *blitzkrieg* on you that would make Hitler look like an angel with wings on. Have you got me, pal?"

He says he has got me.

Right then the fat guy comes in with the brandy an' some cigarettes. I tell him to charge it to my pal Borg.

I take a little drink. Borg says:

"Don't I get nothin', you bastard?"

"Sure, pal," I tell him. "You will get somethin' all right. Because I would like you to know that you cannot call me a thing like that because my mother was a very particular dame an' I have got every reason to believe that she married my old man two months before I was born. So that makes you a heel an' I am gonna push your nose outa the back of your head right now."

He says: "Lay off me. I was only speakin' metaphorical."

I think this out an' I am not sure whether it is a proper sort of apology so I bust him one just in case.

This gives me time to finish the bottle an' when he comes to he starts talkin'.

CHAPTER NINE
SWEET STICK-UP

IT IS about two o'clock when I get through with Borg an' in a way I feel sorta sorry for this guy. Because here he is come over to Paris thinkin' that he is goin' to collect a nice wad of dough from Nakorova for pullin' a very sweet kidnappin' job an' all he gets is a bust in the beezer.

Before I go I talk straight to this mug. I tell him that my advice to him is to stick around the Hotel Mouton until his face heals up an' then to scram out of it an' to get back to New York the best way he can an' to keep his mouth buttoned up. I tell him if I get one crack outa him he'll spend the rest of his life kickin' his heels in Alcatraz. I think he sorta feels the strength of this argument.

I do not think I am goin' to have any trouble with Borg, but I have got an idea in my head that I do not want him kickin' around tryin' to find Nakorova because I do not want him to know Nakorova is dead.

An' I have got another reason. I reckon that Borg was not workin' on his own on this kidnap job. Borg is a very good muscle man but he ain't overburdened with brains. Nakorova wouldn't have been such a mug as to put Borg in charge of the snatch so I reckon there was some other guys in it with him.

But I do not ask him about these guys because that is one question that nothin' would make him answer. Borg is a rat all right but he ain't a squealer an' even if I was to saw his head off he wouldn't give the names away.

It looks to me that if it was good enough for Borg to come over here an' collect his dough then maybe it will also be good enough for the other guys.

So I give him a nice goodnight. I tell him that if the French cops see him kickin' around Paris they will certainly pull him in an' so if he wants to stay outa the can he better keep under cover until the time when his boat goes.

He sorta falls for this. I reckon I won't have any more trouble with the guy.

I leave him drainin' the brandy bottle. I take a cab an' I get around to the Hotel St. Anne. When I get there I have a word with the night guy in the reception, show him my police pass an' tell him to do a little ringin' on the 'phone for the benefit of Mrs. Rillwater. After a minute he says that she would like me to go right up. I grin to myself because it looks to me as if Juanella will not be feelin' so good about one or two things.

When I get inside her sittin'-room she is there waitin' for me. It does not take me very long to see that this dame has been cryin'. She has got a couple side curls outa place—which, if you know Juanella, is a very extraordinary thing—an' there are dark circles under her eyes.

"How's it comin', babe?" I tell her. "Now the thing to do is to relax an' give Uncle Lemmy a little drink, because you an' I are goin' to talk a whole lotta sense. I would also like to tell you that the next time you try a double-crossin' act with me the Day of Judgment will be a walkover compared with what I am goin' to do to you."

She shrugs her shoulders.

"Oh, what the hell!" she says. "I give up!"

She goes over to the sideboard an' brings out the rye bottle. She pours me a little drink an' hands me a cigarette. Then she sits down.

"Well?" she says. "What's eatin' you this time, handsome?"

"It's your turn to do the talkin' gorgeous," I tell her. "But just so's you'll see I'm not tryin' any bluff on you I'd like to tell you one or two things. You went round to see Borg to-night. You took a little packet of dough round there with you. You tried to graft Borg to tell you where Buddy Perriner was, but he wasn't havin' any. An' anyway he didn't know."

She looks at me with her eyes poppin'.

"I was in the next room," I tell her. "That Hotel Mouton is one of those funny places with holes in the wall. After you'd scrammed I went in an' had a little séance with Borg myself. But my arguments were a bit more forceful than yours. He listened to me."

"I bet he did," she says. "I hope you hurt that guy."

"I hurt him plenty," I tell her. "He said I was a bastard."

She looks sorta dreamy.

"I didn't know he had that amount of sense," she says. "Me—I have always thought you was a love-child too. It sounds better that way. Only don't let a little thing like that stop you makin' a pass at me some time when you feel you can get around to it."

"Look, honey," I tell her. "I think you are swell. You got a nifty figure an' you got a sweet temperament . . ."

"An' where does it get me with you?" she says. "So far as you are concerned I could have a figure like Helen of Troy an' you would never worry to find out whether I wore an old-time wrap around or just kept my stockin's up with glue. I reckon you ought to have been an Esquimaux. You're so goddam cold you ain't even *curious.*"

"Juanella, you lie," I tell her. "You thrill me. Every time I look at you it is just like takin' a sleepin' draught. But use your brains. You know my rule. I never mix pleasure with business."

"Hooey," she says. "You are such a goddam liar that you would make Goebbels look like George Washington. Any time that business stops you givin' a dame a tumble I will paint a coupla swastikas on my step-ins an' rush out an' start colonisin' the North Pole. But it's O.K. with me," she goes on. "I just ain't got any luck. I been tryin' to make you for two years an' you'd even believe it if I told you I got cork legs. You still woulda wanta see for yourself."

She gives herself a cigarette.

"So what's the trouble?" she says.

I blow a very nice smoke ring an' I look at her through it.

"I suppose you wouldn't know where your little friend Geraldine is, Juanella?" I tell her.

"No," she says. "All I know is she's not round at the hotel. I wish to God I knew where that kid was."

"Me too," I say.

I stretch out my legs.

"This is one of them nice nights," I go on. "It is sorta full of surprises. I'll give you another one. Sergius an' Edvanne Nakorova are dead."

She don't say nothin'. She gets up, goes over to the sideboard an' gives herself a drink, an' she turns around an' looks at me, leanin' up against the sideboard.

"Sometimes," she says, "I think I am goin' nuts! You're not *really* tellin' me that those two mugs have really departed from in amongst us?"

"That's the way it goes," I say.

She goes back an' flops inta her chair.

"For cryin' out loud," she mutters. "So what now?" She starts thinkin'. "Look, Lemmy," she says. "What happened to these two guys?"

"Plenty," I tell her. "Last night at that supper party Edvanne Nakorova slipped me a note. She told me she wanted to see me. I reckon she was scared.

"O.K. Well I went around to her apartment an' waited for her. She was sorta playin' around on the edge of things tryin' to do a deal with me. She practically admitted that Nakorova had been behind the Buddy Perriner snatch. The next thing was she was goin' around to see him an' try to get him to talk. When I get around there they are both dead. She killed him."

Juanella purses up her lips an' whistles.

"What do you know about that screwy dame?" she says. "An' what the hell did she wanta do that for?"

"Did you know she was Sergius' wife?" I tell her.

She shakes her head.

"No," she says. "But I wouldn't be surprised at anythin'."

"Well, she was," I say. "Edvanne Nakorova was a French woman. I think she was pretty stuck on Sergius too. It would have to be a pretty tough job of work that would make her bump him, but she did it."

"But what for?" she says. "What would she wanta do a thing like that for?"

"She wanted Nakorova to come clean an' spill the beans," I say. "Nakorova wasn't havin' any. He pulled a gun on her an' said if she didn't behave herself he'd give her the works. So she poisoned him an' she poisoned herself afterwards."

"Yeah," says Juanella, "but you're not tellin' me *why*."

"I'm tellin' you now," I say. "Sergius was a Russian an' Edvanne was French."

"So what?" she says. "Does every dame who's not got the same nationality as her husband have to poison the guy?"

"Not always, Juanella," I say, "but this time that's how it was."

I go over to the sideboard an' give myself another little drink.

"Look, baby," I tell her, "I reckon things are movin' pretty fast in this job. Pretty soon there's goin' to be some real fireworks. If you take a tip from me you're goin' to cash in right from the start."

She says: "There's nothin' else to do. This job's gettin' beyond me. What do you wanta know, Lemmy?"

"First of all," I tell her, "you tell me why it was that Willis Perriner went bail for you comin' outa the United States, an' why was it that his attorneys fixed your passport, an' why did you come over here an' start cavortin' around with Geraldine without Larvey knowin' anythin' about it?"

She says: "Well, that's easy. I wanted to pull a fast one on Larvey. Things ain't been so good with us lately. Ever since Larvey an' I have been under that suspended sentence that you fixed for us, business has been bad an' it looked to me that here was a chance to make some legitimate money." She leans forward. "You know Sam Fremer's Bar, Lemmy?" she says.

I nod my head.

"I was kickin' around there one night," she goes on, "an' I heard somethin' I wasn't supposed to hear. Willie Lodz was a bit high. He was shootin' his mouth off to some smart dame he'd got with him. He was tellin' her that pretty soon they'd be in the red, that they were goin' to be worth a lotta money. He mentioned Borg's name. Well, you know Borg. If there's ever been a tough kidnappin' stunt in the U.S. Borg was somehow mixed up in it. He was just born in the snatch business.

"I didn't think anything much about it, but after he's had a few more drinks I hear Lodz say 'Perriner,' an' I get wise. Everybody around town was wonderin' what had happened to Buddy Perriner. I got the idea in my head that he'd been snatched. So I went along an' saw Willis Perriner an' I gave him a little advice."

"Such as?" I tell her.

"Such as that Buddy had been grabbed off by a very tough crowd an' that I thought maybe I could help, that I was lookin' for a little easy dough on the side, that I wasn't afraid of anything an' that maybe I could get into a lotta places where coppers couldn't get."

"Ain't you the little smart dame?" I crack. "So what did Willis say?"

"Willis told me about Nakorova," she says. "He told me that he thought Nakorova was behind the snatch. He also said that he was over her in Paris an' that Geraldine, who was nuts about him, was over here too. He said he'd stake me to come over here to wise up Geraldine as to what I thought, an' tell her what sort of a guy Nakorova really was. He said the thing for me to do was to play this thing on my own, to get over here, stick around with Geraldine, to look after her an' to see that she didn't make a goddam fool of herself with this Sergius guy."

I nod my head.

"An' I suppose it was you who told Willis not to let me know anythin' about it?" I say.

"You're dead right, cutey," she says. "Because first of all I thought if you knew you'd give me the air, an' secondly thought I might be a bit smart an' pull a fast one on you. I reckoned it would be good goin' for me to get that Perriner boy back again right under your nose. Besides I wanted the dough. Anyhow," she goes on, "Willis Perriner was so desperate that he fell for the idea."

She shrugs her shoulders.

"I wasn't to know I was comin' over on the same boat as you," she says. "I spotted you the first day out an' I got plenty scared. I radioed Geraldine that I was on my way to see her from her pa an' that if she wanted to send any message to me she'd better sign it 'The Boy Friend.' I fixed this in case you tried to get at the radio guy aboard. I wasn't so pleased at you bein' on the *Fels Ronstrom*. That was just too tough."

"It mighta been tough on you," I say. "It mighta been tough if I'd had you wiped up for obstructin' me around here. As it is you might be more of a help than a hindrance. Tell me somethin' : Who do you think was in on this snatch? Who were the guys who actually did it?"

"Three of them," she says. "There was Borg, Willie Lodz an' some dame I don't know, some classy dame. You know what that kid Buddy Perriner is—he falls for any woman who's got a nice shape an' a sweet face. So I think they got one for him. It was the dame who got him down to the place where they snatched him."

"You wouldn't know what that dame looks like?" I say.

She shakes her head.

"Why?" she says. "Is she important?"

I grin.

"Listen, honey," I tell her. "I'll tell you something funny. This mornin' when you were gettin' your hair done I came up here an' had a look around your rooms here. I'd already found out that Geraldine had scrammed. I thought she mighta sent you a note or something before she went. I got a pass key from downstairs an' I came up here snoopin'.

"While I was in your bedroom I heard somebody kickin' around in the bathroom. I took a peek through a crack in the door an' there was some fancy dame searchin' around tryin' to find something. Now this dame had a good shape an' a face to match it. She looked as if she might be a nifty number. I wonder if that was the dame that Willie an' Borg used. Maybe she was Lodz' girl."

"How would she be over here?" says Juanella.

"Why not?" I tell her. "Borg talked as much as he knew to-night. He admitted that they'd snatched Buddy, but he wouldn't say who his pals were. If Borg can be over here I don't see why Willie Lodz can't be over here *an'* the dame they used. Anyhow there was some dame up in these rooms, so it looks like its *gotta* be that dame."

She nods her head.

"What are you aimin' to do, Lemmy?" she says. "If Nakorova's dead, what is there to worry about?"

"Plenty," I tell her. "First of all at the present moment we don't know where Buddy Perriner is. Secondly we don't know where Geraldine is."

"Have you got any ideas?" she asks.

"Yeah," I tell her, "but I'm not tellin' you. I'm beginnin' to get some very sweet ideas in my head. The first thing that you've got to get inta yours is that you have gotta play ball, behave yourself. You gotta be a good girl. See?"

"I'm playin' ball," she says. "I feel all washed up. I'm worried sick about that kid Geraldine."

"Me too," I tell her. Because I am too although I'm not tellin' her why.

I give myself another cigarette.

"The point is," I tell her, "that this guy Zeldar who is secretary to this business Nakorova was supposed to be runnin', was around to see me this morning like we arranged. He came round to show me that Nakorova was on the up-an'-up. Now maybe Zeldar knows something about this business an' maybe he don't. We have got to find out. Do you know where he lives?"

She says she does. She says that after I left the party at the Cossack, Zeldar said that he was stayin' around at the Miramar apartments off the Rue de la Paix.

I look at my watch.

"O.K.," I tell her. "This is what you're goin' to do, Juanella. It is twenty minutes to three now. At three-fifteen you ring through to this Miramar dump an' you get Zeldar on the telephone. You tell him you gotta see him. Say you've got some very important information for him. Say he's got to come around to see you right away, otherwise hell will be poppin'."

"O.K. That guy oughta be around sometime about three forty-five. I'm goin' back to the Grand Hotel now, an' I'm goin' to hang on the end of my telephone wire. If you can fix it so Zeldar comes around to see you you ring through to me an' let me know."

"O.K.," she says. "An' what do I tell him when he gets around here?"

"I do not give a damn what you tell him," I say. "Make up something. Tell him some phoney story about Nakorova or Edvanne. Tell him that you can't find Geraldine, an' that you're worried sick. Don't let on that you know that Nakorova's dead.

"Sorta suggest to Zeldar that you are a pal of Borg's an' somehow mixed up in the Perriner snatch in America. See what he says an' let me know. The main thing is to keep Zeldar around here talkin'. You got that?"

She says O.K. an' I grab my hat. I have just got to the door when she says:

"Hey, Lemmy! An' what do I get for actin' as your unpaid stooge. Can't you say goodnight to a girl like a human bein'?"

I go back an' I give her a kiss. She puts her arms around my neck an' just *gives*. I'm tellin' you that this baby has got temperament plus.

When I break away it is like tearin' porous plaster off Grandpa's chest. She says sorta weak:

"There's one thing about you, handsome. You may be a cold son of a so-an'-so but you gotta honey of a technique. Any time you start a harem just give me a job mixin' the sherbert at night an' I'll slay put!"

She puts a curl back in place. Then she says:

"Don't worry, kid. I'm sold. I'll keep this guy Zeldar around here even if I haveta do a fan dance. I'm just another dame whose heart is breakin'. But I'm still smilin'. Scram, Casanova!"

When I get back to the hotel I give myself a hot shower after which I dress an' lay down on the bed an' start doin' some very serious ruminatin' because this mix-up is gettin' to be very interestin'.

With what I got outa Borg an' what Juanella has told me I get this story:

Nakorova goes over to New York an' makes a play for Geraldine Perriner in order to get next to Buddy. He fixes it so that when the time is ripe Borg, Willie Lodz an 'some good-lookin' dame that they are usin' to string the kid along are goin' to snatch Buddy.

O.K. Well, the snatch comes off an' Nakorova beats it for Paris. Geraldine, who still thinks she is nuts about him, comes after him. Willis Perriner gets the jitters about Buddy an' gets the F.B.I. on the job, an' Wilks is told off to keep an eye on things over here.

Juanella Rillwater, kickin' around New York an' lookin' for some pickin's, hears enough of a conversation in Fremer's Bar to put two an' two together an' get wise to the kidnappin' trio. Bein' a smart baby, an' thinkin' that she can do a bit of good for herself, she does not go to the cops but gets along to Willis Perriner an' tells him what she has heard.

Pa Perriner tries to be smart. He don't say anything to the F.B.I. but he fixes with Juanella to come over to Paris *pronto,* see Geraldine, *prove to her* that Nakorova is really a bad guy, an' stick around an' generally keep her eye on Geraldine so that nothin' happens to *her.* He cables Geraldine that Juanella is comin' over on the *Fels Ronstrom.*

I come over on the same boat. I radio Geraldine off the boat an' tell her that I am Hickory an' want to see her. She shows the cable tee Nakorova because she does not know at that time that he is the kidnappin' guy.

An' then she radios Juanella on the boat sayin' that she is interested in me an' signs the radio 'The Boy Friend.' So it was Geraldine who sent this cable to Juanella an' not Sergius.

Sergius now gets wise to the fact that some trouble is goin' to break. He has found out that Rodney Wilks has been stickin' around findin' out a thing or two, so he puts Edvanne in to get Wilks outa the way an' meet me pretendin' to be Geraldine an' stall me along until such time as he can bump me off.

But he does not tell Edvanne that the stuff he gives her will kill Wilks. He says it is just a Mickey Finn that will put him nicely to sleep for a bit, an' she believes him.

Soon after I arrive an' after I have seen Geraldine the first time, Juanella blows along an' tells her what she knows. Geraldine is smacked clean outa the field for a home run. She knows now that Sergius is bad medicine but she sticks around pretendin' to be still stuck on him because she thinks that this way she has got a chance of findin' out where Buddy is. Juanella probably tells her that this is the way to play it because that baby is mad keen to rescue Buddy before me an' touch Willis Perriner for a big hand-out for services rendered.

So everything is all right up to there. Zeldar is put in by Nakorova to prove that he has really got a business an' stall me off for a bit so that they will have time to do something—*what?*

By this time Willis Perriner has heard from the kidnappers. They tell him that they have got Buddy an' that unless he gets the Federal Bureau to lay off they will bump the kid. Perriner goes haywire. He knows if he tells headquarters this they will not take any notice so he sends me that wire direct hopin' I will lay off. As you guys know I pretend to do this.

But there is something screwy about all this. If they have got Buddy an' are waitin' for the ransom why does Sergius take a chance an' get Edvanne to kill Wilks. They must know that whatever else they could have got away with they cannot get away with this. By killin' Wilks Nakorova was spoilin' his own game. *So why did he do it?*

I can guess the answer to that one. Sergius didn't mind havin' Wilks killed because he still thought the could get away with it. He thought he could get away with it so much that he wasn't even scared when Edvanne told him that I was on his tail. He had somethin' up his sleeve that made him feel safe.

An' he told Edvanne what that somethin' was an' she didn't like it an' that's why she killed him an' herself too.

In the meantime Borg an' his pals are worryin' about their rake-off. Somebody has got enough jack to finance Geraldine to try an' graft me to keep outa this job, but they have not got enough jack to pay off Borg an 'the boys who did the kidnappin', so Borg comes over to Paris to get his dough an' for all I know Willie Lodz—who is a sweet murderer who would bump his dyin' grandmother for ten dollars—is over here too an' the dame who was in it with 'em, an' for all I know this is the nice-lookin' baby that I saw givin' a quick once over to Juanella's bathroom—an' what the hell was *she* lookin' for?

But Borg don't know where Buddy is. An' I believed him when he said this because the job has been played so sweet that I reckon Nakorova would not let the actual snatchers know where Buddy was goin' to be finally kept.

An' here is the joke. Supposin' Nakorova has fixed it so that he is the only person who knows where Willis Perriner is sendin' the ransom? Supposin' he is the only guy who knows where Buddy is?

But I reckon I have still got a chance. I reckon that if my little theory about why Edvanne preferred to bump Sergius an' herself rather than *let somethin' happen* is right, then maybe I can still get next to this business. Anyway time will show as the guy said when he sat down on the electric bomb.

An' the last thing is Geraldine. Where is this baby? Why does she suddenly scram off an' leave everybody, includin' Juanella, up in the air? Why don't she let *anybody* know?

Well . . . maybe I know the answer to that one, an' if you guys are as smart as I think you are I reckon you can make a good guess too!

So there you are!

I have just concluded these deep thoughts when the telephone starts janglin'.

I slip off the bed an' grab it. I look at my watch. It is twenty-five minutes past three. Juanella comes through.

"Look, you great big blond an' beautiful beast," she says. "This guy Zeldar is on his way around to see me right now, an' I wish I knew what I am gonna tell him when he gets here."

"Swell, Juanella," I tell her. "You tell him what I told you. Keep him stringin' around for half an hour or so. Keep him there as long as you can."

"Like hell," she says. "It's nearly half-past three. Supposin' this guy tries to make me. What the hell!"

"That's O.K.," I crack back at her. "It wouldn't be the first time that some guy tried to make you an' won a smack on the schnozzle in the attempt. How did he sound?"

"Goddam suspicious," she says. "He wanted to know what the trouble was about an' I told him that Geraldine was gone off some place an' I was worried sick. I said that I thought that she'd taken a run-out powder with Nakorova an' that I thought of ringin' the police department an' gettin' them to put an alarm out. That seemed to get him. He said all right, he'd come around."

"Swell," I say. "An' now all you have to do is to start a big sobbin' act an' keep on talkin' hooey as long as you can, which is a thing that ought not to be very difficult for you, honey-lamb."

"Oh yeah," she says. "An' what are you gonna do in return for all this?"

"Sweet nothin'," I tell her. "Maybe I'll be nice to you one day an' buy you a vanilla sundae."

"Like hell you will," she says. "The only thing that you would give me is something with raspberries in it. But never mind, I'll catch you off your balance one day an' when I do . . ."

"What're you goin' to do to me, precious?" I say.

She tells me. I will not tell you guys what she says in case you are not very broad-minded.

I hang up, ease downstairs, an' get the night desk to telephone for a cab. When it comes I drive around an' stop the cab twenty yards from the Miramar apartments. I walk along an' take a look at this place. It is the usual sort of good class apartment block.

I ring the bell an' after a bit the concierge comes along an' asks what is it. I tell this guy that I am a friend of Mr. Zeldar's an' that he was called out half an hour ago an' that he would like me to wait for him till he comes back.

He takes a look at me an' says all right. He takes me up to the first floor an' shows me into a room. He says that I can wait there for Mr. Zeldar who will have to pass the door on the way to his apartment when he returns.

He then goes off. I give him two minutes an' then I walk along the corridor. There is only one door so I reckon this must be Zeldar's place.

The lock on the door is very old-fashioned an' I open it with a spider key that I carry in my pocket an' go in.

I shut the door behind me an' switch on the light. The place is a four-roomed flat with a sittin'-room an' library. There is a fire burnin' in the library grate an' a lot of papers spread out on the desk. It looks like Zeldar was workin' when Juanella came through.

I look through the papers an' I see that they have got to do with the Nakorova firm—Gloydas, Nakorova & Haal. There are a lotta reports about consignments of rye, bran an' a lotta other like stuff from different Mediterranean ports to Delfzyl—the Dutch place where the firm have got their sub-office. There are a lot of commercial papers an' whatnots but all lookin' very innocent an' I can't find anything that seems to matter very much.

I go into the other rooms an' start runnin' the rule over them but I'm still unlucky. There is nothin' that means anythin' at all. It looks to me like either this Zeldar don't know anythin' about what Nakorova has been play in' at or else he is a very wise guy who keeps things where other guys can't find 'em.

What the hell! I sit down in a chair an' start ruminatin'. I am sorta disappointed because all the time I have had a hunch that I was goin' to find somethin' here that would give me a good lead to work on an' it looks as if I was wrong.

I get up, switch off the lights an' start walkin' towards the apartment door. I am just goin' across the hall when the doorbell rings.

I stick my hand under my coat an' pull the Luger out of its holster, but I put it back again. Because I reckon that the guy at the door is not Zeldar.

First of all Juanella would have kept Zeldar longer than this, an' secondly he wouldn't have rung the bell. He would have had a key. I reckon that the concierge guy, thinkin' that Zeldar was comin' back pretty soon like I said, has left the main door unlocked downstairs, an' the guy outside has just walked in an' come straight up the stairs.

O.K. Well, we'll see.

I switch on the hall-light, take off my overcoat an' hat an' hang 'em up on the hall-stand, stick a cigarette in my mouth just as if I was the guy who lived here, an' open the door.

A tall, thin-faced guy is standin' in the doorway. He is smokin' a cigarette an' his mouth is twisted up in a funny sorta smile. He has got a snub-nosed belly gun in his hand an' it is pointin' right at my navel. He looks like he means business.

"All right, fella," he says. "Just back in. I'll shut the door. An' don't try an' start anythin' or I'll blast your spine out!"

I say thank you very much an' do what he says. He shuts the door behind him an' backs me into the library. He feels around for the switch an' flicks on the light.

"Look, pal," I tell him. "Ain't you got this wrong? Maybe you come to the wrong apartment because I don't think I know you."

He chucks his hat on to a chair. He is still holdin' the gun very close to me.

"That's O.K.," he says. "My name's Lodz—Willie Lodz. I'm stickin' around here until Nakorova turns up. An' I'm gonna stick around until somebody shows me one hundred grand, an' if I don't get it some guy is goin' to get hurt plenty—see!"

CHAPTER TEN
NICE GOING

I STAND there in the middle of Zeldar's library lookin' at this guy Lodz. Believe me I am feelin' so happy that I would not change places with anybody, because my hunch was right. I had a feelin' that I was goin' to find somethin' around in Zeldar's dump. Well, I have found it all right. I have found Lodz.

He says: "Take your weight off your feet an' sit down."

He sees a bottle on a table in the corner, walks over an' gives himself a drink. He is still holdin' the gun on me but he is not worryin' very much because he thinks that I am the guy who lives here, an' because he does not know that I have got a gun under my left arm which is givin' me a very comfortin' feelin' at the moment.

He goes over and stand in front of the fireplace. He is sorta pleased with himself.

He says: "Are you Zeldar?"

I tell him no. I tell him that I am Zeldar's confidential secretary. He grins.

"That's O.K. by me," he says. "Where's Zeldar?"

"He'll be around," I say.

I ask him if he would mind if I smoke a cigarette. I do this just to get him used to seein' me move my arms about a bit.

He says: "No, go ahead."

I put my hand round to my hip pocket an' pull out my cigarette case. I take out a cigarette an' light it but I do not put the case back in my pocket. I sit there throwin' it up an' catchin' it with my right hand.

I say to this guy: "I reckon Zeldar won't be too surprised at seein' you, although maybe he'll be surprised that you had to come here with a gun."

"Oh yeah!" says he. "The dirty double-crossin' bastard . . ."

"Look, Lodz," I tell him as if I didn't like hearin' him call Zeldar that, "ain't you bein' a bit tough? Zeldar ain't double-crossed anybody."

"Oh no?" he says. "Well, some guy's double-crossed me an' if you know anything about me you'll know I'm not a guy that takes that easy."

"Well, what's the trouble?" I ask him, makin' out that I am wise to this business. "What's your grouse? Didn't Nakorova cash in?"

He turns around an' spits in the fire.

"Zeldar knows goddam well Nakorova didn't cash in," he says. "That Russian so-an'-so has been playin' me around. The arrangement was that I got the pay-off in New York. Well, it never turned up. After I done all the work with Borg an' the dame snatchin' that Perriner guy, gettin' him aboard the boat an' gettin' him to see reason, the next thing I find out is that Nakorova has taken a run-out powder an' come over here, an' all I get is a goddam letter. So here I am."

I start blowin' smoke rings. It gives me time to think.

After a bit I say: "Well, did you see him? An' what did he say?"

"I didn't see him," he says. "I couldn't get at that guy. I reckon he's been keepin' outa my way. Last night I got a line on where he was, but I didn't wanta go around there. I didn't know who he'd have with him. I thought maybe he'd have some pals with him. I wanted to get him around to my dump because I had a little idea to talk to him with the butt end of a gun. If I had got my hooks on that guy I'd have popped him. So I telephoned through to his place. Some dame answered."

I nod my head. I reckon this dame was Edvanne.

"What time was that?" I say sorta casual.

"Somewhere around half-past two," he says. "I asked if Colonel Nakorova was around. She said no, that he wouldn't be around—he'd gone. I told her my name was Lodz an' asked her if she'd got any sorta message for me. She said yes she had, that I was to go along an' see Zeldar. She told me what his address was."

I do a big grin inside. I get it. So this guy Willie Lodz rang through to Nakorova's flat after Edvanne had poisoned Nakorova. So she tells him that Nakorova's gone, he's left Paris—which was about right because by that time he was as dead as hell. An' she then pulls a fast one on Willie Lodz. I reckon she knows that Nakorova has not paid these guys. She also knows that she's goin' to finish herself in a coupla minutes, an' the last thing she wants to do before she goes out is to make some trouble for Zeldar. So she tells Lodz where Zeldar lives an' sorta suggests to him that he goes round an' looks after his own interests.

A sweet set-up. I am still sittin' there throwin' up my cigarette case an' catchin' it with my right hand. I shrug my shoulders.

I say to Lodz: "Look, pal, I think you're wrong. I think you've got Zeldar wrong, an' I don't think you need worry about your dough. I reckon Mr. X has been Nakorova. It looks to me like he's been double-crossin' you an' Zeldar."

"I would go as far as to say," I go on, "that when Zeldar gets back here he will be the first guy to congratulate you on doin' a nice job, an' you needn't worry about the pay-off. Zeldar is a nice guy to work for. He lays cash on the line."

This pleases him. His face sorta relaxes.

By this time I have smoked my cigarette nearly down to the end. I throw the cigarette stub away, open my case, take out another one an' light it. I get up an' hold the case out towards him. He puts out his left hand an' takes the cigarette. I snap the case shut, an' just as he is puttin' the cigarette in his mouth I make as if I was goin' to put the case in the breast pocket of my coat.

But I don't. As I get it in the inside of the lapel of my coat I drop it an' grab the Luger outa the holster. His right hand with the gun in it is hangin' down by his side. He has just put the cigarette in his mouth when he sees the gun comin' outa my coat. As he starts to raise his right arm I stick my left foot out an' catch it as it comes up. I am only a coupla feet from him an' as his hand hits my foot I smack him across the dome with the butt of the Luger. He subsides in front of the fire. He is out for ten.

I don't waste any time. I take the gun outa his hand, ease inta the hallway, put my hat an' coat on an' open the front door of the apartment. I go back, get hold of him an' sling him across my shoulder. It is only when I am carryin' him that I feel the sting in my other shoulder from Edvanne's bullet.

I switch the lights off, get outa the flat an' close the door behind me. I start easin' down the stairs as quick as I can because I reckon that if I meet Zeldar on the way the game is up. All the way down I am prayin' that Juanella will have kept this boyo stickin' around.

I am lucky. I get outa the front door an' on to the street. It is as dark as hell. I turn down a side street an' go walkin' along, lookin' around to see if I can find a telephone booth. I reckon it is lucky that it is so dark otherwise I might meet some guys who would have wondered what I was doing.

Five minutes afterwards I find a 'phone box. I slam Lodz on to the floor an' prop him up against the side of the box. Then I ring through to the Sûreté Nationale. I tell the night guy who I am. I also tell him to get in touch right away with Chief Inspector Erouard. He says if I will hang on for a minute he will put me through to Erouard at his private place. I say O.K.

I stand there hangin' on waitin' for Felix. When I look down I see that Willie is beginnin' to stir, so I put my foot on his face an' smack his head back against the wall. He decides to do a little more sleepin'.

Two three minutes afterwards Erouard comes on. He sounds as if he has just got outa bed.

"Look," I tell him, "I have not got a lotta time to talk to you, because plenty has been happenin' around here."

I tell him I am talkin' from the 'phone box an' where it is. I tell him about Willie Lodz an' I ask him to send a police wagon around here to pick up this boy an' smack him in the cooler till further orders. I also ask him to send a coupla police guys around to Zeldar's apartment to wait for that boyo, to pick him up an' then to hold him on some phoney charge until he hears from me again. He says O.K. He says it looks as if things are movin'.

I say: "Are you right, pal? You'd be surprised!"

I then ask him to get through to the Paris airfield, to get a plane waitin' for me an' to give the pilot a clearance so that he can take off directly I arrive. He says he will also fix that an' that maybe sometime when I have got a few minutes to spare I will let him know what is goin' on because he is sorta curious. I tell him that I reckon I will be back in two three days.

I also tell him there is one other little thing he can do for me. I say that I have got to send a dame around to see him within the next few hours. I tell him that her name is Mrs. Juanella Rillwater—the dame Briquet has been tailin'—an' that she is playin' for us. I say that I am goin' to give her some instructions that she will tell him when she gets along. I say that this dame will be doin' a job of work for me an' I will be obliged if he will give her co-operation. He says this is all right with him an' that he thinks my methods are unique even if they are startlin'.

I tell him he don't know the half of it an' that when I see him again I will give him a story that will make his ears flap so much that he'll have to tie 'em back. Then I hang up.

Willie is still sleepin' peacefully. I go over his pockets an' find a wallet an' some letters. I stick 'em in my coat pocket. Then I yank off the telephone cord an' his scarf an' I truss him up like a chicken.

After which I scram.

I don't reckon that Lodz has had a very good evenin'.

It is nearly five o'clock when I get back to the Dieudonne. Juanella is yawnin' her head off an' lookin' very nice in a peach colour crepe-de-chine negligée.

She starts talkin' but I tell her to lay off an' relax an' to give me a drink because I am goin' to be busy.

She gives me a shot of rye an' rings down to the night guy for some coffee. After which she lays herself down on the settee an' looks sulky.

I start goin' through the papers an' things I took outa Lodz' pockets. Among 'em I find this letter:

My friend—There is not the slightest need for you to worry because everything must work out excellently in Paris. When the result is secured the money will be there. Be patient and tell your charming friend to be patient too. She will soon be wearing diamonds!

The possibility of a double-cross—as you so tautly put it—will be obviated by the fact that, if necessary, the second screw can be turned here in Paris, a process that my associates can look after. If things get too hot here their London organisation which is as well prepared as the others can function.

This makes everything simple. Your fears about our young friend being tough are groundless. Even if he is not afraid to die the second screw must make him agreeable. If you feel you must—come over. You can see me by arrangement. But take care. The only thing that worries me is Edvanne. You will guess why. If you come to Paris be careful. In her presence discuss only our American arrangements. If you do come bring your charming friend with you. She would melt the hardest heart.

Sergius.

I start grinnin'. I am beginnin' to see daylight at last. I reckon that this letter that Sergius wrote to Lodz in New York, when Willie started worryin' about his dough, tells me plenty.

The coffee comes up an' Juanella pours it out. I give her a cigarette an' tell her to sit back an' listen.

"Here's the way it is," I say. "I am now goin' to scram outa this city an' depart into the wilderness, an' you gotta be very careful to do exactly what I tell you. Otherwise you might find yourself attendin' my funeral."

She says what the hell an' where am I goin'.

"You mind your business," I crack back. "But I reckon to be back here within four or five days an' with a bit of luck I'm gonna have good news for all. Here is the way I see this job:

"Sergius Nakorova was not the tops in this kidnappin' business. Sergius was only a stooge workin' for Zeldar. Zeldar is the big boy.

"Sergius is put in at New York to make a play for Geraldine an' when he has done this to hire some guys to snatch Buddy Perriner. He puts in Willie Lodz, Borg an' Lodz' girls. But at that time Lodz don't know that there is anybody else in the game except Sergius an' the Russian does not wise him up.

"Willie an' his pals snatch Buddy an' Sergius comes over here knowin' that Geraldine will come after him.

"The next thing is that Wilks gets wise to what is goin' on an' I am due to arrive. Sergius gets his orders that he is to get Wilks outa the way, otherwise he is not goin' to be paid his cut, an' he is worryin' about this because he has already heard from Lodz, who is wantin' his dough for the kidnappin', an' Sergius has not got it.

"Sergius has written Lodz this letter that I got here sayin' that the job is O.K. an' that the money will be here when the results are secured. He tells Lodz for the first time about havin' associates in the job an' Lodz gets nasty an' comes over. He brings his girl friend with him—who is the dame I saw searchin' around in your bathroom—although what the hell she expected to find I don't know.

"In the meantime Edvanne has bumped Sergius an' herself. Why does she do this? She knows damn' well that Sergius has planned the Buddy kidnappin' so it is nothin' to do with that.

"Well, I'll tell you why she did it. She did it to stop Sergius doin' somethin' else that was on the ice an' because she had got wise to what was behind this kidnappin'."

"O.K., Sherlock," says Juanella. "All right. Well, supposin' she did get wise to Sergius. Supposin' there was somethin' else behind this kidnappin' an' she didn't like it, what does she have to kill *herself* for? Why didn't she turn Sergius in? She'd have made things pretty easy for herself with you if she'd done that."

"Good reasonin', Juanella," I tell her. "But that's the interestin' part of the situation. That was the point that was worryin' me. Well, I know the answer to that one, an' I've already told you what it is. Edvanne bumps Sergius because she'd got wise to the truth of this story an' she bumped herself because she thought she couldn't stop what Zeldar an' Sergius had planned to happen."

Juanella shrugs her shoulders.

"Maybe I'm stupid," she says. "But I still don't see it."

"Use your brains, Juanella," I tell her. "Look, what do guys kidnap other guys for? They kidnap 'em for dough, don't they, to get ransom money? O.K. Will now, look at this job. Buddy Perriner is nicely kidnapped so all they gotta do is to put the ransom note in an' wait for Willis Perriner to pay. Well, do they do that? No, they don't. They have to do a lot of other things as well. They have to get Geraldine Perriner over here in Paris, after which Willis Perriner hears somethin' that makes him send me a cable tellin' me to lay off.

"Naturally, I thought that somethin' was a demand for a ransom, but it wasn't."

"Why not?" says Juanella.

"First of all," I say, "because they haven't got any ransom money. Ain't Willie Lodz an' Borg an' Lodz' dame shoutin' their heads off because they can't get their money?

"An' another thing," I go on, "is Geraldine. Geraldine's disappeared, ain't she?"

"That's right," she says. "An' so what? Maybe I'm dumb but I can't see this thing."

"Of course you can't, honeybunch," I tell her. "Well now, think again. First of all Geraldine knew all about Sergius Nakorova. You told her all about him. You'd proved to her that he made a play for her merely for the purpose of kidnappin' Buddy. You know darned well that she stuck around with him afterwards only because she thought she might find out where Buddy was.

"Well, then she disappears. But she wasn't snatched. Nobody carried Geraldine off. She just walked outa the hotel with her luggage an' she don't say one goddam word either to you, to me or anybody else. Why?"

"All right," she says. *"Why?"*

"Because she was told not to," I tell her. "Because Buddy Perriner wasn't snatched in order to get a ransom at all. Buddy Perriner was snatched in order to make him *do somethin' an' to make his father do somethin'.* Look"—I show her the letter I found on Willie Lodz—"see what it says here: *'Your fears about our friend being what you call tough are groundless. Even if he is not afraid of death the second screw* must *make him agreeable.'*

"This is a lovely kidnappin'," I tell her. "They grabbed Buddy Perriner off because he's got to do somethin'. Then they get in touch with old man Willis Perriner an' they tell him what *he's* gotta do. They know Willis Perriner will do it because Buddy has been snatched an' he's afraid they'll bump him. But they've got to have a second screw— the thing that is goin' to make Buddy do what he's told."

Juanella looks at me, her eyes poppin'.

"Jeez!" she says.

"You get it, don't you?" I say. "So what does somebody do? Some-body rings up Geraldine on the telephone at the Hotel Dieudonne, tells her to pack her bags an' fly over to England. They tell her to do it right away without seein' anybody or speakin' to anybody. They tell her that if she don't do it, they're goin' to bump Buddy. So she's got to do it.

"So the job is this: They got both the Perriner kids. They got Geraldine in England, they got Buddy somewhere else. If Buddy don't do what he's told they tell him they'll kill Geraldine. If she don't do what she's told they tell her they'll bump Buddy. If old man Perriner don't do what he's told, they'll bump both of 'em, which is what I think they will do in any event because they've *got* to."

Juanella don't say anything. She walks over to the sideboard. She pours out a coupla drinks an' she brings 'em over. She gives me one.

"Well, here's to them two kids," she says. "God help 'em."

"I hope so too," I tell her. "But the job ain't too bad up to date. Maybe there's a chance."

"What are you going to do about Zeldar, Lemmy?" she says. "When that guy came around here he was as cool as a cucumber. I told him I was worried sick about Geraldine. I said that I reckoned the best thing would be for me to go to the police here. The guy never batted an eyelid. He said that maybe that would be a good thing for me to do, but that I needn't bother to do it. He said he was goin' down to-morrow mornin' to see your friend Erouard at the Sûreté Nationale about some enquiries they was makin' for you, that he'd tell 'em himself. It looks to me like that bird had got his getaway all set."

I grin.

"Don't worry about him," I tell her. "I reckon he is grabbed off by now. I fixed with Erouard to have some cops waitin' for him when he went back to his apartment, which is a very lucky thing for me because I do not want that guy on my tail where I am goin'."

"What are you goin' to do, Lemmy?" she says.

I grin.

"I am goin' to take a little trip to Delfzyl in Holland," I tell her. "When I was at Zeldar's apartment to-night lookin' through his papers, I couldn't get an idea. The only things I found there was some consignment notes for some cargoes of rye shipped from Mediterranean ports to Delfzyl in Holland, an' Delfzyl is one of the branch offices of the Gloydas, Nakorova & Haal business. It didn't mean anything much to me at the time, but it means plenty now."

"So you got an idea?" she says.

"I got a big idea," I tell her. "Look, not so long ago I took a look around Rodney Wilks' room. Somebody had searched that place. They'd been over it with a tooth-comb, but they overlooked one thing. Rodney had left a message for me. There was a note written on the back of an envelope in pencil. I couldn't make head nor tail of it because sometimes I am so thick that I can't even see my own nose. The note says:

"'*Before seven will you have it straight and how much?*'

"I've been thinkin' about that goddam message ever since I saw it. It was so obvious, so simple that I couldn't see what it was. But comin' around here it hit me just like a steam-hammer."

Juanella sits up straight. She is lookin' excited.

"Well, what does it mean?" she says. "Do you tell me or don't you?"

"I'll tell you," I say. "*Before seven*. Well, ain't my Federal Identification Number B 47 on this trip? Ain't that the number I put on every wire I send to headquarters to show 'em it really comes from me? Well, that's what Rodney meant. It was to show me that the message was meant for me.

"The next thing: '*Will you have it straight?*' Well, what is it that you have straight? There's only one thing that I ever had straight in my life an' that's rye whisky—*rye*. An' the third thing: '*And how much?*' When I have a drink of rye whisky how much do I have— four fingers, don't I? An' Zeldar is a guy who can't use four fingers on his left hand.

"So there is Rodney givin' me the works. He sends me a message. He tells me that the place where the rye goes to is the place I want, an' he tells me that the guy I wan is Zeldar—the man with the four stiff fingers."

Juanella gets up. She goes over an' looks through the curtains. There is a streak of dawn in the sky.

"Watch your step, Lemmy," she says. "I reckon if these guys get their hooks on you they won't be so nice to you."

"You're tellin' me," I crack. "But if you think I am goin' into Holland as Lemmy Caution, you're wrong. I'm goin' to be Willie Lodz chasin' my money. I reckon the only people who've seen Willie in this job are Nakorova who's dead, an' Zeldar who will be in the cooler here. Maybe I can pull a fast one with these other guys."

"Well, I wish you luck," she says. "An' what do I do?"

"Right now you get me some notepaper," I tell her.

When she brings it I sit down an' I write a long letter to my old pal Detective Inspector Herrick of the Special Branch at Scotland Yard, London, England. I tell him the whole story as far as I see it. I suggest to him that he takes a look around London, finds out if there is some sort of branch office of the Gloydas, Nakorova & Haal syndicate, an' puts on the screws to see if he can get his hooks on Geraldine. An' I tell him to work fast because it is goin' to be very important.

When I have finished this letter I seal it, an' I give it to Juanella. I tell her to get along, after she has had a couple hours' sleep, an' see Erouard at the Sûreté Nationale. I tell her to arrange with him for her to be flown over to England. When she gets there she is to go right along an' see Herrick. She says O.K.

I pick up my hat an' I scram. When I am goin' outa the door I realise that Juanella must think this is a serious business because she does not even ask to be kissed.

CHAPTER ELEVEN
THE BRAIN BABY

OUTSIDE my window I can hear a lot of guys clatterin' along the cobbles, so I reckon it must be some more of these Dutch reservists goin' on their way to Gröningen.

I switch off the light in my bedroom an' look out. It is as dark as hell outside an' the wind is whistlin' around this old-time town makin' funny noises.

I fix the window curtain back in its place an' go back to the dressin' table an' take a look at myself. I reckon that I look pretty well like a guy would think Willie Lodz looked like if the said guy did not know Lodz.

I have got on a black fedora an' I am wearin' a very nice suit with a pale blue silk collar an' a bow tie with big points an' a diagonal stripe. I have not shaved my chin very closely an' it is a bit blue an' makes me look good an' tough.

But I am not feelin' quite so good because this is a chancy business. First of all I have got inta this country on my own American passport, but I am registered in this hotel as Willie Lodz of New York.

So I am O.K. just so long as some enthusiastic Dutch copper does not ask me to show him my passport. If he does, the way things are blowin' around here, with Mister Hitler's boys just over the other side of the frontier, an' everybody lookin' for trouble, I reckon they will throw me in the clink as a suspect as soon as they look at me.

Even if I was to tell 'em who I *really* am it wouldn't do me any good.

What the hell!

Maybe you've seen some of these old time pictures of Dutch towns that guys in the Middle Ages usta paint. O.K. Well if you have, multiply 'em by each other an' you will have a good idea of this town Delfzyl. Before this war it didn't matter a hoot because it is a place with only about ten thousand inhabitants an' an old fort that nobody uses very much except to lean up against. There is a good harbour an' guys wear funny trousers so now you know all about it.

An' there is so much goddam funny business goin' on around here that everybody is in a state of jitters all the while wonderin' who's doin' what an' why.

I go over to the cupboard an' give myself a shot of rye outa my last bottle. Then I get out the Luger an' stick it in the holster under my arm.

I reckon I will get movin'.

After I have been walkin' for ten minutes the moon comes up an' makes things a bit easier. I am easin' along very quickly, keepin' in the shadows, because there are police an' army sentries posted along the highways leadin' down to the harbour an' docks an' these guys are liable to get very curious if they see a strange face.

I am also prayin' very hard that the guy in the American vice-consul's office with whom I have had a coupla minutes' confidential conversation this afternoon has not handed me any incorrect stuff about where this Gloydas, Nakorova & Haal dump is, because I have a feelin' that to-night is my big night.

I turn off the last street on the right on the harbour road an' look for the white post. After a bit I see it. I look across the road an' there sure as a gun is the dump.

It is a little two-story house painted white an' across the front I can see the letterin' *Gloydas-Nakorova-Haal.*

I wait for a minute an' then I slip my hat over one eye an' start to cross the road an' just when I begin to do this the door opens an' two people come out.

I get back into the shadow an' wait. They come halfway across the road an' then turn up towards the town. It is a man an' a dame. The guy is a big guy an' the woman has a nice shape an' walks so it is pretty to watch her.

I go after 'em. Maybe the guy is Gloydas, an' if he is then he is the guy I want.

They are takin' their time. They just go strollin' along an' I see that the dame has now put her arm through his, so it looks like they like each other.

They turn off right an' then left an' then go into a lighted doorway. When I get up to it I see it is a tavern. I push open the door an' take a look inside. It is the usual sorta Dutch tavern with a wooden floor an' oak panellin' an' beams, tankards around the walls an' some old pictures. The sorta place that American tourists like to get their pictures taken in so that they can show 'em way back home in Oshkosh.

There is a gallery runnin' around the place about eight feet off the floor with a staircase leadin' up to it on one side. Opposite me in the middle of the wall is a big open fireplace with a swell fire burnin' an' under the gallery right the way round are oak tables.

I take a look around an' I nearly get heart disease. The guy I have been followin' is sittin' at the table under the gallery farthest away from me. He has got his back to me. Sittin' on the other side with her head towards him talkin' very seriously is the dame.

An' it is the dame that I saw searchin' around in Juanella's bathroom at the Hotel St. Anne in Paris. An' I am bettin' all the tea in China to a poke in the snoot that this is Lodz' girl.

I get outside good an' quick an' lean up against the wall. After a bit I look around an' find a nice doorway on the other side of the street. I go over there an' park myself an' do a little heavy thinkin'.

About fifteen minutes later they come out. They walk up the street an' I go after 'em. They go right back to the main street, walk down it for fifty yards an' then turn left. When I go round the corner I can see the guy standin' on the step of a little hotel talkin' to the dame an' by the looks of it he is wishin' her goodnight.

After a bit she goes in an' he starts comin' back my way. I get outa the way quick an' duck down some alley until he has gone past.

Well . . . I reckon that I ain't got anything very much to be pleased about. I have come along to this dump hopin' that I am goin' to pull something as Willie Lodz an' right here is the dame who is goin' to be able to tell the world that I am certainly not that guy!

I stand there thinkin'. I light myself a cigarette an' ruminate on the strange things that can happen to a guy just any time he don't want 'em to.

Then I make up my mind. I chuck my cigarette away an' turn down the street towards the hotel. It is a little *pension* sorta place with ferns in window boxes outside.

I go in. On the other side of the hallway is an office with a glass window an' some plump guy is sittin' there dozin' with a big pipe hangin' out of his mouth.

I ask him if he speaks English an' he says *Ja*. I then say that I am an American who is lookin' for some friends of mine that I was expectin' to meet up with an' that I think that there has been a mix-up in our hotels. I ask if I can take a look at his register an' see if they are here, an' while I am doin' this I am prayin' that he is not goin' to ask me what their name is.

I am lucky. He shoves the register over to me an' tells me to look for myself.

I get it. There is only one name there that can be the dame. She has got room No. 15 an' she is registered as Miss Ardena Vandell of New York City, New York, U.S.A.

I give an exclamation as if I was very pleased. I tell the old guy that this is my friend. He seems as pleased as I look. He says shall he send up an' tell her. I say no if he wouldn't mind I would like to give her a big surprise because this Miss Ardena Vandell is a close relation of mine an' she will be tickled pink to see me.

He grins some more an' says go ahead, that the room is on the first floor.

I light myself a cigarette an' walk up the stairs.

Outside No. 15 I take the Luger outa its holster an' hold it under my coat. Then I tap on the door. After a minute she opens it. This is the dame all right. This is the baby I saw in Juanella's bathroom!

The passage I am standin' in is very dimly lit but the light in the room behind her is bright. She stands there sorta framed in the doorway. Lookin' at her I get the idea in my head that this guy Willie Lodz must be a good picker of dames. She stands there with her eyebrows raised lookin' me over.

I show her the gun.

"Just ease in quietly, baby," I tell her very softly, "an' don't make any noise. I wanta talk to you."

She looks plenty surprised but steps back inta the room. I go after her an' close the door behind me. I put the gun back in its holster.

"Sorry about that gun business, Ardena," I tell her. "But I didn't want you to start shoutin'. You see I'm supposed to be an old friend of yours."

She goes over to the fireplace. There is a big fire burnin'. She turns around with her back to it an' stands there lookin' at me. She is as cool as a cucumber. She puts her hands behind her back. I have told you guys that this dame has got a swell figure, but that wasn't the half of it.

She has got hair as black as night, deep blue eyes, a swell skin, an' her features are one hundred per cent. marvellous. It also looks to me, by her general attitude, that she is pretty tough. I put my hat down on a chair an' get myself a cigarette. I offer her one an' light it for her. I am thinkin' that nothin' very much short of an earthquake would surprise this baby an' maybe not that.

"Let's get down to cases," I tell her. "I got an idea, Ardena, that both you an' me are in a little bit of a jam, as you are Willie Lodz' girl friend you will be very sorry to hear that he is in even a worse one. That's why I am here."

She sends a stream of smoke out of her nostrils slowly. Then she says:

"So Willie is in a jam, is he? That's very interesting. And who are you?"

I'm all ready for her.

"Way back in 1932," I tell her, "Willie Lodz was in trouble with the Michigan State police over a highway robbery. There was another guy in it with him—a clever guy called Hoyt. The Michigan cops got Willie but Hoyt got away with it.

"I'm Charlie Hoyt," I go on. "I usta be a pal of Willie's. Maybe you heard of me?"

"I have heard of you all right," she says. "But tell me about Willie."

"Willie is in the cooler in Paris," I say. "I don't think I am guessin' far wrong if I sorta suggest that Willie was in Paris to collect the dough over the Perriner snatch, an' that he sent you along here for the same reason, because he is a clever guy an' he would know that if he couldn't get the dough in France maybe *you* could get it here.

"Well, I reckon Willie lost his head. I met up with him one day in Paris, where I've been stickin' around for the last year or so, an' he told me about this snatch. He said that he might need my help in gettin' his dough, he said he'd cut me in on the job. Well, I reckon he gets sorta reckless, see? He thinks he is goin' to collect this dough from some guy named Zeldar, so he goes along with a gun. But somehow the Zeldar guy gets wise an' tips the cops off an' they get Willie.

"Four days ago Willie gets hold of a lawyer who sees him in the jail an' sends out a letter to me. In this letter he says that his girl—meanin' you—is down here in Delfzyl, that I'd better get along here an' see if I can give you a hand. He reckons maybe things will be a little bit tough around here."

She smiles.

"I think he was right," she says. "Would you like a drink?"

I tell her yes. She goes over to the sideboard an' she pours me out a drink. Then she says:

"I don't want to disbelieve you, Charlie, but I'd like to make quite sure that you're being straight with me. Tell me a little more about this business."

"I'll tell you so much you'll be surprised," I say. "I wish I'd brought that letter that Willie sent me outa the cooler. It would make your hair stand up. These guys have double-crossed you an' him to hell."

She raises her eyebrows again.

"Yes?" she says. "How?"

"Look," I tell her, "here's the low-down: Some time early this year that guy Colonel Sergius Nakorova an' some other wise guys work this job out. The first thing is that Buddy Perriner has got to be snatched, an' the first move in that game is for Nakorova—who is a swell lookin' guy—to go over to U.S. an' make a play for Geraldine Perriner, who is a very temperamental sorta kid, an' who falls easy.

"The second thing is that if an' when Nakorova gets the job goin' an' it looks as if Geraldine is fallin' for him, he shall get some tough boys to snatch Buddy Perriner.

"Well, everything goes very well. Nakorova gets Willie Lodz, Borg an' you to fix the snatch job, but the dirty dog leads you all up the garden path. He lets you all think that this is just goin' to be an ordinary snatch, an' that when you get Buddy aboard that boat an' got him stuck wherever it was he had to be stuck, a ransom note would be put in, Willis Perriner would pay up, Buddy would be sent back an' you guys would all cut in on the dough.

"That's what Nakorova *said*. The dirty double-crossin' so-an'-so."

"I see," she says sorta casual. "So there was something else behind it? Go on, Charlie."

I take a deep breath an' start prayin' that I am not goin' to slip up in my story. This dame is testin' me out, puttin' me through it to see if I am really wise to what Willie is supposed to have told me.

"You bet there was something behind it," I say. "Work it out for yourself. When Buddy is snatched Nakorova hangs around for a bit, makes love like hell to Geraldine so that she don't know which way she is pointin'. Then he scrams over to Paris. Before he goes he fixes with her that she shall go after him. A coupla weeks later she gets on a boat an' goes to Paris.

"In the meantime Willis Perriner is not feelin' so good. He calls in the F.B.I. an' they send some fella called Wilks over to France to find out what's goin' on. In the meantime I reckon Borg an' Willie an' you are wonderin' where your dough is, an' the next thing that happens is that Willie gets a letter from Nakorova tellin' him that the dough will be all right eventually when some result or other is secured in Paris. Maybe Willie showed you that letter?"

"What then?" she says.

"The last thing that happens," I tell her, "is that Willis Perriner sends some dame, Juanella Rillwater, Larvey Rillwater's wife—maybe you've heard of her—over to Paris to wise up Geraldine about Nakorova. She does this an' Geraldine gets wise.

"Well, you would have thought that Geraldine would have packed her grip an' gone home. But she don't. She disappears. Willie told me that he reckoned she'd gone to England. Well, do you see what I'm drivin' at?"

"Not quite," she says. "You tell me."

I say: "It looks to me like the whole thing is a plant. It looks to me like Sergius Nakorova never intended to put in a ransom note askin' Willis Perriner for money, because he didn't want money. *He wanted something else.*

"After Willie an' Borg an' you have fixed this kidnap stunt an' got Buddy on this boat they're through with you. They never intended to pay you a cut. Snatchin' Buddy Perriner was only the first move in the game. The next move is to get that boy to do somethin' they want him to do, an' they got a swell way of makin' him do it."

She nods her head.

"You mean Geraldine?" she says.

"That's right," I tell her. "It is stickin' out a foot that Geraldine disappeared because these guys who are behind Nakorova told her she'd got to disappear. They told her she'd got to go to England. They told her that if she didn't they'd slit Buddy's throat, so she had to go.

"So there's a sweet set-up for you. Willis Perriner has got to do what he's told because they've got Buddy. Buddy's got to do what he's told because they've got Geraldine. Geraldine's got to do what she's told because they've got Buddy. You an' Willie an' Borg get sweet nothin'. You're all washed up an' they're through with you, an' there ain't anything you can do about it. An' how do you like that!"

She starts smilin', an' I am tellin' you guys that although she has got a very sweet mouth an' lovely teeth, that smile is very ominous. She takes up my glass, walks over to the sideboard an' gives me another drink.

"It looks as if you're all right, Charlie," she says. "You know your stuff." She starts smilin' again. "But I wouldn't like to say that we were all washed up. I've got an idea in my head that when I walk out of Delfzyl I'm taking some money with me. And I am very glad you've turned up. Maybe I am going to need a little help."

I grin at her.

"You're tellin' me," I say. "Maybe you're goin' to need a whole lotta help. Another thing," I go on, "I don't like this place. It is too dark an' it is sorta dreary. It smells ominous to me."

She goes back to the fireplace.

"What was your idea in coming down here?" she says. "That is supposing you hadn't met me?"

"It wasn't my idea," I say. "It was Willie's. In this note Willie sent me he told me that he reckoned you'd be around here sometime, an' that if I was to run inta you I was to introduce myself an' join up with you an' make the best of a bad job. He said that if I didn't meet up with you here, it might be a very good idea to try an' see these guys who was behind Nakorova. Maybe Gloydas or Haal or Zeldar. He said that when I saw 'em I could tell 'em that I was representin' him, that I wanted that dough an' that if I didn't get it maybe I would shoot my mouth off an' start a little trouble for them. He said that he reckoned they might be a bit tough about this"—I grin at her—"but then Willie knows me—I'm tough too."

"I'm glad of that," she says, "because I think that somebody will have to be very tough before this job is through."

She takes a cigarette outa the box on the mantelpiece an' lights it. Then she turns round an' looks at me.

She says: "Supposing your idea is right about there being something else behind this snatch except getting a ransom, what do you think they're after? If the pay-off wasn't going to be money what was it going to be?"

I grin at her.

"I'm not quite certain," I say, "but I'll make a coupla guesses." I blow a smoke ring. "You tell me somethin'," I go on. "Have you been down to the harbour here?"

She nods her head.

"Well, I haven't," I tell her, "but I'll take a bet with you that there are two or three of the Perriner Line cargo ships anchored there right now."

She smiles.

"You're right again, Charlie," she says. "There are two of them."

"The second thing is, I'm bettin' my best pair of shoes that Buddy Perriner was brought over here on one of those boats, that you guys fixed it with some of the crew that that kid was either doped or sandbagged, hidden away on one of those boats when they went to sea. An' I reckon he's around here somewhere."

She moves away from the fireplace an' starts walkin' about the room. I can see she is thinkin' very deeply an' I am bettin' an old penknife I got against the Federal Bank Reserve that she is wonderin' just how far she can play along with me.

You guys have gotta realise that I have put up a very sweet story to her. She is believin' that I am a pal of Willie Lodz' all right, because if Willie had met me sorta casual in Paris, an' if I had been an old-time pal of his an' good enough to be in a highway stick-up with him, then I am just the sorta guy that he would write to just as one final chance to get his dough.

An' Charlie Hoyt is just the guy to get the dough. He has got a record in the U.S. that would make Jesse James look like a Sunday School superintendent's favourite aunt.

After a bit Ardena goes back to the fire an' sits down in the big arm-chair. She leans back an' puts her hands behind her head an' looks at me. I give her a sorta casual once-over an' it hits me very hard that Willie Lodz must have some very nice technique to get himself a dame in this class. I tell you she is tops an' she is cool an' easy an' unhurried an' non-flusterable. Also I like the way she has got her hair done, an' when it comes to ankles she can give points to Geraldine an' Juanella any day, but don't say I said so.

She gets up. She stands there lookin' at me, smilin' prettily. She says:

"Listen, Charlie, I'm going to trust you. It looks as if I've got to. But take my advice and don't try any funny business with me otherwise I am going to throw you to the wolves—don't make any mistake about *that*."

I think I will clinch this deal.

"Look, Ardena, I'm puttin' my cards down. I can't go back to the States because they still want me for killin' that goddam copper in the Michigan stick-up that Willie and I pulled in '32, see? Well, I had a bit of dough but I've done it. I'm broke. I've got to get a stake from somewhere. I wanta clear out some place where there ain't any war goin' on an' where a guy can do a little quiet drinkin' an' get around with a doll now an' again. That's how it is with me, an' so far as I am concerned you will get some very square dealin'. You got me?"

"All right, Charlie," she says. "We'll call it a deal. Candidly," she goes on, "I'm glad you're here because I'm a little bit scared myself. These people are a little steep if you know what I mean . . ."

"Such as?" I ask her.

She grabs another cigarette. Then she goes over to the sideboard an' gives herself a straight one. The way she sunk that whisky was an eye-opener.

She says:

"You've done pretty well with what Willie told you in that letter and what you've thought out for yourself. But you don't know the half of it."

"Go ahead," I say. "Put me wise to this thing. Maybe I can think of somethin'."

"This job was originally planned in England," she says. "I was over there with Willie. We were keeping out of the States for a bit. Things were a bit too hot for us.

"We met Nakorova and his wife Edvanne. Nakorova put the job up to us as a straight snatch and nothing else but. All we had to do was to get the Perriner kid.

"We went over to New York to get ready for the job. Then it looked as if there was going to be a war and Sergius told us to lay off and that he would give us the tip. We hung around for some time and then he told us to go right ahead as planned.

"It was easy. Old Perriner was up to his eyes making war stuff that he wanted to sell to the Allies if war was declared, an' Buddy was stuck down there in the works working like steam and he didn't like it. When the time came I made a play for him. He fell for my line and I got him to the place where the boys picked him up and the job was done.

"Willie still believed that everything that Nakorova said was right. But I was beginning to get suspicious. First of all it looked funny to me to stick Buddy on one of old man Perriner's ships. Then I found out that Nakorova had gone to all the trouble of getting half a dozen men on the boat on his pay-roll, so that Buddy Perriner could be sneaked aboard an' kept hidden. *Why?* When he could have taken off to some place in Mexico and the old man stood up for a couple of million. It would have been easy.

"Well, I know what happened," she says. "Gloydas told me. He told me to-night."

"Yeah," I say. "It looks as if you an' this guy Gloydas are pretty good pals."

She gives me a wink that is full of meanin'.

"How else was I to play it?" she says. "I was here on my own. Willie's all washed up and I'm playing my own hand.

"I told Gloydas that Nakorova had done Willie down for our dough, and that I'd come along to see if there was any pickings. Gloydas has got an idea in his head that he likes my kind of woman. He says that if I hang around for a bit and play ball and keep nice and quiet he'll take care of me."

"Very nice work," I tell her.

She takes another cigarette an' gives me one.

"This Nakorova-Gloydas combination have got brains," she says. "Lots of 'em. Listen to this:

"Sergius Nakorova was no mug. While he was playing around with Geraldine in the States he found out plenty. Through Buddy he found out that old Willis Perriner knew goddam well that a war was comin' along and he was dead keen on the Allies getting away with it. Also he was betting on Roosevelt's Neutrality Act going through. Willis Perriner's scheme was that directly the Act was passed he was going to send those ships to sea and they were to sail for England and deliver the stuff. Perriner schemed to get around the 'Cash and Carry' part of the Act by selling the ships as well as the cargoes to the English and by putting neutral crews aboard. That's where he made his mistake. Half a dozen men in the crew of the *Maybury*— the biggest ship—were put in by Nakorova. They were the boys who took Buddy aboard, kept him out of sight and told him to keep his mouth shut if he wanted to go on living.

"When the time was right and the ships were at sea, and Nakorova safely in Paris, the ransom letter was delivered to Willis Perriner.

"This letter did not ask for money. It said that if Willis Perriner wanted to see his son alive again he was to radio the ships that they were to run into this port and to await further orders. And he was to tell the captains that they would get those orders from Buddy Perriner, here in Delfzyl."

I get up an' go over to the sideboard an' pour myself out another drink.

"You was right when you said these guys had got brains, Ardena," I tell her. "They got brains an' they got nerve, but when you come to work it out if everythin' went all right they are not takin' much of a chance. I reckon there's some sweet dough in this for this bunch."

She looks at me.

"Sweet dough! Do you know what's on those boats?"

I shake my head.

"There's over two hundred airplanes on them," she says. "Two hundred of the very latest fighters and bombers, with all the equipment, all ready to be assembled. There's over three million dollars worth of stuff on those two boats. An' you know what they aim to do with it, don't you?"

"That's easy," I told her. "They just sail round the corner outa Delfzyl Bay inta the River Ems. Everybody knows the Germans had the Ems deepened two years ago to take big ships. All they gotta do is sail round the corner over to the other side of the Ems an' they're in Germany."

"That's right," she says. "And those are the orders that Buddy Perriner has got to give the captains aboard those two boats. That's the orders he'll have to give."

I put down my glass.

"Well, it's a nice job," I tell her. "An' nice dough, an' it's even nicer for 'em now they won't have to pay Nakorova."

"Why not?" she says.

I gave her a big grin.

"Nakorova's dead," I tell her. "His wife bumped him off an' then killed herself. Nakorova made a mug outa her too. Like you an' Willie an' Borg she thought this job was just a snatch. Then she found out the truth. She got scared. She wanted to try an' get Nakorova to lay off because, even if Edvanne Nakorova was a bad dame, she was a good Frenchwoman, an' France is at war with Germany.

"But Nakorova wasn't havin' any. He told her that he was goin' through with the job an' that if she didn't like it he would give her the works. So she killed him. Then she killed herself because really she was dead-nuts on him. She was fond of that guy an' he just broke her heart by tryin' to make her into a traitor to her own country.

"She was a hot dame," I go on, "but in her own way she earned a *croix de guerre* that she won't ever get. Also she had a pair of ankles that are nearly as nifty as those you're sportin'."

I reckon that one pleases her. She gives herself another cigarette. She is smilin'.

"That's what they call retribution in the story books," she says. "Well, have you got any ideas?"

I shrug my shoulders.

"Look, Ardena," I tell her, "we're in a tough spot. What can *we* start here? Maybe we might get this guy Gloydas in a corner some place an' talk to him with the butt end of a gun, but is that goin' to help?"

She shakes her head. She stands there lookin' inta the fire. After a bit she says:

"Charlie, we've only got one chance. It's no good believing anything these guys say. Gloydas told me that if I stick around here he'd look after me. Well, I wouldn't like to believe him. Once they get those ships round into the Ems River tied up to a German wharf, Gloydas will probably tell me to take the air. I wouldn't put it above him. If we're going to look after ourselves there's only one way we can do it."

"Such as what?" I ask.

"Look," she says. "Figure it out for yourself. The two Perriner boats—the *Maybury* and the *Mary Perriner*—are tied up here in a harbour in a neutral country. They've got small crews aboard them, but they're not American boys and we can't expect any help from them. They're good sea captains, I reckon, but beyond that they haven't got much sense. None of those people are any good to us. As far as the Dutch authorities are concerned here, everything is in order. Holland isn't at war with Germany an' Willis Perriner is quite entitled if he wanted to to sell any stuff he wants and to deliver it in the Ems River.

"But there is just one point for us. Buddy Perriner has not yet given the orders for those boats to leave here an' go round. The captains have had their orders by radio from Willis Perriner. Perriner had to tell them that they were to take their orders from Buddy Perriner here. They won't clear from the harbour until they get them."

"That's right," I say. "So what?"

She smiles.

"Look," she says, "this business started as a snatch. I reckon it ought to finish as a snatch. Everybody has been snatching somebody right through the whole game. Buddy was snatched. Geraldine's been snatched."

She comes an' stands lookin' at me.

"Look, Charlie," she says. "What about you and me doing a little snatch? What about snatching Buddy Perriner before he gives those orders?"

CHAPTER TWELVE
IT CAN HAPPEN

I SIT there lookin' at her with my mouth open, because I am beginning to think that when it comes to nerve this baby is the high spot.

After a bit I say: "Ardena, I reckon you're right. It looks to me as if the only chance there is of gettin' any dough outa this job is to snatch Buddy. But when we have snatched him what do we do with the mug? This ain't Chicago, honey, this is Delfzyl, Holland."

"I know," she says. "I've got to think something out."

"There is another thing," I say. "Supposin' we get away with this business. Supposin' we grab Buddy an' put him on ice somewhere. I reckon this Gloydas bunch is goin' to be good an' annoyed. Gloydas might get plenty tough with you."

"He might," she says. "But they'll still be short of a coupla million bucks or so, and he's going to think of that, hey? It is obvious that they're not going to get any money until they deliver that cargo, and they know those captains won't clear the ships until they've got orders from Buddy."

She thinks for a minute. Then she says:

"It might not be so difficult at that. If we were to grab Buddy and hide him away some place, Gloydas would be in such a bad spot that I reckon he would be prepared to cash in on account. Then after we'd got the dough we could telephone through to him and tell him where Buddy was."

"Well," I say, "that sounds all right. It *might* work that way."

She thinks for a minute an' then she says:

"This thing's got to be worked out carefully. Anyhow we can't do anything until we've found out where Buddy Perriner is. One thing is certain and that is that he can't be far away."

She smiles at me sorta archly.

"I'm having lunch with Gloydas to-morrow," she says. "Maybe I'll vamp him a little bit. He's feeling so certain of this job that I think he'll be inclined to talk. Where are you staying?"

I tell her I'm stayin' at the Falconer Guest House.

"All right," she says. "Now look, you get back there. Stick around there until you hear from me. Don't show your face on the street any place. If I'm lucky with Gloydas to-morrow, and find where Buddy is, I'll get a note round to you some time to-morrow afternoon, because we've got to get a move on. If we're going to do this snatch, it's got to be done soon."

"Why not?" I tell her.

"All right," she says. "You wait at your place until you hear from me."

I get up.

"So long, Ardena," I say. "I reckon you're a very swell dame. Believe you me, Willie Lodz knew what he was doin' when he picked a girl like you."

She looks at me an' I see that her eyes are not blue—they are violet. She says sorta soft:

"Why worry about Lodz, Charlie? He's just a past chapter in my life." She goes on sorta demure: "I'm beginning to think you're not so bad yourself."

I grin.

"Swell goin', Ardena," I tell her. "I reckon I've seen worse dames than you too." I sling her a hot look. "I could go for you in a very big way," I say.

She smiles. Did I tell you she had the swellest teeth?

"All right," she says. "Well, we can leave the love stuff. We've got some tough business to do first."

She goes over to the sideboard an' pours out two drinks. She brings 'em back an' gives me one.

She says: "Well, here's to us. I hope we can pull it off, an' I hope you've got it in your head that we've got to either leave this job alone or get away with it. If either of us makes a mistake we're properly in the cart."

She puts her glass down on the table.

"Get this, Charlie," she goes on. "So far as the authorities here are concerned everything that the Gloydas bunch are doing is ordinary straight business. This is a neutral country an' if an American firm wants to deliver war stuff to the Germans that's O.K. If we start something and then slip up we haven't got a dog's chance. We're a couple of crooks with bum records who are tryin' to pull a fast one to get ourselves a little jack on the side. If Gloydas gets wise to what our game is we'll find ourselves stuck in a Dutch cooler an' then shipped back to U.S."

"I got all that, sister," I tell her.

She puts out her hand an' I give it a squeeze.

"That's all right then," she says. "I'm depending on you, Charlie. Good luck to you and keep your feet dry!"

I grin at her. "You're tellin' me," I say.

I slip her a big wink an' I scram.

I go back to my hotel an' I go to bed. I think it has been a very nice evenin'!

It is twelve o'clock when I wake up. I go over to the window an' look out. It is a nice cold day with a little bit of sunshine. I give myself a cigarette an' I go back to bed. I lay there lookin' at the ceilin' thinkin' about this dame Ardena.

After a bit I get up, take a bath, have some lunch an' stick around smokin' cigarettes an' drinkin' *Advocaat*. I reckon it will not be a good thing for me to be seen outside this dump in daylight.

I sorta visualise this baby havin' lunch with Gloydas. I am wonderin' how far she is bein' successful in pumpin' that bird, but I have got an idea that she will not have a lot of difficulty about that. First of all Gloydas will not be afraid of shootin' his mouth because they have got everything so tied up that practically nobody can stop 'em doin' what they want to. Secondly Gloydas is stuck on this dame— which does not surprise me at all because she is a doll that anybody could be stuck on—an' that bein' so he will be inclined to shoot his mouth to her plenty. He will want to show her just what a lot of hundred per cent. guys they are. If Ardena don't get the whole bag of tricks out of that guy then I'm a Dutch bulb-grower with artistic leanin's.

After a bit I go up to my room an' I write a long report on all this business to the Director of the F.B.I. at Headquarters, Washington. I stick this report in a thick envelope an' I enclose my F.B.I. Identification Card because I reckon that if anything goes wrong an' I get myself in a jam I do not want the Dutch authorities creatin' international hell by wantin' to know what a U.S. "G" man is doin' kickin' around in Delfzyl raisin' all sorts of hell with no authority.

I seal up the envelope, stick the flap down with some sealin' wax, put it in another envelope with a note addressed to the American Consul here. In this note I tell him that unless I get in touch with him before a week is out he is to send off the letter to the Director of the F.B.I. because I reckon if he don't hear from me in a week's time maybe I shall be pushin' up daisies some place.

I go downstairs an' I tip the porter to send this around to the Consul's office right away, after which I get myself a chair an' stick it in the hallway of the hotel an' I sit down an' smoke. Because you guys will realise that if Ardena writes to me here she is goin' to address the letter to Charlie Hoyt an' you will also realise that I am registered in this hotel as Willie Lodz, an' I do not want any mix-up.

At half-past three, just when I am feeling good an' bored, I see a boy comin' along the street with an envelope in his hand. I ease outa the hotel entrance sorta casual an' I stop him ten yards or so away from the door. I ask him if he has got a note for Mynheer Charlie Hoyt because I am that guy. Luckily for me this boy is a bit of a sap an' don't argue about it. He gives me the envelope an' scrams.

I go up to my bedroom an' tear it open. Inside is the letter from Ardena. It says:

Dear Charlie—Everything is turning out swell. I had one hell of a lunch with Gloydas. This guy is so certain that this job is in the bag and that nothing can stop it coming off that I didn't have any trouble getting him started talking. The thing to do was to stop him!

If we're going to pull anything we've got to do it to-night. Gloydas says that the two ships will have to clear the harbour at half-past one to-night so as to get the Ems tide. They are big ships and want handling.

There is only one thing that is worrying Gloydas and that is the pilots. Each ship has got to have a pilot to get around by Borkum Island and swing back into the Ems River on the German side. Gloydas says that the trouble is that a lot of the Dutch pilots around here won't take any shipping into German wharves—they're afraid of British air-raids—and he wants to get hold of a couple of guys who are not going to be too curious. I am going to meet him later to-night down at the Spruithuis Tavern down at the harbour. He says that he reckons we can find a couple of pilots who can do with a little jack and who are not going to ask too many questions.

And anyhow these men have got to be aboard the Maybury and the Mary Perriner at one-thirty sharp as the boats will be cleared from the harbour about ten minutes after that. This will give you the time limit. We've got to work fast.

I am wise to where Buddy Perriner is. If you keep on straight down the dirt road that leads past the Nakorova-Gloydas-Haal docks office, you will come to some marshland. A mile along this road is a house standing away back from the road on its own. Perriner is inside. Apparently he is fed up but O.K.

To-night, at one sharp, the two Captains are goin' along there to get their orders from Buddy. Buddy is being very careful to do what he's told because he has been informed exactly what is goin' to happen to his sister if he don't. He's frightened sick about that.

He has also been tipped off that when he has given the necessary orders he will be left behind here in Delfzyl on his own and can then get over to England how he likes and rejoin his sister. They have also told him they will tell him where she is.

This is just a lot of hooey to keep him quiet because they are going to take him along on one of the boats. Anybody would have known this because it is a cinch that they would not leave that guy behind here to start shouting his head off.

There is only one way for us to play this job. Here it is: You will have to get along to that house between twelve and twelve-fifteen o'clock. There are a couple of guys there looking after Buddy. You'll have to fix these two somehow. Then you'll have to talk some sense into Buddy and you'll have to do it quick. If he won't listen to reason you'll have to slug him.

I reckon that by twelve o'clock I will have ditched Gloydas. I do not think I shall be free until then because Gloydas aims to fix the two pilots as late as he can to-night so as not to give them too much time to get around talking before the boats sail. I have fixed myself up with a hired car and I reckon to be along outside the house wait-

*ing to pick you and Buddy up at twelve-thirty sharp. Once we have
got him into the car the rest is easy.*

*I have arranged a swell hide-out down on this side of the docks
where we can take him. Once we are there all we have to do is telephone through to the house where Buddy is now—I have got the
number—and tell Gloydas that if he likes to send us along our dough
we'll tell him where Buddy is—and they can pick him up and still have
time to get on with the job and get away in time to make the tide.*

*If they try any funny business about our cut all we have to do
is to rush Buddy along to the U.S. Consul's Office, slam him inside,
blow the whole works, stop the boats leaving and give an imitation
of two good little crooks who are trying to stop an American guy
being snatched into Germany with a coupla million dollars worth
of war supplies. I reckon we'll get a reward from somebody even
if it's only from old man Perriner!*

*Your job is to stick around in your hotel and not move until
to-night. The two guards up at Buddy's place will be tough I expect
but that ought not to bother you. If you have to bump them why
worry. But you can't waste any time about it. If they won't listen
to reason quick you've got to fog them and beat it. Time is the thing
that matters.*

*And you've got to have Buddy sprung by twelve-thirty. I will be
there with the car. Watch your step and don't make any slip-ups
and maybe we'll still be doing a little heavy spending on the old
White Way before long.*

Well, I'll be seeing you. Keep your feet dry.

Ardena.

I read the letter through two or three times. Then I tear it up and
throw the pieces in the fire. I light a cigarette and I do a little heavy
thinking. First of all this Ardena dame has got brains all right and
she is being a great help to me, because I do not see there is anything
wrong with this scheme of hers from my point of view. I think it is
a swell scheme for me because when we have got Buddy fixed up in
this place she has got for him, I reckon it will be a very easy thing for
me to deal with the lot of 'em, because my idea is to ditch Ardena an'
then rush Buddy along to the Vice-Consul's office and hold the boats
up. I reckon I can still throw a spanner in the works.

I give myself a big grin because I can just imagine what Ardena is going to feel like when she finds that instead of pulling a last-minute snatch with Charlie Hoyt, she has for once in her life been doing a job of work for Lemmy Caution of the Federal Bureau of Investigation.

I get myself a drink an' sit there thinkin' what goddam mugs crooks are. All the time they are tryin' to double-cross some legitimate guys out of their hard-earned jack an' all the time they only succeed in double-crossin' themselves.

Just take a look at this job from the start.

Nakorova, workin' hand-in-hand with the Zeldar-Gloydas mob, hired Willie Lodz, his girl Ardena an' Borg to snatch Buddy Perriner. He does not tell them what is really behind the job. But when they have done their bit he four-flushes them for their dough.

Borg an' Willie Lodz come over to Paris—each one without tellin' the other—to try an' collect off Nakorova or Zeldar or anybody else they can separate from the money. Ardena—Willie Lodz' girl, who seems to have more brains than the rest of them—does a bit of snoopin' an' comes direct to Delfzyl after her *cut*. She is quite prepared to double-cross Willie for his share an' give it to me just because he is stuck in the cooler in Paris an' out of action *pro tem*. She's a sweet thing—ain't she?

Nakorova also tries to double-cross his own wife. He gets her to stand in on the snatch game an' pretend to be his sister. Then She finds out what is behind this job an' threatens to turn him in to me if he don't lay off. He won't have it so she bumps him an' herself. Well . . . there it is an' a nice little story it is too an' it makes me think. . . .

Because it is still workin' the same way an' here am I right up to my neck in a snatch plot with Ardena an' I am goin' to double-cross her, an' I am aimin' to do it so swell that she won't know what's hit her!

I get to thinkin' that the guy who said that crimes does not pay was one hundred per cent. right. Which is a very comfortin' thought, only the worst thing about it is that you cannot get crooks to believe it—otherwise it would be a very swell sayin'.

I light myself a cigarette an' lay down on the bed an' start thinkin' about Juanella. I am wonderin' if this dame has made London all right an' whether she has contacted Herrick. An' if so whether he has got a line on where Geraldine is.

I reckon this will be a tough job for him an' I hope he has got a move on an' got that dame safe because if he don't and anything goes wrong here they will bump her as soon as look at her. I reckon this mob is pure poison.

But I have got confidence in Herrick. I worked with that guy on a case one time in England an' he certainly has got what it takes to make a police officer.

Anyhow I am not feelin' so good about Geraldine because you guys will realise just as well as I do that they would have bumped her anyway. Because anyhow, it is not reasonable to suppose that they are goin' to let anybody have the chance of openin' their mouths after this job has been pulled.

An' although it may be tough, this is the idea that I have got to get into Buddy Perriner's head when I get at him. Once I can make him believe that in any event he won't see his sister any more he is more likely to come quietly an' not start any argument.

This maybe will not be so easy because I have always found it a very tough business indeed to get any guys to believe you when you are actually tellin' the truth an' meanin' it.

I remember some dame that I met up with when I was doin' a job with the Mexican Government down in Chihuahua. This dame was tops. She was the rattlesnake's rattles. She had shape, seduction, *joie de vivre, je ne pais quoi,* allure, oomph an' what-have-you-got. What I mean is she was a swell dame. She was positively *attractive.*

Well, she finds somethin' in my character that appeals to her. Every night we usta sit on the corner of the patio rollin' our eyes at each other while I told her the sort of bedtime stories that a dame would really like to hear on the radio. Every now an' then she would hand me out a kiss that was so goddam determined that it woulda make a tank start goin' backwards.

An' every night when I reckoned that things was gettin' a little too sultry for Lemmy I usta take a peek round the edge of the veranda an' say "Carissima, I can see your husband comin'." An' she usta say: "Lemmee, my toreador, go—my heart will follow you an' stab you with each step. *Adios Caro mio!"*

After which I usta scram.

But one night I took a look around the corner an' sure as shootin' her old man *was* comin' that way an' lookin' as if he'd just been bitten by a coupla whip-snakes. I reckon he'd heard about me!!

I do not like this one little bit, so I give the baby a big heave an' I say "Carissima, I must scram because I see your husband approachin'."

An' what happens?

Just because I *am* tellin' the truth on this occasion she does not believe me. She says: "No . . . you always say that. It is a lie. I will not let you go."

An' by this time I have got away from this baby her old boy has arrived an' is doin' a knife throwin' act which was practically cuttin' my chassis to ribbons. If that guy hadn't run out of knives I would probably be in strips to this day.

All of which will show you mugs that you gotta be very careful when an' how you tell any woman the truth. Because even if it is sometimes good she won't like it.

I have never yet met up with a dame who would not rather have a real honest-to-goodness dyed-in-the-wool, custom-made goddam lie—providin' it was a nice one—than the truth. Work it out for yourself. An' if you don't believe me, try it. An' any time I see any of you male guys walkin' around with a black eye an' a bump on your dome that looks like you been bombed with an old-fashioned cannon ball I will know that you been pullin' a George Washington act on the girl-friend.

Because I will tell you guys somethin' that is so logical that you can practically set it to music an' sing it in your bath. If a dame is beautiful she *don't expect* to be told the truth an' if she is ugly she don't *want* to be told the truth. If a dame is clever she wants to be told she's beautiful an' if she's beautiful she wants to be told she's clever, an' if she's beautiful *an'* clever then you gotta tell her that she's got a line an' a technique that makes Helen of Troy, Messalina, Mae West an' the girl who usta do the belly dance at the Moulin Rouge look like a troupe of performin' jackals.

An' if she's beautiful *an'* clever an' has got technique as well—then I give up. An' my advice to you is to cross your fingers an' get yourself a fast train to Oshkosh good an' quick because a dame like that is probably too good for anybody except a guy with armour plated feelin's an' no hope.

But if by any chance you know any dames like the above I would very much like some telephone numbers, because I am one of them mugs who are so used to steppin' in where angels fear to tread that I have developed a sorta cast-iron temperament an' am always prepared to try anythin' once—and maybe twice if I like it.

You got me?

I wake up at quarter to eleven an' start preparin' for action. I take a look at the Luger, examine the ammunition clip, stick on my hat an' overcoat, take one little drink outa the rye bottle an' scram downstairs.

In the hallway I meet the porter. I tell him that I am goin' for a little stroll around before turnin' in. This guy is a nice guy an' speaks English very well except that it sounds like his tongue was stuck to the roof of his mouth with carpenter's glue.

I get talkin' to him about the Dutch language an' start askin' him questions. I ask him the Dutch for this an' that an' he is very obligin'. I remember some of the words that he tells me because I reckon I am goin' to want 'em later.

Then I scram.

I reckon I have got an hour to get busy in.

I start walkin' down towards the harbour an' when I get down there I ask some guy where the *Spruithuis* is because I reckon I am goin' to do a little checkin' up an' see if that dame Ardena is around with Gloydas like she said.

When I get there I see that this dump is an old-fashioned sailors' tavern down in one of the little harbour streets. I take a look into the main bar-room, which is filled with sea-farin' guys of all sorts an' sizes, all talkin' about the war. Over on the other side of the room is a half-open door an' through it I can see some people sittin' around tables an' drinkin'.

I go over to the bar an' order a glass of *schnapps*. When I have got it I ease over to the door an' take a peek through into the other room.

Over in the corner I can see Ardena lookin' like a million dollars. She is sittin' at a table with Gloydas. On the other side of the table are two heavy, square lookin' guys in jerseys an' sea-boots. One of 'em has got a woollen cap on an' looks like Captain Kidd's great-grand-son, an' the other guy is a shorter fella in a big blue wind-breaker jumper. I reckon these two guys are the pilots who are takin' the boats out for Gloydas.

I stand there behind the door watchin' 'em. The two Dutchmen are drinkin' beer out of mugs but Gloydas an' Ardena have got a bottle of champagne in front of 'em, an' by the looks of it Gloydas is carryin' just about as much as he can hold. He is very red in the face an' laughin' an' talkin' like hell. Ardena is playin' him along an' noddin' her head at him, an' the two Dutchmen are lookin' at him like he was somethin' very strange from up-country that nobody had ever seen before.

I lean back against the wall an' start sippin' at the glass of *schnapps*. I get to thinkin' that this Ardena baby has surely got next to Gloydas all right. She has been puttin' some overtime in on that mug an' he is certainly takin' a night off.

Well, maybe this is understandable. He thinks maybe that he has got everything fixed very nicely, that there is nothin' else for him to worry about an' that it is O.K. for him to sit back an' take a little drink.

But I am not feeling so good. I go back to the doorway an' take another look. Gloydas is leanin' over the table. The two Dutchmen are sittin' down now an' they have all got their heads close together. Then Gloydas starts feelin' in his pocket an' brings out a packet of dough. He slips it over the table an' the biggest of the two guys grabs it.

Then they all start shakin' hands. All except Ardena who is very busy fillin' up Gloydas' glass.

The two sailor guys finish their drinks, get up, button up their coats an' start walkin' towards the door. I stand back against the wall of the bar-room. It looks like it is all fixed up an' these are the two pilots who are goin' to do the job. When they go past me I take a quick peek at 'em. They are tough-lookin' guys with faces tanned from sea-air an' salt water. As they go clumpin' outa the bar in their big boots I get to hopin' that one of these days they will run on a big rock an' stay there.

I take another look through the door. Gloydas is sittin' back in his chair. His face is as flushed as a tomato an' he is squeezin' Ardena like he was a bear.

I move away, across the bar-room, an' scram. I am not feelin' so happy. Why the hell does Ardena want to get Gloydas so cock-eyed that he don't know what he is doin'? What is the big idea?

She an' I have planned to snatch Buddy. Then we was supposed to hold up Gloydas for the dough before we told him where Buddy was. Well what is the idea in gettin' Gloydas so goddam drunk that he does not know which way he is pointin'?

I have told you guys before that everybody in this case has been double-crossin' everybody else.

Ardena has been plannin' to double-cross Gloydas an' I reckon to pull a fast one on her.

But what does this new business mean? What is that baby doin' gettin' him so high that he will not know what the hell he is doin?

At the back of my head I have got a funny idea. I am wonderin' whether Ardena is plannin' to double-cross me!

Hell . . . I reckon it is too late to start askin' questions.

Whether she is on the up-an'-up or not I am goin' through with the Buddy snatch if I can.

So here we go!

CHAPTER THIRTEEN
SNATCH-AS-SNATCH-CAN

WHEN I get outside I start walkin' away from the harbour. I make a good *détour,* come around, an' pick up the road I was on the night before. I walk along quickly, keepin' in the shadows until I come to the Gloydas-Nakorova-Haal office. I go right past it and strike the dirt road like Ardena said in her note.

When I get about a mile down the road I see the house. It is a two-story dump standin' back well away from the road. There is a wall round it about thirty yards away from the house but there is no sort of cover, because all around the place is flat marshland an' even the road I am walkin' on is wet from the dykes.

I reckon that it is lucky it is a dark night otherwise any guys in this house could see me comin'.

I get off the road an' start walkin' towards the wall. I ease around to the back an' look for a gate or an openin' but I can't find one.

I take a look at the wall. It is about eight feet high an' easy. I jump for the top, catch it an' pull myself up an' over. I drop on the other side.

Standin' back in the shadow of the wall I take a look at the house. It is as dark as hell an' the shutters are all pulled. I can't even see a glimmer of light anywhere.

I start walkin' over towards it. Then I work around to the front. There are two or three plank steps leadin' up to a sort of wooden veranda that runs around the front of the house. On the other side of this veranda is a door.

I give a hell of a cough an' start walkin' up the wooden steps. I make a lot of noise doin' this an' I bang on the door two or three times.

Nothin' happens. After a bit I start bangin' again. I wait an' listen. Two or three minutes go past an' then I hear some steps comin' towards the door inside.

The steps stop. Then some guy says in Dutch: "Who is there?"

I start rememberin' the words the hotel porter told me. I say in a very gruff voice to cover up my lousy Dutch:

"This is the harbour police."

There is a pause for a second or two an' then I can hear the guy openin' the door.

I take a step back. As he opens the door I step forward an' bust him one. I give him a sleepin' draught on the jaw that woulda sent most guys off for half an hour. He goes over with a crash but starts gettin' up again. I reckon I do not want any trouble with this guy so I slip the Luger out of its holster quick an' crown him one on the dome with it. He goes down like a log—makin' a helluva lot of noise doin' it.

I am wonderin' where the hell the other guy is. I close the door quietly behind me an' stand there listenin'. I can't hear a thing.

Then I start movin' forward but I have only gone a step when a light flashes in my eyes.

Right in front of me is a flight of wooden stairs leadin' up to the first floor hallway. On the top of these stairs is the other guy. He has got a flash-lamp in one hand and a gun in the other.

I reckon that he has seen his pal is knocked out, an' I reckon I got to work fast. I take a quick shot at the lamp with the Luger an' get it. Then I bend down in the darkness an' grab hold of the unconscious guy. I hold him up in front of me an' as the guy on the stairs looses off with his gun I drop the guy an' give a big groan.

It works. The bozo on the stairs thinks he has got me. He starts comin' down. When he gets to the bottom he pauses for a minute. I reckon he is feelin' around for a light switch.

I am right. As he flicks the switch down I go for him with my head down. I run at him an' hit him in the guts so hard that it looks like I was going right through him. Just to make quite certain of this guy I smack him a mean one over the brains with the gun-butt. He flops down.

I look at the first guy. He is shot clean through the pump so I reckon it was nice for me that I was holdin' him in front of me.

I look around. There is a room over on the right of the hallway. I take a look in. It is dark an' all the shutters are pulled. I pull the dead guy over into this room an' park him there. Then I go back for the other mug an' drag him in.

I tear a lump off his shirt an' ram it down his mouth. Then I get the belts off him an' the other guy an' truss him up. When I have finished with him he looks like a chicken. I reckon he is safe enough.

I shut the door, cross the hallway an' start walkin' up the stairs. At the top I flick on my cigarette lighter an' take a look around. There is a passage in front of me with a door at the end. The door is closed but I can see some light comin' from under the crack.

I gumshoe along the passage very quietly. I have got my lighter in my left hand an' the Luger in my right. When I get to the door I give it a helluva kick.

It flies open.

In the opposite corner of the room, sittin' behind a table playin' patience, is a young guy with blond hair an' a fancy moustache. He puts the cards in his hand down on the table.

I go over an' give him a big grin. I say:

"Mr. Buddy Perriner, I believe?"

He says: "That's right. Who are you and what the hell do you want?"

I grab a chair an' stick it down in front of the table. I say:

"Now listen: Don't argue, don't start askin' questions. If you wanta get out of this keep your ears open an' your mouth shut. I am goin' to do some quick talkin'. There's no time to be wasted."

He gives a sorta grin.

"My name's Caution," I tell him—"Lemmy Caution of the Bureau of Investigation, United States Department of Justice. You can guess what I'm over here for, but just in case your brain's a bit muzzy I'll tell you:

"Your father was framed inta sendin' orders by wireless to two of his ships, that were at sea with cargoes intended for England, to sail inta Delfzyl, Holland, to await further orders. You know what's on those boats—airplanes!

"O.K. Sergius Nakorova, who made a play for your sister so that they could get next to you, had you grabbed off by Willie Lodz, Ardena Vandell an' Borg. They let your old man know that if he didn't do what they said they'd bump you. You were stuck on one of the boats an' you were brought here.

"In the meantime Nakorova has got your sister over to Paris. From there they get her to England. They tell her that unless she plays ball an' does what they want they're goin' to slit your throat. They tell you that unless you do what you're told they'll bump her.

"O.K. Well, I don't wanta tell you any lies so I'm not tellin' you that your sister's safe because I don't know she's safe. Maybe she is an' maybe she's not. But I got word to the English police four or five days ago. Maybe they've got her—I don't know. But you can take this as read that if they haven't found Geraldine, whatever you do or whatever you don't do you won't see her again."

I lean across the table.

"Look, kid," I tell him. "This is tough, but you gotta listen to reason. Do you think that after you've given your orders as representative of the Perriner organisation to these two captains who're comin' around here to-night, to take those ships around into the Ems River an' deliver those cargoes inta Germany, they're goin' to let your sister go—that is if they've still got her. *They've* got to bump her, see? Have you ever known of any kidnappers who let a victim go after they got the ransom through?"

He says: "What is it you want me to do?"

"Only this," I tell him. "I just dealt with the two mugs downstairs. I had a bit of trouble with 'em. One of 'em's dead an' I have slugged the other one. They are nice an' quiet now anyway. At half-past twelve some dame is bringin' a car out here. We're goin' to get inta that car an' we're goin' to scram.

"There's a funny angle to this story. The dame is Ardena Vandell—Lodz' girl. The dame who vamped you so's they could snatch you. They've been done down for their dough by this bunch. She thinks I am Charlie Hoyt—a pal of Willie Lodz. The idea is that we snatch you again before the captains get here, an' hold 'em up for our dough. That's what *she* thinks. I'm not doin' that. When we leave here we're goin' straight to the American Vice-Consul's office in Delfzyl. I am goin' to knock that guy up an' slam you inside. You'll be under the protection of the American flag. We shoot the whole story to the Consul an' we arrest those two boats. We stop 'em leavin' this port. You got it?"

"I've got it," he says.

He gets up an' walks over to the fireplace.

"What a damn' fool I've been," he says.

I grin at him.

"You're tellin' me, Buddy," I crack. "But listen, you ain't the first guy that's fallen for a dame. An' I can sympathise with you in fallin' for that dame Ardena Vandell. She's got something."

He says: "You're right. Gee, what a mug I was to fall for that blonde."

I don't say anything. I look at him.

Then I say: "Well, it can't be helped now. Get your hat—we'll get goin'. I wanta get away from this dump. There is only one road leadin' to this place from Delfzyl. We'll walk down it. Maybe we'll meet the dame drivin' up."

He puts his hands in his pockets. He looks sorta obstinate.

"I don't think I'm going to do that," he says.

"Oh, no!" I tell him. "An' why not?"

He shrugs his shoulders.

"Look," he says, "I've been told all sorts of fairy stories by all sorts of people. Now *you* come along. You say you are a 'G' man. How the hell do I know if that's true or not? You don't seem to realise that I'm in a jam."

"Don't be a goddam fool, Buddy," I tell him. "Of course you're in a jam an' I'm tryin' to get you out of it. I don't want you to start thinkin'. All the thinkin' you've done so far has been wrong. You do what you're told. We're goin' to get outa here."

He shakes his head.

"I'm not goin'," he says.

"Oh, no?" I tell him. "An' why not?"

He looks at me. He grins. He's not a bad-lookin' guy. I feel sorta sorry for him.

"Work it out for yourself," he says. "All this business has happened through me. They've got my sister through my damned stupidity, and I reckon this business is going to break the old man's heart. I am not looking forward to seeing him again. He's going to be very tough.

"But this isn't an ordinary kidnapping. These guys aren't out just for money. They're not the usual sort of kidnappin' thugs. Apparently they want to get the cargo into Germany. Well, I'm not certain that they won't keep their word to me. After all, all they want is those airplanes. They've told me that when the captains get their orders to-night, they are going to leave me here till two o'clock. After that I shall be free. They're going to give me some dough to get over to England. They're going to tell me where Geraldine is.

"But they told me if I didn't, just what would happen to Geraldine, and it wasn't very nice."

"Look, mug," I tell him, "do you think these guys are goin' to keep their word to you? If they've got Geraldine whatever happens they'll bump her. Are you such a dyed-in-the-wool goddam idiot that you believe they're goin' to let either you or your sister go walkin' about bawlin' this story out. For God's sake," I tell him, "have some sense. Here is a story that would make front page news in every newspaper in the world. Damn it, for all you know it might even bring America in this war."

"You're right," he says. "It might. But I'm not taking any chances. I don't particularly care what they do to me. Whatever's coming to me I can take. Maybe I deserve it—but I have got to think of Geraldine. If what you say is right and they've still got her, and I clear out of this, then they certainly will do what they said to her. But if they're telling the truth and I play ball with them, maybe Geraldine's got a chance. My old man can build some more airplanes for the Allies, but he can't build himself another daughter. For once in my life I'm being unselfish. I'm only thinking of Geraldine and I'm staying right here."

I give a big sigh. The joke is I can understand this guy. He's feelin' lousy. He feels he's been a bum. He thinks whatever he does is goin' to be wrong. The main thing is he's worryin' about his sister. I get up.

"O.K., Buddy," I say. "You've got to decide, because, if you're not comin' with me I'm gettin' outa here. If those guys found me around here they wouldn't be so nice to me."

He nods his head.

"Look," he says, "if you're a 'G' man you get out of here while the going's good. I'm staying. Whatever happens to me you can tell my father that anyway I did what I thought was best."

"O.K., pal," I tell him. "I'll tell him that. So long."

I go over to him an' I put my hand out. As he puts up his own hand to take it I get hold of it with my left hand an' I give him a smack on the kisser that you coulda heard in Japan. His knees fold up an' he goes down on the floor. I am tellin' you this guy has got a hard jaw because all the skin is off my knuckles. I get down on my knees an' get his arm around my neck. I get my shoulder under him an' yank him up. I reckon the best thing I can do is to get outa this dump, walk along the road until Ardena comes along, an' I hope she comes along good an' quick because if this guy comes to I shall have to keep sockin' him until I meet up with her.

I stick him in the chair. He flops there with his hands hangin' down by his sides an' his head back. On the mantelpiece at the other end of the room I can see a flash-lamp. I grab it, go out inta the passage an' start lookin' in the other rooms. I can't find anything except in one room there is an overcoat an' a hat hangin' up. I bring these back, stick the overcoat round his shoulders an' the hat in the pocket. I get him outa the chair an' across my shoulder.

I stand there in the middle of the room an' take a look around this place. I give a big sigh of relief. Maybe with a bit of luck I've cleaned this job up. Maybe in half an hour's time, after I have dealt with my little friend Ardena an' got down to the Consul's office I will start puttin' the screws on these guys so hard that they will wonder what's got at 'em. I give myself a big hand. I am feelin' good.

I turn around an' start walkin' towards the door. I have just taken a coupla steps when it opens. I stand there with my mouth hangin' open an' I am so goddam surprised that I nearly drop Buddy on the floor because, standin' in the doorway with a coupla guys behind him, is the boyo whom I did not expect to see—the guy who I thought was safe in the can in Paris—Zeldar.

He has got a Mauser pistol in his hand that is pointin' at my stomach. He is smilin'. He looks quite happy.

"Good evening, Mr. Caution," he says. "I'm delighted to meet you again."

I do not know if you guys have ever felt that your guts was turnin' over an' over because that is the way I am feelin' right now. I stand there lookin' at this sonofabitch with his pointed nose an' self-satisfied grin an' I woulda given a coupla fingers off one hand to be locked up in a room with him for about half an hour with no guns an' no referee.

What the hell! It looks like this is the end of the story, that I am all washed up, that I have just been tottin' around, stoogin' about the place, plannin', schemin' an' plottin'—for what? Just sweet nothin'.

I turn around an' drop the kid back on the chair. He is beginning to come to. I turn my back on Zeldar an' start pinchin' Buddy's nostrils to help him to come around.

He opens his eyes.

He says: "I'm not goin'. I'm tellin' you I'm not goin'!"

I laugh.

"You're tellin' me," I say. "Take a look around you, you big mug. I reckon you're dead right. You ain't goin' an' I ain't goin' an' nobody's goin'. We're all washed up."

The two other guys come into the room behind Zeldar. He is still standin' there smilin', holdin' the gun. I take a look at him. Somehow he looks bigger an' straighter. When he was in Paris he looked like a mediocre sort of guy, with his shoulders a bit bent, but now he is standin' up an' lookin' like something that matters.

One of the guys who has come into the room sticks up his hand an' says to Zeldar: *"Heil Hitler."* Zeldar says *"Heil Hitler"* an' the other guy says *"Heil Hitler."* So that's that!

One guy says "Congratulations, *Herr Kapitan.* I am sorry we missed you. We were waiting for you as arranged. Then the Fraulein Vandell telephoned that we were to come here."

"Excellent," says Zeldar.

He comes over to me an' frisks me. He takes my gun an' hands it to one of the guys. He says:

"Take Perriner out of here. Take him into the next room. The masters of the two ships will be here at any moment. Perriner will give them their orders. After that you will prepare to leave."

The guy clicks his heels. The two of them go over an' grab Buddy. As they are takin' him out, Zeldar says:

"Herr Perriner, I would stress the necessity of your giving to the captains the exact orders which have been indicated to you. They are to deliver their cargoes and land with their crews at the main Ems Wharf. They will await the arrival of a tug from Delfzyl which will pick them up and bring them back, with their crews and you, to-morrow. If you carry out your instructions in the spirit and the letter you will be in England with your sister in two days' time. You understand?"

Buddy nods his head. They take him out.

Zeldar comes over to where I am sittin' in the chair. He stands there lookin' down at me.

"It would give me the greatest pleasure to shoot you—you American swine," he says. "You have caused me a certain amount of inconvenience. However, it would not be wise to deal with you here."

He lights a cigarette.

"I have an excellent scheme for you, my friend," he goes on. "I propose to land you with the cargoes. You will find that life—as long as it lasts—in one of our concentration camps is not conducive to your own rather light-hearted method of thinking. We have an excellent system for people like you in Germany."

I made a very rude noise at him. He comes over an' smacks me across the face so hard that he nearly knocks me off the chair. But he don't stop smilin'. I reckon this Zeldar can be a very tough guy in a very quiet way.

"You will also be surprised and possibly not too pleased to know," he goes on, "that the ultimate success of our little scheme is in part due to you. Candidly, I did not intend to come here to Delfzyl to superintend the final details. But for you I should have remained in Switzerland where other plans require my attention."

He sits down on the desk an' rolls the cigarette smoke around his tongue.

"I suppose you thought it clever to get the Rillwater woman to telephone me in Paris, to ask me to go round at that ridiculous hour in the morning and see her. It did not strike you that I might regard it as suspicious that she should want to discuss the sudden departure of Geraldine Perriner from the Hotel Dieudonne with *me*. However, I am of a curious nature so I kept the appointment. I wished to hear what she had to say. She informed me that she proposed to get into touch with the French police."

He shrugs his shoulders.

"That, of course, did not suit me," he goes on. "I decided that the time had come for me to leave Paris. I also decided that it might be clever not even to return to my apartment. But on my way to the station—again merely to satisfy my curiosity—I passed that way and watched the arrival of the police officers who so carefully concealed themselves in the doorways of neighbouring houses to await my return." He gives a big horse laugh. "I hope they are not still waiting.

"You will have to get up very early in the morning to catch Alphonse Zeldar," he says. He clicks his heels. "Otherwise *Kapitan* Emil Mienschmidt—officer of the Reich Intelligence Service—at your disposal, Herr Caution."

He makes me a sarcastic sorta bow.

Then he goes over to the door an' bawls out in German. One of the other guys comes in.

"The ships' captains are on their way here, *Herr Kapitan,*" he says. "They will be here in a few minutes."

"Excellent," says Zeldar. "Now we will remove this gentleman into the room farther down the passage. There is still something I wish to say to him."

The guy pulls a gun an' prods me along the passageway. We go into a room at the other end. It is a well-furnished room an' there is a fire burnin'.

Zeldar strolls in. He has still got the Mauser in his hand. The other guy scrams.

"Make yourself comfortable, my dear Herr Caution," says Zeldar. "Because you will not be comfortable for very much longer."

I do not say one word. I am watchin' like a cat to see if I can get some sort of break. I reckon if I don't my number's as good as up.

Zeldar goes over to the corner an' opens a cupboard an' takes out a bottle an' a glass. He gives himself a drink. I sit myself down in a chair that is up against the wall. I sit there watchin' him.

"I do not wish to add insult to injury," he says with a grin, "but I cannot refrain from telling you how invaluable have been the services of the rather ridiculous people we have employed in this affair. The joke is that we have paid nobody. Money is very valuable to my country to-day but apart from that point it seems to me humorous to consider that no one has received a pfennig for services rendered. Yet in spite of the fact these fatuous American crooks *insist* on helping me."

I feel like takin' a big kick at myself. I reckon I know what he means. I reckon that streamlined hell-cat Ardena Vandell has sold me out properly on this job. That baby has been playin' with the hare *an'* the hounds an' I reckon that I am the hare all right.

I put on an act.

"I reckon I gotta hand it to you, Zeldar," I say. "You been the smart guy from the start. I reckon you had us all weighed up and ditched before we even got goin'."

"That is kind of you," he says with a lousy grin. "Very kind. I am sure I appreciate your congratulations."

He walks over to me an' he smashes me one in the pan. I go off the chair. When I get up I am wonderin' if I have got any jaw left. I flop back on to the chair.

He strolls over to the fire an' pours himself out another glass of *kümmel*.

"You are entirely correct, my friend," he says. "As you so aptly put it you *have* been ditched from the start. You have all been very foolish, but *one* of you is such a fool that the rest of you are entirely and absolutely outclassed."

He holds up his glass.

"Here's to the biggest fool of them all," he says. "The most stupid creature that ever walked."

He looks at me.

"I give you the health of the Fraulein Ardena Vandell," he chuckles. "The best friend the Reich ever had."

He sinks the drink.

I say a very rude word to myself. I knew it. I oughta been wise from the start.

That goddam dame has sold me out.

Chapter Fourteen
THE WORKS

I sit there lookin' at my shoes an' thinkin' about four hundred an' different things at once; but mainly, strange as it may seem, I am thinkin' about dames, an' I have never, in all my life, met up with a cheaper little double-crossin', chisellin', two-timin' four-flusher than this Ardena Vandell. An' how!

As a twister she is the complete tops. I reckon that if this baby was ever wrecked with her old mother on some uninhabited island she would steal the old girl's gold-stoppin's out of her teeth while she was asleep an' try to sell 'em to a shark—an' I reckon she would give the shark the short end of the deal.

Me—I have met up with a whole lot of dames. I reckon that dolls of every shape, sort an' description have projected themselves across my flowery path ever since I been wearin' trousers. I have met bad dames an' good dames. I have met 'em thin, fat an' outsize. I have met dames who cried to get what they wanted, dames who went out after it with a gun, dames who tried the pleadin' act an' dames who get what is comin' their way by swingin' a mean hip an' lookin' arch.

But this Ardena is somethin' new. She makes all the rest look like the amateurs' hour. She is the world's biggest pain in the neck to me.

What I mean is I do not like her at all.

I take a look at Zeldar. He is standin' there smokin' a Turkish cigarette an' sippin' at the glass of *kümmel*. But when he is smokin' he puts the glass on the mantelpiece, an' when he is drinkin' he puts the cigarette down so that all the time he can hold the Mauser on me. I reckon that he is usin' a great deal of self-control to stop himself shootin' so many holes in me that I would look like your grandmother's nutmeg grater.

An' the only reason that he is not presentin' me with a pound or so of lead slugs is that he feels it ain't indicated just at this moment and also because he has probably got somethin' worse on the ice for me—like he said.

He throws his cigarette stub into the fire an' looks at me. He looks like the cat that has got a mouse where it wants it. He says:

"I am sure, Herr Caution, that the peculiar and ever-present sense of humour for which I think you are rightly distinguished, will be tickled if I tell you just what fools you all are—especially your friend the *Fräulein* Ardena.

"And realise also that if this young woman had used the slightest particle of common sense she could have upset my plans without much difficulty. She suffers, like most of her sex, from an entire absence of brains."

In spite of myself I am sorta interested. I want to hear just what that baby has been up to.

I say: "So she made a mug out of herself, hey? What did she do?"

He smiles and shrugs his shoulders.

"It was not my intention to come here to Delfzyl at all," he says. "I had proposed that my *aide Gloydas*—who is at the present moment sleeping off a fit of drunkenness—for which he will pay very dearly in due course, damn his undisciplined soul!—should conclude my arrangements and see that the cargoes *and* our young friend Buddy Perriner were safely delivered. I proposed to remain peaceably at Zurich where I have other urgent and important business.

"But apparently in the meantime the *Fräulein* Ardena Vandell arrived here in Delfzyl for the purpose of endeavouring to get for herself some or all of the money that she thought was due to Lodz, Borg and herself for their part in the kidnapping of Buddy Perriner.

"She made the situation clear to Gloydas. She introduced herself to him and explained quite frankly what she was after. Gloydas, who is not quite an idiot, had sufficient sense to communicate with me by telephone and I came at once to Delfzyl, arriving here to-night to keep the appointment I had made with him.

"I found him at the *Spruithuis* almost dead drunk having been seduced into this lack of discipline by the charms of Ardena. For this, as I have already said, he shall pay dearly. He shall rejoin his regiment in our Fatherland and learn to obey orders.

"For the moment, with Gloydas *hors de combat,* I was a little perturbed. But once again someone whom I least expected to do it came to my rescue—none other than the charming Ardena."

He starts laughin'. It seems as if the joke is a good one. He has a really swell laugh. I get around to feelin' that I would give twenty years' pay to kick the bastard's teeth down his throat.

"Forgive my mirth," he goes on, "but the joke is really exquisite."

"Go on," I tell him. "I can hardly wait."

"Ardena," he says, "introduced herself to me. She informed me that she is the lady friend of Mr. Lodz to whom we owe a great deal of money, that she has come here for the express purpose of getting that money, and she has already made herself useful to Gloydas and that if I do not want someone to put a spoke in my wheel I had better consent to pay her off."

He puts the glass on the mantelpiece and pours some more *kümmel* into it.

"Naturally," he says, "I found myself very interested. I wondered how this young woman could feel herself entitled to threaten *me*. I told her so. She then informed me that a perfect plan had been made which would upset all my arrangements and that unless I was prepared to play ball—as she put it—the plan would be carried out."

I sit up. Can you beat that one! So all the time I was kickin' around wastin' my sweetness on this dame she was plannin' to frame me. An' it wasn't a bad frame-up either. She tells me that story about snatchin' Buddy an' holdin' these guys up just so that she has a lever to get dough outa them. The fact that she is ditchin' me in the process don't mean a thing to her. This Ardena is a honey, I'm tellin' you!

Zeldar goes on:

"So I agreed," he says. "I promised her, on my word of honour as an officer, that immediately the ships docked at the German Wharf on the Ems River she should receive her share. Well . . . the poor girl was foolish enough to believe this. Then she unfolded an amusing story.

"She told me how an acquaintance of Willie Lodz had turned up here in Delfzyl and contacted her. She told me that this man had been sent by Lodz who, owing to some ill-luck, had been imprisoned in Paris. She told me that this gentleman was an individual by the name of Charlie Hoyt and that he was even now on his way to effect the rescue of our young friend Perriner.

"Needless to say she informed me of this for two reasons. First to prove that she had told me the truth when she had said that she was in a position to upset my plans, and secondly because—very naturally—she wanted her friend Charlie Hoyt 'taken care of.' In other words, having made use of him, she wanted him out of the way.

"I acted promptly. I came here at once with my men and I have the pleasure of discovering that this mysterious Charlie Hoyt is none other than my old friend Herr Caution, the 'G' man, the man who never lost a case, who always gets his man. Forgive me," he says, "if I laugh again."

"Don't you worry about me," I tell him. "You have a laugh while you can still control your face muscles. One of these fine days I'm goin' to take a poke at you an' when I get through with you your pan is goin' to look like the map of Poland."

He laughs out loud.

"You do not even annoy me, my friend," he says. "Because I propose to give myself a great deal of amusement with you later. When we are aboard and when I have a little more time at my disposal I will tell you some of the processes we use on the occupants of our concentration camps. This should amuse you. You will realise that there is much for you to look forward to."

He drinks some more *kümmel*.

"So you will see, Herr Caution, that crooks like our friend Ardena never learn anything by experience. In order to do you out of your share of the money that Gloydas was supposed to pay for the release of Buddy Perriner she gives away the whole of your little plot without so much as a tremor of the eyelid. And the joke is that she really believes that *I* am going to pay her some money!"

"Which of course you are not goin' to do," I say. "You're goin' to do her down for it, like you caught Nakorova an' Lodz an' Borg. Ardena may be a double-crosser but she's a child in arms compared with you, you cheap lump of German boloney."

"When in Rome do as the Romans do," he says. "Incidentally, when the time comes, when Ardena can also be told exactly what is in store for her, I propose to tell her how very near she was to success. It was the business of the fool Gloydas to arrange for pilots to take the boats out to-night. Apparently he made his arrangements before he became too drunk to talk. If our so charming friend had handed Gloydas over to the nearest Dutch policeman and had a ten minutes' conversation with the American Consul here I have no doubt that she could have very effectually spiked my guns.

"The American Consul would have taken steps to stop the ships leaving Delfzyl, and I have no doubt that, in spite of the fact that she took part in the kidnapping of your young friend Perriner, Ardena would have secured some sort of reward. Instead of which . . ."

"Instead of which you've got her workin' for you," I say. "An' when she's done workin' for you you're goin' to ditch her like you ditched the rest of 'em."

"Once again, Herr Caution," he says, "you show the greatest acumen. But what else can I do?" He spreads his hands. "As much as I should like the *Fräulein* to go on living, such a process is impossible. She knows too much. She could talk too much. And when she finds that there is no money for her I am certain that she will be *most* annoyed and would naturally desire to talk—*if* she got the chance. I shall see that she does not."

He draws some smoke down into his lungs an' blows it out again, slowly. He is enjoyin' life.

"I shall deal with her in due course," he says, "as quietly and efficiently as I dealt with Sergius and Edvanne Nakorova."

I sit up again.

I say: "So it was you who bumped Sergius and Edvanne. It wasn't Edvanne—it was *you*!"

"But of course," he says, smiling. "What did you expect? Surely you do not expect my country to entrust me with delicate and, shall we say, dangerous missions unless I had the ability to carry them out delicately?"

He takes a chair, twists it around and sits across it. This guy is so pleased with himself he could burst.

"I am not quite a fool, Herr Caution," he says. "I realised from the start that we were playing with fire so far as Edvanne Nakorova was concerned. She was a Frenchwoman, and Frenchwomen are notoriously patriotic. I never trusted Nakorova to keep the information about the second part of our scheme to himself. I knew that at some time or other he would, in a weak moment, disclose to her what our real plans were and what the Perriner ransom was actually to consist of. I knew that at some time or other I should have to deal drastically with Edvanne Nakorova and probably with Sergius as well.

"And I realised that the time had come during that little supper party that Sergius gave at the Cossack Café," he says, smilin' like a jackal. "I realised that it was not possible to have Herr Caution dashing about Paris making enquiries which, to say the least of them, would be inconvenient.

"Also, I noticed something else. You left early. I saw no good reason for this. Soon after Edvanne made an excuse to go. I came to the conclusion that Sergius had talked too much to her, that she knew too much, that she was going to confide in you. I realised that the death of your colleague Rodney Wilks had already disturbed her."

I nod my head.

"So you were responsible for the Wilks job too," I say. "You gave that stuff to Sergius an' he didn't know it would kill Wilks?"

"Exactly," he says. "I told Sergius that the mixture would make Wilks feel sufficiently ill to have to leave Siedler's Club immediately. It seemed the most tactful way to deal with the matter. Anyhow, Sergius believed it. But then Sergius was also a fool."

He gets off the chair an' walks back to the fire. He stands there, preenin' himself. He is thinkin' that he is goin' to be berries with Adolf when he gets back to Germany an' gets himself a couple of tons of Iron Crosses.

"When Edvanne left soon after you had gone," he says, "I took the liberty of going after her. I followed her. When she left her flat I followed her round to Sergius' apartment. She did not know that I had a key. I went in after her, and, standing in the hallway, heard a very interestin' conversation between herself and Sergius. Apparently she was pleading with him to tell you the whole story, and it looked as if he was on the verge of consenting.

"Well . . . it was all very simple. I crept out of the hallway, closed the front door of the apartment behind me and then rang the bell.

"Sergius answered it. He asked me in and I began to talk about our proposed interview with you which you will remember we had planned for the next morning.

"Sergius was sitting by the fire and Edvanne was stretched out on the couch—looking as delightful as she always did. We talked most amicably for some time, and then I went over to the table and mixed drinks for us all. Luckily I had with me some of the stuff that had been used on Wilks. It is extremely potent. I mixed some with the drinks for Sergius and Edvanne.

"Then I proposed a toast and we all drank."

He sighs.

"My delightful Edvanne died immediately," he said. "But Sergius was more difficult. He dropped his glass and tried to shoot me. I did not know he was carrying a pistol. Luckily the poison took effect before he was able to carry out his purpose.

"Then I amused myself by reconstructing a little scene for your benefit. I laid Edvanne out very carefully on the lounge and put her glass by her side as if she had herself placed it there after drinking. I imagined that you would conclude that she had poisoned Sergius and herself rather than allow him to continue to plot against her beloved France."

He smiles across at me. I reckon this guy has got the devil lookin' like Father Christmas.

"I have no doubt that she would have killed Sergius," he says. "But she would not have killed herself. I wanted them both dead. I never believe in leaving any evidence."

I get up sorta casual. I take the chair an' spin it round in front of me. He puts the gun up as I move, but when he sees that I am just twiddlin' the chair around he settles down again.

"Well . . ." I say, "I reckon you are the berries. I reckon you are one hundred per cent. I was goin' to say that I have seen things like you crawlin' out from under damp rocks when the sun comes out, but on second thoughts that would be complimentin' you."

I take a deep breath.

"You got me beat," I go on, "just because you got that gun. But havin' the gun is not goin' to stop me talkin'. I think that the guy who invented the word lousy musta been thinkin' of you. I reckon you would make the lowest sonofabitch of a murderin' thug look like somethin' off the front of a Christmas card. You are so goddam lousy that I would not even throw you to a shark because the shark would get poisoned. An' the other thing is . . ."

I throw up the chair in front of me with my right hand, push it at him an' sail in after it. My luck holds. One leg of the chair catches his pistol arm as it comes up.

I let out with my foot an' get my heel on to his shin. He goes red with pain. I come over with my right an' bust him one on the kisser that smacks his nose as flat as a pancake an' busts both his lips. I bring a left arm short jab over before he has got over the first one an' catch him in the guts. Then I kick the chair outa the way an' bring my knee up inta his stomach just for luck.

He goes down inta the fireplace an' his head wins a sweet smack on the iron fender. I get hold of him by the collar an' yank him up an' I fetch him another one that they musta heard over in England. I busted him such a mean bust on the beezer that I can hear my knuckles crack.

He goes careerin' across the room. I go after him. Outside I can hear a lotta noise, but I am so goddam angry with this heel that I am thinkin' of nothin' except fixin' a beauty treatment for him that will make him look like he had his lousy pan run over by a seventy-ton tank.

I get hold of him by the door an' spin him around. I have got an idea that I will stick this guy on the fire just to get a little nice warmth into his entrails. As I turn around the door opens an' some-body catches me a smack over the brains department that puts paid to me all right.

The room goes round an' round an' everythin' goes nice an' dark. I fade out.

When I come to I am lyin' up against the wall over by the table. There are a coupla million stars dancin' in front of my eyes an' I reckon that the guy who cracked me over the dome must have been usin' a piece of old iron.

Far away I can hear a telephone ringin'. Then when I get my eyes to stay open I can see Zeldar sittin' on a chair on the other side of the room with a wet handkerchief tied around his snoot. That sight is pleasin' anyway.

The telephone goes on ringin'. Suddenly I realise that it is just above my head on the table. Every time it rings the sound sorta goes through me an' echoes in my nut like sleigh bells. I am not feelin' so good.

One of Zeldar's guys comes over an' pushes me outa the way with his foot. He starts talkin' into the telephone, standin' just over me. He is sayin' *Fräulein* this an' *Fräulein* that an' it looks like he is talkin' to Ardena.

After a minute he stops talkin' an' turns around to Zeldar. He is holdin' his hand over the mouthpiece.

"It is the *Fräulein* Vandell, Herr Kapitan," he says. "She says everything is in order. She is speaking from the wharf where our ships are docked. She says that everything is well, that the pilots are aboard an' that the ships are ready to clear."

Zeldar grunts.

"Excellent," he says. "Tell her to go aboard the *Maybury*. Tell her that we are coming down now and that I look forward to drinking her health."

By this time I have pulled myself together. I reckon that I have still got half a chance. You guys will realise that there is damn' little love between me an' Ardena, but she is a dame an' I reckon that if I can give her a tip she might still be able to duck outa this business. If she can, then maybe she will do a little talkin' an' even if Buddy an' I are good an' stiff by this time there's a chance that sometime somebody will get this so-an'-so Zeldar.

The guy at the telephone is still talkin' to her. He is standin' just on my left. I lean back against the wall, pull up my legs an' shoot 'em into his stomach as hard as I can. He gives one helluva howl an' drops the telephone. I grab it.

"Ardena," I yell, "this is Charlie. You've been framed. Scram kid . . . scram!"

I hear her say: "Aw . . . nuts to you!" an' they are on to me. Zeldar an' two other guys who have come in. The guy I kicked is still lyin' on the floor holdin' his stomach an' writhin' about.

They get to work on me. Me—I have been in some very tough corners but when it comes to really givin' a guy the works I hand it to these three guys.

After they have tried most other things, one of 'em gives me a sweet kick under the heart. I fold up an' go out. Everything gets nice an' dark again.

When I open my eyes I feel like the wreck of the *Hesperus*. Both my eyes are half closed, an' my head is achin' like somebody was playin' a tom-tom inside it.

I try to move my hands but it's no soap. When I look down I see that somebody has stuck a very nice pair of steel bracelets on my wrists.

I take a coupla deep breaths just to see if I got any ribs left. Anyhow I can breathe all right. By this time I am able to see outa one eye. I take a look around.

I am lyin' up against the wall in some sort of cabin or deck house. I reckon I am aboard the *Maybury* all right. From somewhere below comes the throb of a ship's engines. There is a dim light on in the cabin an' I can see the portholes are all curtained in with black stuff. It looks like we've cleared Delfzyl.

I look across the cabin. On the other side, handcuffed like I am, I can see Buddy.

I run my tongue over my lips. I can feel that I got one or two teeth missin' an' my lips are bust. My tongue feels as if some guy has been scrapin' it with a bit of old iron. Between you an' me I am not feelin' quite so well thank-you-very-much.

I say: "Well, Buddy, how're you goin'?"

"I'm O.K.," he says.

He grins across at me. I reckon he is not a bad kid.

"It looks as if they've been pushin' you around a bit," he says. "I'm damn' sorry, Caution. This is all my fault."

"What the hell," I tell him. "Me—I have never been a one for post-mortems—especially when it looks as if that is what is waitin' for us."

He says: "So it's like that, is it?"

"Yeah," I tell him. "That's how it is. I had a little talk with our pal Zeldar. They got somethin' on ice for us. He reckons to stick us in some concentration camp but I'm bettin' we won't I even get there. I don't think I like that guy. He's not a nice guy."

I start thinkin' about Zeldar an' I grin.

Buddy says: "What the hell have you got to be pleased about?"

"Nothin' very much," I say. "Except I was thinkin' of what I done to Zeldar before they got to work on me. You oughta see that guy's mug. I reckon that his girl friend will have a fit when she sees him."

"Well, that's something," he says.

He shuts up because somebody is unlockin' the door.

A guy comes in. It is one of Zeldar's guys. He has got an overcoat on an' he has got one hand in a pocket.

"Gentlemen," he says, "the *Herr Kapitan* thinks that you might care to join him in the saloon. You will, I am sure, be very glad to know that we have cleared Delfzyl. The *Herr Kapitan* thinks you might like to be amused on your journey. You will please get up and walk along the deck. If you attempt to speak to anyone or make one suspicious movement I shall shoot you. You understand, gentlemen?"

We get up. When I get on to my feet I fall over again an' have to start in on the gettin' up business a little more slowly. I reckon that I am just one big bruise.

We go outside an' start walkin' along the deck with Zeldar's guy behind us. The boat is a big one but I cannot see many guys aboard. I reckon they are takin' these boats around to the Ems with just half a dozen hands.

It is as dark as hell. There is a bit of wind an' the noise of the ship an' the sea.

I get to wonderin' what Zeldar has got ready-eyed for us.

I reckon that whatever it is I am not goin' to like it!!

CHAPTER FIFTEEN
YOU'D BE SURPRISED

IT IS not so easy walkin' along the deck with a pair of handcuffs on. The boat has got a little bit of a roll on an' I do not feel too steady on my legs.

Suddenly Buddy gives a lurch an' cannons inta me. The guy behind me sticks the gun in my back an' nearly knocks me over. Buddy gives him a helluva kick on the shins. The guy then crowns Buddy with the gun butt an' the kid goes down on the deck. He lies there groanin'.

"The pig can stay there," says the guy with the gun. "That will serve as a taste of what is going to happen to him."

He starts cussin' in German.

He prods me along the deck, down a companion way an' along a passage. He opens a door an' shoves me inside.

It is a nice little saloon-cabin, an' there is a very sweet little party goin' on inside. Sittin' around the table are Zeldar, Ardena an' a couple of other mugs. There are some bottles of champagne on the table an' everybody seems good an' happy. Ardena—that smart hell-cat—is sittin' back smokin' a cigarette an' lookin' as if she had done somethin' clever.

Zeldar says: "Franz, where is the other fool?"

Franz starts crackin' off at Zeldar in German. He is tellin' him that he has smacked Buddy over the nut for gettin' fresh.

Zeldar laughs. "So our young friend has misbehaved," he says. "Well, he will soon have ample opportunity to learn discipline."

He tells the guy to go back an' chuck some water over Buddy. After he has done this he is to bring him along. The guy clicks his heels an' scrams.

Zeldar fills Ardena's glass an' gives her a big smile. Then he fills up his own an' the other guys'.

I plank myself down on the velvet covered seat runnin' along the far side of the cabin an' watch 'em.

I am feelin' a little bit sorry for Ardena. Here is this silly dame swillin' champagne an' thinkin' she is on top of the world when all the time she is sittin' on a volcano that is goin' to burst plenty in a minute. But I reckon that Zeldar is gettin' a kick outa playin' her along an' makin' her think that she's been goddam clever.

He raises his glass.

"I drink to your health, *Fraulein,*" he says. "And I have a unique little surprise in store for you." He points over to me an' grins. "Do you recognise your friend?" he says.

She smiles back at him.

"That's Hoyt," she says. "Charlie Hoyt—the poor mug!" She holds up her glass. "Here's to you, Charlie," she goes on. "I'm sorta sorry that I had to take you for a ride. But that's the way it goes. A girl has got to look after herself these days!"

They all start laughin'. Zeldar says:

"*Fraulein,* you are missing the cream of the jest. That is *not* Charlie Hoyt."

He gets up an' makes me a bow.

"Allow me to present to you Herr Lemmy Caution, a famous Federal Agent of the United States Department of Justice—the individual you *thought* was Charlie Hoyt."

She looks at me with her mouth open. I have never seen a dame so surprised in my life. Then she starts laughin'. She has a good time. She laughs fit to burst her ribs an' they all join in. I told you that was goin' to be a very nice little party.

"Consider, my charming Ardena," cracks Zeldar. "Our friend here arrives in Delfzyl and persuades you that he is Hoyt and you believe it. How colossal! He is planning to double-cross you, and you, in turn, succeed in double-crossing him. And you do not even realise that he is a member of your delightful country's Department of Justice. I think the picture is unique. It is a superb situation for everyone except the unfortunate Caution and the unfortunate Buddy Perriner."

He gets up an' comes across to me. He stands lookin' down at me.

"American swine!" he says.

He throws the glass of champagne in my face.

"O.K., Zeldar," I tell him. "Have a good time while the goin's good. One day somebody or other is goin' to catch up with you an' things won't be so hot. Another thing," I go on, "what has somebody been doin' to your nose? You never looked anythin' else except a lousy sonofabitch anyway, but now, with that double-sized schnozzle that you got yourself an' them two black eyes you are positively good-lookin'. An' all I wish is that the guys who pulled me off you had been a minute or so later. I woulda burned the pants off you—you . . ."

I tell him just what he is. I call him some very carefully selected names that woulda steamed up even a deaf guy.

He steps back an' he clocks me. He busts me one on the nose that made me see the swellest firework display I have ever got for nothin'. Then he goes back to the table an' sits down.

Then Ardena gets up. She strolls over to me. I reckon I am not lookin' quite so good. My nose is bleedin' like hell an' what with one thing an' another I cannot even see straight.

She says: "Well, for cryin' out loud. Is this my big day or is it."

She stands, lookin' at me, sippin' champagne.

"Even when I thought you was Charlie Hoyt," she says, "I didn't like you. You was just another heel thinkin' he was bein' clever and musclin' in on somebody else's territory. But at least I thought you was an honest-to-goodness crook."

She gives a big laugh.

"So you're a 'G' man," she says. "Well, isn't that just too too marvellous. Personally, if you hadn't got a lot comin' to you I would take a bust at you myself, you lousy, crawlin' gum-shoein' dick. Have a drop of liquor, big boy."

She holds up her glass an' pours it over my face. It stings like hell but anyhow I get a taste of the stuff an' I'm tellin' you it was good liquor.

She goes over to the table an' fills up her glass. She says to Zeldar:

"Am I the lucky little dame or am I? Just imagine, if I'd gone through with the idea that I put up to this mug he woulda scotched me an' chucked me in the cooler. Oh boy . . . what an escape!"

She gives herself a drink.

Zeldar says: "Exactly, *Fraulein*. From that point of view you have been extremely lucky." His voice changes. "I hope your luck will hold."

She looks at him.

"What do you mean by that crack, Mister Zeldar?" she says. "I don't like the way you said that."

He shrugs his shoulders. He is grinnin' like the devil.

"My delightful, my charming Ardena," he says, rollin' the words around his tongue. "I must tell you that I specialise in making fools of people. I am so expert in the art that I am afraid I have even indulged in the process with regard to your sweet self. You understand?"

She flops down in her chair. She sits there lookin' at him.

"Listen," she says. "Just exactly what is this? You aren't tellin' me that . . ."

"My dear," grins Zeldar, "I *am* telling you—as you put it—that there is no money in this business for you. There is no money in it for anyone—except ourselves. But cheer up. You will not be too badly off in Germany. I have no doubt that there are ways in which a lady of such great personal charms as yours will be able to—shall we say— exist. You may have a little difficulty in settling down to your new life but I am sure I you will adapt yourself to it. Fill up your glass and forget such mundane things as money."

In spite of the fact that Ardena is a double-crossin' little heel, I feel a bit sorry for her. She sits there, lookin' at him with her jaw hangin'. Zeldar and the other guys are smilin' like a lot of jackals that have just found a nice juicy corpse lyin' around.

She says sorta quietly: "You don't mean that there's goin' to be no pay-off?"

Zeldar fills up her glass.

"I am afraid not, my dear," he chuckles. "There will be no pay-off. You are now receiving my best thanks for services rendered and a few glasses of excellent wine. That is all you are going to get."

She flushes pink.

"You cheap, chisellin' bum," she howls. "What the hell is this! If you aren't goin' to pay me off what the hell did you bring me on this goddam boat for? What's goin' on around here?"

"Hush . . . hush . . . little one," he croons at her. "It will do no good for you to excite yourself—except perhaps that it amuses us. *Of course* you had to come on this little trip. First of all without your aid I should never have been able to reach the pilots that the fool Gloydas had secured for our little trip, and surely you did not imagine that I was going to leave you behind in Delfzyl? Oh no . . . you might have talked. You will be much safer with us."

"My God!" she says. "You mean . . ."

"I mean that you must prepare to make a long stay in Germany," says Zeldar. "There you will learn to control yourself. While you behave you should be not too uncomfortable. If you do not behave you will be made to learn discipline."

He looks at his pals with a self-satisfied smirk.

"I leave no loose ends untied," he says. "There will be no evidence of our operations. Caution and Perriner will be liquidated and you, *Fraulein,* will remain in Germany. Now drink your wine and be cheerful. Did not our great German philosopher say that women were intended merely for the relaxation of the warrior. *That* is their business and that only. Make yourself expert, Ardena. It will be the better for you."

She says a rude work at him. For a moment I think that she is goin' for him. She is so steamed up that I reckon she woulda liked to bump that sneerin' guy.

Just at the moment the door opens an' Franz pushes Buddy in. The kid don't look so good. He is drippin' with water that somebody has chucked over him an' he has got a bump on the side of his head like a Roc's egg.

Ardena takes one look at him an' jumps over. She gives him a smack across the kisser that sounded like a whip crackin'.

"You lousy mug," she shrieks. "If it hadn't been for you an' your goddam nerve in fallin' for me an' gettin' yourself snatched, I would never have got myself in this jam. I would like to bust you to bits. I would like to . . ."

She is almost stranglin' with temper. Buddy, who is still swayin' about an' is not so good on his feet, starts to say something but she clocks him again. He falls over against the cabin wall an' lays there. Zeldar an' the others are laughin' their heads off. I reckon this is as good as a play to these guys.

I say: "Why don't you pipe down, Ardena? You got what was comin' to you. Didn't they tell you that crime don't pay?"

"Shut up, flatfoot!" she yells. "Otherwise I'll get busy on *you*!"

She sits down again. Then she says:

"Oh, what the hell! Life can be goddam tough."

She puts heir head between her hands an' starts cryin'.

Zeldar looks at his pals an' grins.

"I hate to see these tears, *Fraulein*," he says, "but you will probably feel a little better, a trifle calmer, afterwards."

She starts dabbin' at her eyes with her handkerchief. Then she shrugs her shoulders. She gives a bad imitation of a smile.

"Oh well," she says. "I can take it!"

She pours herself out another drink, picks up the glass an' swallows the champagne. She throws the glass across the cabin. It smashes against the wall just by my head.

Me—I am feelin' tired. My head is achin' like hell. I take a look at Buddy. He is lyin' against the cabin wall on the other side. He don't look so good either.

I get to thinkin' about dames. Not that it is goin' to do me any good, because I reckon that nothin' is goin' to do me any good now, but because if ever you are in a tough jam an' it is no good tryin' to get yourself out of it, you might as well think about dames. It sorta takes your mind off things.

I think of all the tough, silly dames that I ever come across in my life an' I come to the conclusion that I have never met a dame who is so goddam silly as this Ardena. She is such a mug that she has practically double-crossed herself.

Also I reckon that she has had a drink too many. Her head is noddin' an' in a minute I reckon she is goin' right off. She puts her elbow on the table an' leans her head on it an' groans.

An' the sight of her don't make me feel any better. The boat is pitchin' an' tossin' like hell. I reckon it must be damn' stormy.

An' when I think this I have to clamp my mouth shut tight to stop myself yelpin'.

I have got an idea.

I sit back against the cabin wall an' the boat gives a roll that sends a coupla glasses off the table. It must be a helluva sea runnin' because the *Maybury* is a big boat.

I am watchin' Zeldar like a cat. I am waitin' to see just how soon he will get it but he is sittin' back holdin' up a glass of champagne, smokin' a cigarette.

Then the guy sittin' beside him gets up an' finishes his drink. He is lookin' a bit funny. He goes over to the porthole an' he pulls the curtain aside. He looks out. Then he turns round an' he is just startin' to say somethin' when Ardena lets go a howl.

She has got one leg stuck out an' I can see a ladder right down the front of her stockin'.

"For God's sake!" she says. "Look at that . . . that's the second pair to-day. I reckon I'm goin' to leave off wearin' stockings. To hell with it!"

She sits there lookin' at her leg an' I'm tellin' you it is *some* leg. I get to thinkin' of the night when Edvanne pulled that fast one on me about havin' a run in *her* stockin'.

Then the guy who has looked outa the porthole starts shoutin'. He bawls:

"Herr Kapitan . . . Herr Kapitan . . . We are at sea! This is not the Ems River!"

Zeldar's eyes pop. He spins around in his chair. Ardena says in a cold sorta voice:

"Stay where you are, Zeldar. If anybody moves they get it!"

She has pulled a gun outa her stockin' top. She is lookin' as cool as an iceberg.

What the hell *is* this!

She starts talkin' to Franz. She is talkin' in German. He hesitates for a moment an' she moves the gun. Then he comes over to me. He unlocks the handcuffs.

"Take the guns off them, Mr. Caution, please," she says.

"You watch me, sister," I tell her. "I can hardly wait."

I get up an' stretch myself. I am creakin' all over. Then I ease around the cabin collectin' guns, an' I am not too gentle in handlin' Zeldar.

Zeldar leans across the table. He says to her:

"You fool, you must be mad. You will pay for this. You will . . ."

She smiles at him.

"If anybody's doing any paying it's you, *Herr Kapitan* Meinschmidt," she says, an' I notice she is talkin' very pretty English. "The trouble with you is that you come to conclusions too quickly. . . ."

"Such as?" I ask her.

"Such as that I was Ardena Vandell," she says. "If any of you people had taken the trouble to find out you would have known that Ardena Vandell is a blonde. That's why I had to set about Buddy when he was brought in. In another minute he would have given the game away by *not* recognising me."

"That's O.K. by me," I tell her. "An' now, if it ain't rude just who are you?"

"I'll come to that in a minute," she says. "In the meantime you might get Buddy Perriner out of those bracelets and give him a drink. I want to talk to him."

I go over to Buddy an' yank him up. I take off the handcuffs an' give him a shot of champagne outa the bottle. He is beginning to look almost human. Then I give myself a little treat. I go up to the guy Franz who has done all the pushin' around an' I clock him. I bust him a sweet one that sends him spinnin'. I am beginnin' to enjoy life!

Then I go an' lean against the cabin wall. I have got a gun in each hand an' I am just waitin' for an excuse to drill one of these so-an'-so's.

I take a look at the dame. She has taken Buddy's handkerchief outa his pocket, poured some champagne over it, an' she is bathin' his face with it. Me—I give a big sigh. I reckon that I could do with this dame givin' *me* a little champagne behind the ears.

"Mr. Perriner," she says, "I am a representative of the British Government. The pilots aboard this ship and the *Mary Perriner* are not Dutch pilots. They are English naval officers."

She turns to Zeldar an' hands him a sweet smile. He is lookin' at her like he had been poleaxed twice.

"You really are a very stupid person, *Herr Kapitan* Meinschmidt," she says. "Just about as stupid as Gloydas. If Gloydas had been a little more astute he would have noticed that a British drifter came into Delfzyl harbour because of bad weather two days ago. He would have noticed that she moored near the *Maybury*. To-night, when you allowed yourself to be stampeded into rushing off to catch Mr. Caution before he could effect Buddy Perriner's rescue and so very kindly left it in my hands to see that the pilots went aboard the ships, you could not know that, at the same time, the British drifter's crew went aboard too. It was quite easy in the darkness.

"At the moment both the ships are in our hands.

"Thank you . . . *Herr Kapitan!*"

I get it. So that was why she was vampin' Gloydas. That was why she was gettin' around with him when he was fixin' the pilots. What a baby! She hocked his drink an' put a couple of her pals in. She goes on talkin' to Buddy:

"At the moment we are west of Rottum Island in the North Sea," she says, "an' it is my duty to acquaint you, as the representative of the owners of these ships, with the legal position of the *Maybury* and the *Mary Perriner*. Within half an hour we shall be picked up by British torpedo boats. The two ships will be arrested by the Contraband Control. We have evidence that they are carrying cargoes intended for the enemy."

Buddy grins.

"No, ma'am," he says. "The cargoes were intended for England. My father always meant the airplanes to go to the Allies. He took a chance and put the ships to sea before Roosevelt's Neutrality Bill was passed. The fact that the cargoes *nearly* went to Germany is my fault. . . ."

She gives him a smile.

"And that of Ardena Vandell—the *real* one," she says.

She turns around and says to me:

"Mr. Caution, would you be good enough to go up to the bridge and tell our pilot to make the necessary signal to the *Mary Perriner*. He will instruct the captain. Then if you will come back we will deal with our German friends here."

"O.K., sweetness," I tell her.

When I get to the cabin door I turn around and take a look at her. She is sittin' back with her legs crossed holdin' her gun on the boys with one hand an' puttin' a curl back in place with the other.

I say: "Hey, kid . . . what's your real name?"

She shoots me one of them quick little smiles.

"My name's Georgette," she says. "I'm glad to meet you, Lemmy."

I grin at her. I remember the night when I first met up with her in the hotel room in Delfzyl. The night I told her I was Charlie Hoyt an' she kidded me she was Ardena Vandell.

"Georgette," I tell her. "I think you're swell!"

She starts fiddlin' with the side curl again. She says:

"Thanks, Lemmy. You're not so bad yourself!"

Zeldar comes up for air. He gives a snort an' hollers:

"This is a neutral ship. This is a United States ship. It is neutral territory. I am a German officer and I demand to be put ashore in a neutral port!"

Buddy gets on to his feet. He ambles across to Zeldar an' he says in a nice quiet voice:

"You're wrong—you *bastard*! My father sold these ships with the cargoes to England. The sale was made to an English firm before they ever left America and you know it. These ships are English and you're on an English ship, and how do you like that!"

He pulls back his fist and he smacks Zeldar a hard one. Zeldar gives a sigh an' flops.

I open the cabin door. Before I step out I take a look at Georgette. She is still playin' with that side-curl.

I reckon I would like to play with it myself.

We are rollin' along. The sea is as rough as hell an' every time I try to take a step along the deck I have to give an imitation of a slack wire performer.

Away on our port side is the torpedo boat. She is ploughin' through the sea, cuttin' the waves in half. She eases along, slippin' through the water like a graceful dame. She reminds me somehow of Georgette—very slim, very nice to look at an' goddam tough!

Up on the bridge is the English naval guy. I grin to myself. The last time I saw this guy was in the *Spruithuis* tavern when Gloydas took him an' his pal on as pilots. I give him the works.

Comin' back I get to thinkin' that a lot of mugs think these English palooks are slow. But don't let 'em fool you. I remember these two guys easin' out of the *Spruithuis*, clatterin' past me, talkin' to each other in Dutch an' generally behavin' like a coupla heavy Schnapps-drinkin' Delfzyl pilots.

An' all the time they are stickin' around, workin' with Georgette. An' they have got a drifter stuck in the harbour with another dozen guys aboard waitin' for a chance to get on to the two Perriner boats without upsettin' the Dutch authorities. An' I give it to 'em. I come along as Charlie Hoyt an' this smart English dame realises that I am the answer to the maiden's prayer. I am just what she is lookin' for. She uses me to get Zeldar an' his boys outa the way just at the crucial moment an' then she slips her own people aboard. Nice work!

An' there are mugs who think the English can't put on an act.

I get along to the companion way an' go down to the cabin. Georgette is standin' in front of the mirror powderin' her nose. The others have gone.

I wonder where she got the powder-puff from. I suppose she got it outa the *other* stockin' top. I get to thinkin' that it is an amazin' thing the amount of stuff that a dame can carry stuck in the top of her silk stockin's. Besides her legs I mean.

"Listen—you world-famous Secret Service agent," I tell her. "I gotta little business to settle with you."

"Yes?" she says. "Well, go ahead. I've got a pot of tea coming along. Would you like a cup?"

Here is another thing that makes the English a great race. Every time some British guy gets himself run over, or shoots somebody, or goes inta war, or blows somebody up or does some other goddam thing, he always has a cup of tea—before *an'* afterwards. I know it ain't in the history books but I am prepared to bet a blue silk garter that some dame once give me for showin' her the way home in an earthquake to a coupla million dollars that when Julius Caesar landed in Britain he found the local mob sittin' around the foreshore fillin' the football coupons an' drinkin' tea outa sea-shells.

I get serious.

"First of all, Georgette," I tell her, "I would like to congratulate you on bein' a very smart number. I think you got plenty. But there is one little thing that you an' me have got to get right. This guy Zeldar belongs to me. That cheap faerrin' is my meat an' I'm takin' him back to the States with me when I go an' stickin' him up in a Federal Court on about seventeen hundred different charges. By the time I am through with that lump of German sausage I am goin' to get him electrocuted so many times that they will run out of juice. See, honey?"

She shakes her head.

"Nothing doing, Lemmy," she says. "I've got him and I'm keeping him. And I'd like a cigarette, please!"

I give her one.

Some guy—one of the crew—brings in a pot of tea an' planks it on the table. He looks plenty scared. These guys are not very used to bein' pushed around on a rough night at sea.

She starts pourin' herself out a cup of tea. I think she has got her nerve all right.

"Look, honey," I tell her. "Don't get me wrong, but you just have not got the right end of this. *I* want this guy Zeldar. I was on to him first. Besides which I got something on him that you have not got. I got a murder charge. This is the guy who was responsible for poisonin' my side-kicker Rodney Wilks in Paris."

She puts down her cup. She is still smilin' sweetly at me. When she smiles she shows a dimple. I think this baby is sorta cute even if she is argumentative.

"Honey," I tell her. "You gotta see this my way. First of all I would like you to know that I am a very obstinate sorta guy an' I am very fond of gettin' my own way. I was on to Zeldar in Paris an' he's mine. So don't let's argue."

She shakes her head.

"*We* were on to Zeldar *before* he went to America," she says. "We were on to him and Nakorova and Willie Lodz when they were planning the job in England. That's why I went over to the States where I picked up Ardena Vandell—Lodz' girl—after they had got Buddy—and got the story from her. She had an inkling of what was behind the kidnapping. She was scared stiff.

"That suited me excellently. I knew Zeldar was in Paris waiting for Nakorova to go over there. I knew that once Nakorova arrived in Paris Geraldine would follow him over. Obviously they were going to get her too."

"What!" I holler. "You knew that they were goin' to grab off Geraldine in Paris an' you never did a goddam thing to stop it. Say, what's the matter with you? You oughta join the F.B.I. in the States for a course of trainin'."

"Do you think so, Lemmy?" she says, sorta sweetly. "But you see there was no need for me to worry about Geraldine. We'd arranged all that."

She pauses. This dame is takin' my breath away.

"It was obvious that Zeldar would force Geraldine to leave Paris," she says. "He was already worried about getting away to Zurich—you see we've been starting quite a lot of things that were worrying the Gloydas-Nakorova-Haal syndicate both in Zurich and Delfzyl.

"I knew that Zeldar would eventually instruct Geraldine to go to England under threat of what they would do to Buddy. Quite obviously she would be sent to agents of his somewhere in Great Britain. That was why I waited for Zeldar to move. We wanted to get those agents. I kept under cover but I kept close to Geraldine at the Dieudonne. Directly Zeldar instructed her to fly to England I telephoned through to London and arranged things. Two of Zeldar's people met her at the airport and our own people were waiting there too.

"They got Zeldar's last two agents in Great Britain and you'll find Geraldine living quite comfortably at the Savoy Hotel."

I draw a deep breath. Me—I am beginnin' to feel *hurt*.

She smiles at me so sweetly that she almost breaks my heart.

"You know, Lemmy dear," she says. "You really ought to come to England and take a six months' course with the Special Branch!"

I give a big sigh.

"O.K.," I tell her. "Well, maybe you were the smart baby there, Georgette. But what the hell was I to think? When Geraldine disappeared I reckoned that Zeldar had got her. I reckoned he'd sent her to England. And I was entitled to think that because I reckoned that if she'd been able she would have sent a note around to Juanella Rillwater—the dame who was supposed to be lookin' after her."

"Oh *that* . . ." she says, sorta casual. "Well, that's exactly what she did do!"

"For cryin' out loud!" I say. "Well, Juanella never got that note. Otherwise she woulda told me."

"Of course, Lemmy dear," she coos at me. "But you see, I knew that Geraldine had sent a note to Mrs. Juanella Rillwater at the Hotel St. Anne. It cost me exactly fifty francs to get the information from the Dieudonne page boy. So I just went round before him to the Hotel St. Anne and waited until Mrs. Rillwater went out, and then I went upstairs, got into her room—I'm rather good at door locks—and collected the note when it arrived. Candidly, I didn't know exactly who and what Mrs. Rillwater was and I wanted to find out."

"O.K.," I say. "I get it. I was there myself. I came up to Juanella's room to take a look around. You were in the bathroom. You were takin' bottles outa the cupboard an' lookin' at 'em and puttin' 'em back again. I saw you through the crack in the door. That's why I sneaked out."

"How funny," she says sorta arch. "You see I saw you when you were in the sitting-room. So I went into the bathroom. I hoped you wouldn't find me there. I opened the cupboard door in the bathroom so that I could watch you in the mirror on the door. I saw you looking through the crack in the door. So I got out quick. I left for Delfzyl right away."

I give another sigh. What do you *know* about this dame!

"Well, honey," I tell her. "It's no use belly-achin' about it—I gotta have Zeldar. So you might as well make up your mind."

She shakes her head.

"No, Lemmy," she says. "I've got first call on him and I'm going to keep him."

"Yeah," I tell her. "An' what are you goin' to do with him? You got nothin' on him. You may know what he was plannin' to do but you got nothin' on him that you can hang him over. I know you guys. You'll keep him around in some prison till the war's over an' then you'll spring him an' he'll get away with it."

She shrugs her shoulders.

"Look, Gorgeous," I tell her. "This guy Zeldar is poison. He killed Rodney Wilks. But he didn't do it himself—Edvanne Nakorova did it. But I can't prove it an' nobody will ever be able to prove it. He killed Sergius an' Edvanne Nakorova. He told me so himself. But if he went to trial for it he would deny it an' nobody could hang it on to him. He covered up too well. He's too damn' smart.

"O.K. Then there's us. You heard what he was goin' to do to Buddy Perriner an' me. An' what about *you*? You heard what he had on the ice for you, didn't you? Listen, kid, you gotta tell your people that Zeldar belongs to me. I got something on him. Kidnapping over a state line is a Federal offence an' you can send a guy to the chair for it. Anyhow he would get life."

She shrugs her shoulders again.

"How can you prove that he was behind the kidnappin' of Buddy?" she asks. "Sergius and Edvanne Nakorova are dead. Willie Lodz and Borg will keep away from the States. Ardena Vandell has already gone to Mexico. You'll never get any actual evidence against Zeldar on those counts. Nobody is going to talk. The actual business was done by Lodz, Borg and Ardena. You can prove nothing.

"This is one thing you don't get, Lemmy," she says. "And I'm sorry for it. But that's how it is."

I get up.

"Well, honey," I tell her, "it looks as if I am beat this time. I will now take a walk around an' see what is happenin'. Maybe you will rustle up a little coffee in the meantime."

She says she will get along to the galley an' see the guy about some coffee.

I go up on deck. The wind has died down but the sea is still rollin' us about plenty. I have to hang on to things. I stand over by the rail peerin' ahead an' gettin' an occasional glimpse of the torpedo boat.

Just then the *Maybury* gives a lurch an' I have to grab hold of the rail. My hand touches a bit of chain. I look down an' see that this is the part of the rail that is taken out when they run the gangways out to land people. There is a chain an' a bolt to hold the rail secure.

I slip out the bolt. I give the rail a little push an' it gives. I fix it so it looks all right but I still leave the bolt out.

I ease down the forward companion way. I stick around in the dark till I see Georgette come back from the galley. Then I go in an' get a box of salt from the guy in there.

I go to the bottom of the companion way an' I take outa my pocket a flask of whisky that I have got off the captain. I drink half of it an' then I put a helluva lot of the salt in the flask.

I go up on deck an' climb up to the bridge. Buddy is talkin' to the naval guy who is lookin' after the ship. I give him a big wink an' go down to the deck. He comes down.

"Buddy," I tell him, "I been thinkin' about that guy Zeldar. I do not like that guy. I think he is a very mean guy."

Buddy tells me what he thinks about Zeldar. It sounded very nice an' well thought out. I take out the whisky flask.

"Look, kid," I tell him. "I think that this guy Zeldar might like a little drink of whisky. Maybe he'll be feelin' like it. Maybe he'll take a big pull at this flask an' if some lousy guy had put some salt in it I reckon that Zeldar might feel a bit funny in the stomach. See?"

He says he sees.

"Well," I go on. "Supposin' he was feelin' sorta sick an' wanted some air, an' somebody took him over by the rail just over there on the lee side. An' supposin' the rail fell out while he was leanin' on it. I reckon that would be just too bad, don't you."

Buddy says yes, he reckons it would be very bad. Then he asks me if I got any whisky.

I give him the flask.

A spot of moon has come out. It looks swell. I am beginning to feel very nice. Beyond the fact that my nose is as tender as a piece of steak an' I am bruised all over from the dressin' down I got from Zeldar's mugs, I am still able to sorta take an interest in things.

Another torpedo boat has come up an' away behind us, rollin' about, I can see the *Mary Perriner*. I reckon it will be very nice to take a walk on a piece of dry land.

I go downstairs to the cabin. Georgette is sittin' there with the coffee pot. I get to thinkin' that here is a dame that has got practically everything it takes an' then so much that you couldn't add it up.

I put on a very sad sorta face. I sit down an' I look like a guy who has just been gypped for his last nickel.

She says: "What's wrong, Lemmy?"

I shrug my shoulders.

"Nothin' much," I say. "But I am a very proud sorta guy an' I feel like ten cents. Here am I supposed to be an ace investigator, an' I been stoogin' along on this business while you have been makin' rings around me. *I'm hurt*. I just don't know what to do I'm so hurt."

She falls for it. She says:

"Lemmy, without your stooging as you call it, we couldn't have done a thing. If you hadn't turned up in Delfzyl and pulled that Charlie Hoyt act on me I could never have got Zeldar's confidence. I could never have got our own men aboard the two boats to bring them out into the North Sea. You've done a marvellous job."

I shake my head.

"It's no good," I tell her. "I'm finished. The guys I've been used to workin' with will be takin' a mike at me the whole time. I shall have to resign. There's nothin' else for it but that. My career is ruined."

I am doin' so well that I reckon I am goin' to make myself cry in a minute. I get up an' lean against the wall lookin' like a Roman gladiator who has just put his head in a lion's mouth an' discovered that it ain't a stuffed lion.

She comes over to me. She puts her hands on my shoulders and she says:

"Lemmy, I'm surprised at your takin' this thing like this. But you've done a good job. And I owe you a lot."

"Yeah," I say. "Do you mean that?"

She says she means it.

"O.K., Georgette," I say. "Then this is where you pay your bill. Even when I thought you was Ardena Vandell I was nuts about you. You are my favourite chemist's prescription. You are the apple sauce on the pork spare-ribs. Any time you are around you can do anything you want with me an' I give up about Zeldar. You can have Zeldar an' I will not say another word about it."

I have already told you guys that I am a very poetic sorta cuss an' right now I am feelin' that poetry is everything to me I because the way that Georgette gets inside my arms is nobody's business. Me—I have very seldom struck a dame who was tops at her business an' who could, at the same time, put so much into kissin' as Georgette.

Right in the middle of this affectionate co-operation Buddy comes in.

"A terrible thing has happened," he says. "Zeldar has fell overboard."

Georgette looks at him and then at me with her eyes wide open. "How?" she says.

"He had some whisky," says Buddy. "I was sorta sorry for him an' I gave him a drink. He didn't feel so good so I took him up on deck. He was leanin' up against a rail an' the rail fell out."

She says: "Didn't you do something about it? Didn't you shout 'man overboard'?"

"Yes," says Buddy. "But I got a sore throat an' I couldn't shout very loud. Nobody heard me. It's a terrible thing," he says, "but maybe it's for the best."

I nod my head.

"Maybe you're right, Buddy," I tell him. "But I'm sorry."

"Me too," says Buddy.

The mug is grinnin' like an ape.

He has a cup of coffee an' scrams.

I say: "Georgette, there is the hand of fate. Just when I have agreed that you can have Zeldar the mug has to fall overboard. Ain't that just like life? You never know what's goin' to happen from one minute to another."

She comes over to me. There is a lot of mischief in her eyes. She says:

"You didn't know anything about Zeldar fallin' overboard, did you?"

I look at her in surprise.

"How could I know, honey?" I tell her. "I was here all the time. I got an alibi."

"Like hell you have, Lemmy," she says. "And how was it that Zeldar came to be feeling ill. Let me give you a word of advice. The next time you put salt into whisky don't leave any on the lapel of your coat, you big sleuth!"

I don't say a word because whatever I have done in this business, this dame has got me beat. Standin' there lookin' at her I get around to thinkin' about some guy who said that English dames had not got anything very much. This guy musta been missin' on all six cylinders.

I also get to thinkin' that now that Zeldar has had that little accident, everything will be very nice an' maybe I can get a month or so's leave an' hang around in England.

Because I am a guy who is very keen to learn anything that is goin' an' I reckon that maybe Georgette might be able to teach me somethin' else.

An' any guy who says that he cannot learn from a dame like Georgette is missin' some very interestin' education.

You'd be surprised!

THE END